MONTANA HITCH

MONTANA HITCH

RICHARD WHEELER

Thorndike Press • Thorndike, Maine

Library of Congress Cataloging in Publication Data:

Wheeler, Richard S.
   Montana hitch / Richard Wheeler.
      p.   cm.
   ISBN 1-56054-144-X (alk. paper : lg. print)
   1. Large type books. I. Title.
[PS3573.H4345M66   1991]   91-9815
813'.54—dc20   CIP
   $16.95

Thorndike Press Large Print edition published in 1991
by arrangement with M. Evans and Company, Inc.

Large Print edition available in the British Commowealth
by arrangement with Peekner Literary Agency.

Cover design by James B. Murray.

The tree indicium is a trademark of Thorndike Press.

This book is printed on acid-free, high opacity paper.

For Tracy Dunham

Chapter One

Abner Dent topped a gentle roll of prairie, saw his house a mile off, and hated it. The great white monster thrust arrogantly from the earth, defying man and nature. Even from where he sat his horse, Abner could make out its broad veranda along the south side, and the cupola with its weathervane on top. It didn't belong there. It sat upon land Abner didn't even own, land the government had yet to survey. It crushed his ranch like a hundred-ton anvil, squeezing life from it day by day. Once he'd loved it, found joy in it, built it for his bride-to-be with all his dreams of bliss permeating its splendid rooms. Oh, where had the good times gone? Where had joy fled?

The familiar bitterness rose in him again, as it always did when his thoughts returned to Eve. His wife. Whose bridal gift had been that house and a raft of extravagances his outfit could ill afford. But that wasn't all that crabbed at Abner now, as he glared dourly at the homestead. His tall, angular, jet-haired bride, plucked from a hurdygurdy up in Maiden, had turned out to be no wife at all. And Abner had no solution for it other than patience, which is what he summoned now,

7

as he sat his horse, staring ahead at the whited sepulcher of all his dreams.

He set the matter aside, as he always did. There was little point in fretting about something he couldn't change. Just now, it was all he and Henri could do to keep the nine steers and the old bull he was driving from snaking back to the herd. His métis boy had gotten better but still was no drover, and the two of them were barely a match for those big, sneaky steers that seemed to understand they'd soon be steaks on platters up at Maiden.

Henri was all Abner could afford, and he could barely pay Henri his twenty and found. Abner could never put the proper French inflection on the half-breed's name, and ended up calling him Hungry, which probably fit him better anyway. Hungry Billedeaux. Together they drove those scheming cattle eastward across the Judith Basin grasses toward Abner's home place. Tomorrow they'd begin the three-day drive up to Maiden, the gold and silver camp high in the Judith Mountains forty miles away.

Zimmerman wouldn't like that bull, but he'd take it. They all demanded beef up there. Abner had a contract with the Maiden butcher to deliver ten beeves at the beginning of each month. Zimmerman wanted more, but Abner Dent couldn't raise them fast enough. Not with a herd of five hundred, he thought, thinking of his expanding neighbors, especially Marvin Trump to the north. And Eve. Especially Eve.

Dreams never quite work out, he thought. Some sort of mailed fist in the universe smashed most dreams to smithereens, or twisted them to death. His, for instance. He lifted his gaze from a dawdling brindle long enough to feast his spirit on what lay about him. From the moment he first saw the Judith country in '79, he'd loved it. Buffalo still ran thick then, but they'd been shot away by 1882, well after he'd built the cabin and run his first odd bunch of longhorn cows, worn-out oxen, six retired milkers, and some bought shorthorn calves. Not much of a start, but something from nothing. He'd started penniless and built it all with hard work, sacrifice, and a ruthless determination to track down every predator and rustler, two- and four-footed, that disturbed his growing herd.

Here in the Judith Basin he'd found the richest grasses he'd ever seen in this northern country, hip-high, waving in the summer breezes. Off to the east rose the dark, ponderosa-clad Judiths, rich in gold and silver. Southeast, the ridge of the Snowies. To the north, the Moccasins lay easterly and the Highwoods dim on the northwest. And to the south and west, the Little Belts. All wilderness, and the summer home of the Blackfeet from time immemorial. The distances had stirred something in him, and he knew where he'd settle. He'd raise beeves here, even if he was miles from markets, even if the Judith was one of the coldest places in the Territory.

That was before Maiden, and the Maiden lady. His mind went blank and turned inward. The grand vistas, the lush spring grasses and snowpatched blue ranges all disappeared. He glanced at Hungry, seeing how the lad was holding up. Hungry slouched in his battered saddle, a Texas castoff, as weary as the lineback dun mustang he rode. Half French, half Cree, a child of the fur trade, now long gone. All over this north country one could find Cree and Assiniboin and Blackfeet with French names, sometimes Scottish names. Trappers' names.

Abner couldn't afford a regular Texas cowboy like himself. But a man couldn't run a spread alone, especially an open range spread surrounded by predators. He could have afforded a couple or three Texas drovers, and might have had a herd of a thousand by now — if things had gone a little different.

Still, he hung on. His neighbors didn't like it, hauling ten beeves each month off the open range, out of mixed herds, and driving them to market. Trump especially. It looked like theft. Abner snorted at that. He'd been the first on the Judith, but in a year or two others had come in and built their own herds, often from any slick calf they could throw to earth — most of them Abner's calves. Abner's response to their suspicion had been blunt:

"Marvin, I gather my steers regularly at the end of each month, good weather or bad. You send your rep over and have a look at the beeves."

Trump had muttered and done nothing, preferring suspicions and doubts to finding out truth. Abner had started another practice, too. Each time he reached Maiden and penned the steers in the yard behind Zimmerman's butcher shop, he'd gotten the town marshal, Francis Matz, to look at the brands and give him an inspection letter. But that had never stopped Trump and the rest from muttering — and mavericking.

The sun caught the west side of his house and scorched it white until it shimmered against the dark grasses around it. Just beyond it coiled the brass band of the Judith River. His house but not his place. He squatted, like everyone else, waiting for the government to survey the area. That house didn't belong there yet. All the rest who'd come to the Judith Basin had built soddies or log places, temporary, not risking anything better until they could own the ground under them. And not wanting to pour precious capital that could buy cattle into a mere shelter. There were empires to build in the Judith, for those willing to survive in sod or log cabins.

Odd how the sun caught his house. Beyond, over the Snowies, slate clouds were building into May showers, and the sky had turned indigo. But his house blazed and shimmered, as golden light toyed with it, making it seem even larger. It was the only frame house in the basin. Big, too, with three bedrooms upstairs, a summer kitchen, kitchen, parlor, dining room, study, and water closet. The only indoor water closet in the basin, as far as he knew. With an oak commode and a vitreous white porcelain flush tank with a pull chain high above. That had taken some doing — a driven well, a windmill, and a reservoir on the knoll behind the house to supply gravity feed. It worked most of the time, except when it froze or the wind didn't blow for a week or two. That's when Eve complained.

The house stared back at him, defying him. The log cabin had been comfortable enough and inspired dreams. But this thing, this monster before him, had ruined dreams. Still, it was his, bought and paid for with beef, two-thirds of his herd, including mother cows.

Bought and paid for and maybe — if he endured — a sign of what would come. He might enjoy it someday, this thing that could sink the Bar D. The house was a fine one, a famous one, an astonishing one for a man not yet thirty. But a man shouldn't have to hurry his dreams.

He reined his orange gelding at the gate of the pole corral, and slid to earth, feeling pain in his saddle-bent legs. He swung it open, hearing spooky steers scatter behind him. Irritably, he clambered into his saddle to help the inept lad keep the beeves from snorting clear back to the open range they'd been hijacked from. In a minute he'd turned them back and shoved them in, seeing the flat sun lance their sides. The red and brown and yellow and black-spotted critters bawled, wanting water, too dumb to find it where the big pen angled down to the icy river. Abner studied them a moment, pleased they were in good flesh after a hard winter, pleased that he'd deliver good weight to Zimmerman this time. Every penny counted.

Several times, especially in cool weather with a tailing wind, he'd driven the cattle to Maiden in two days. Usually it took three, and the cattle had lost little weight en route because Abner always pushed them slowly. After delivery, he and Hungry allowed themselves a beer or two and some fun at the saloon, unrolled their soogans in the rear of the butcher shop, and hastened home the next day. It had been a hard grind, delivering once a month, winter and summer. But it had brought cash, desperately needed credit and hard money.

"Mister Dent, I'll go wash up and rest now," Hungry said. "I'll be over in an hour or so, when Mrs. Dent is ready."

Abner nodded. It was a game they played. It didn't salve Abner's anger much, but it helped. Hungry lived in Abner's original cabin, now a bunkhouse a hundred yards from the great white house. He ate with the Dents, summoned to meals with a triangle of bar steel, hanging from a post.

He watched the lad unsaddle the thin dun and brush the damp, matted hair where the saddle had pressed down. Abner had taught him that; taught him to care for his mounts. Hungry had known nothing about horses or cattle or ranching. Wearily, feeling pain lance him, Abner undid his own cinch and pulled the damp saddle free, dropping it over the top rail of the pen. He looked over his tired gelding, feeling hocks and pasterns for heat, checking shoes and hoofs. The horses faced a hard trip beginning at dawn. Satisfied, he ran the animal into a smaller pen next to the cattle, and waited. Hungry found a pitchfork and speared prairie hay from a stack, and carried it to the pen. Abner nodded and turned toward the house, knowing Eve sat out on the veranda watching him, the way she always did in clement air.

He slapped dust from his jeans with his sweat-stained gray hat, not wanting to dirty the great house any more than it was. She watched him, her sharp-edged face blank. He clambered up the stairs to the veranda, seeing a jumble of books and magazines, Harper's and The Woman's Home Companion and rolled newspapers that had come all the way from the East.

"There's nothing to do," she said.

He kept his counsel. Something in her features still warmed him, and he smiled faintly, half-pleased that she wore her new yellow dimity she'd had made at Fort Benton. She ordered things there from a seamstress who had a dressmaker's dummy just Eve's size. Her long jet hair hung loose over her breast, reminding him of raven's wings. She was almost beautiful, and it always amazed him that she had chosen the homeliest cowboy in the Territory.

He glared at the mound of unread rolled-up papers and resented the extravagance. But it had been like that from the beginning. Up in Maiden she'd smiled and teased and flirted, and he had never imagined what would come.

"We'll be off in the morning," he said.

Her skeptical lilac eyes lit up.

He kicked the last dirt off his boots and pushed through the door into a house that scarcely seemed lived-in. She'd draped sheets over the parlor settee and chairs. He padded uneasily across an ashes of roses rug, and into the grimy kitchen, illumined by the low westerly sun, whose rays caught the clutter of pots and plates at the drainboard and enlarged the pile until it looked menacing. He'd never gotten used to it, but he had found no remedy.

Wearily he poked a finger into the stove reservoir and found it mostly empty and the water cool. He crumpled one of her unread newspapers, The Boston Transcript, and jammed it into the firebox in the side of the Majestic range, and then added the last of the kindling from the woodbox in the summer kitchen, and lit it with a sulphur match. He drew water from the faucet, grateful for the gravity feed, and poured buckets of it into the stove reservoir. It would take a while. An acrid smell of sulphur lingered.

This fancy house of his had a dining room instead of a table in the kitchen, and there, on the oval oaken table, he found the residue of breakfast and her lunch. She'd had eggs.

She'd even managed to steal them from the hens, he thought. He picked up the yolk-coated Haviland bone china plate, her cup and saucer and the dirty silver and hauled it to the drainboard and dropped it in the zinc sink.

She'd complained about not having help, and it had become a sore point between them. He wiped the crumbs off carefully, not wanting to have to get out the Bissell carpet sweeper and scrape around the dining room. Once he'd hoped he could afford help for her someday, but now he didn't care. At the rate things were going, he'd end up being someone's help instead of hiring help.

He checked the fire in the range and found it crackling and the black castiron surface heating up nicely. But it was still too cold to make a drop of water bounce and spit. He slid out the back door toward the icehouse built into the low slope to the west, and pulled open the massive door. Cold smacked him, leftover winter from the ice he'd sawed out of the Judith River. He'd salvaged some meat from a heifer that had died birthing, and cut through loin with a hacksaw he kept there for the purpose. He remembered to pick up some of the wrinkled potatoes. That would do. He felt too tired for a fancy meal.

He tried not to think about all this, the hollowness of it, the disappointment. But it

17

crept into him anyway, filling him with gloom. Everything there was to say had been said long before, and now words dropped off cliffs. Still, he hoped. She'd been eager to please him once, long ago. Maybe she would again. People grew, changed, deepened. And there still were good things, happy moments, when she came alive and her eyes glowed. That's when he forgot how homely he was, how lumpy his face, how his ears stuck out like prickly pears, and how his Adam's apple, sharp enough to cut butter, bobbed when he spoke. Those few joys had made the rest bearable. Ugly and stubborn; that's how he branded Abner Dent. And with a long fuse. It didn't pay to blow up all the time. He hardly ever got mad, and he wondered idly what would happen if he ever lost his temper, really lost it. The thought made him uneasy.

The smell of hot castiron met him in the kitchen, and he knew he'd have a meal soon. He poured cold water into a tin kettle, added a little powdered soap from Bollanger's store in Maiden, and scrubbed the rime from yesterday's cooking from it. He rinsed it with lukewarm water from the stove reservoir, threw the water out on the lawn, and then started more heating in the kettle while he scrubbed the potatoes.

He heard the front door close, knew she

was coming, and bit off the words he wanted to say. His only helps now were patience and forgiveness, and those had grown thin.

The tallow in the spider on the range had turned to clear liquid, so he sawed the hunk of loin into thick steaks, aware that she was watching him from the kitchen door.

"I'm tired of meat and potatoes," she said.

"You could change that."

"You promised me help."

"I don't remember it. And I can't afford it now. We're sinking."

Abner had a sense that this conversation repeated a hundred others verbatim, and he wondered why he let the thing continue on. He'd choked back too much pain for his own good.

"I don't want to get my dresses dirty," she said. "You'll get someone for me. You always do."

He salted the steaks, checked the potatoes in the kettle, and then drew hot water from the reservoir into a dishpan and began washing dishes.

"Eve — these expenses are eating into my broodstock. It's like eating the seedcorn."

In his rolltop desk in his study lay a stack of bills he couldn't pay. Dressmaker's bills. Invoices from Fort Benton and Maiden and Lewistown mercantiles, for bolts of cloth, perfumes, ostrich-feather hats, lantern-show slides, Wedgwood teapots, hair curlers, salts, elixirs and patent medicines, an herb she liked called pennyroyal, and God knows what else.

"I know," she said, and it surprised him. Once in a while he thought maybe, just maybe . . .

"Sure it's lonely, Eve. Not like Maiden. Not like being in a dance hall with a hundred people every night. I know that. But if you could just — slow down for a while. We have to build and that takes time, Eve. In a year or two we could have a lot more. Build the herd back and then we can afford —"

"Can I go to Helena?"

He gaped at her. "I can't afford that."

"There's nothing to do here, and I'm lonely. You're gone all day and no one comes. Just a month." She smiled. "I'll buy something for you."

Abner shook his head. "Don't even think of it."

"I need a parasol."

He wiped the plates with a dirty rag — there'd been no time to catch up with laundry — and set the dining table with them, adding fresh-washed silver and glasses. On the wood range, the potatoes bobbed in boiling water, and the redolence of frying steaks began to fill the great house.

She stood watching, like a calculating crow.

"You could get things from the pantry, Eve."

"My dress cost thirty dollars."

How well Abner knew. The bill lay on his desk. "There's an apron," he said, knowing her answer.

"You promised me."

He wasn't sure what he'd promised her. A lot less than she claimed; he knew that.

"We're losing calves," he said abruptly. "Someone's rustling them. I've got cows with sore bags. I don't have help enough to keep watch. Someone's stealing and I'm going to get him. When I get back I'm going to do something about it. I think I know where to start. Dixie Lacy."

She nodded, not very interested.

"I don't want you buying anything now. Not a thing. I'll tell the merchants not to honor — doggone it, Eve. Would you just help a little? For a while? Just stop ordering things? For us?"

"Of course I'll help you, Abner. Of course I will."

"Will you really?"

She smiled. "I promise."

Some of the weariness left him then. Her crooked grin had always melted him. Maybe there'd be a way. He needed a year. At least a year in which she didn't spend one damned dime.

"Eve," he said, and reached to her, drawing her to him. She didn't resist, and even slid her arms around him. "I need that," he whispered in her ear. She smelled of some perfume. Lilac, he thought. Yes, lilac. Like her eyes. "I want you to be happy, Eve."

"That's nice," she said. "I do, too."

He smelled charring meat and plunged toward the range to flip the steaks. Fat spat at him, stinging his wrists. He whirled to the pantry for the pickles, pulled a loaf of his bread from its box, snatched butter from the ice-house, stabbed potatoes from boiling water, and finally forked meat onto a platter.

She smiled at him from her seat at the table.

He banged the triangle outside the door knowing the clang would summon Hungry. The sallow lad hastened toward the house and settled himself at the dining table, eyeing the heavy steaks, potatoes, uncut bread, and butter.

"You sure cook a great feed, Mrs. Dent," Hungry said to Eve, who had already assaulted her steak like a vulture.

Chapter Two

She spotted Dixie at noon, riding down the river, and felt a swell of irritation blossom in her. He had kept her waiting. Usually he arrived magically, an hour or two after Abner and Hungry left for Maiden with the month's batch of cattle. She studied his progress from her white wicker chair on the veranda, resisting the temptation to rush out to him. She'd learned long ago never to do that; never to be too eager. It meant losing control of situations.

Dixie always sent shivers through her because something frightful lay just beneath his infectious joy. He possessed everything with his soulful brown eyes. When he looked at something, a cow, anyone's wife, a ranch, a horse — he already owned it. She had to be careful around him, and not let him think that he owned her. No one owned her.

He paused on his blood bay beneath a willow, absorbing the Dent ranch, the windows, the barn, the dugout, and finally her on the veranda, noticing her white sateen dress and white highbutton shoes and white lace parasol. She never dressed like that when Abner and Hungry were around, but it excited her to be so elegant and sit outdoors on the shaded broad porch like Kentucky gentry and wait for Dixie that way. Later, she'd dress in her new lace-sleeved pink dimity and cook him supper. She didn't like to cook, but sometimes she had to.

Dixie steered the blood bay toward the corrals in the thick quiet, and let himself into the barn. She couldn't see him there, but she knew he would open the rear door, pitch hay to the horse, and leave its saddle on but loosely cinched. He would also open the gate of the pen behind the barn, giving him instant flight with no obstacles. For all his reckless joy, Dixie Lacy lived carefully and planned his every move, including swift escapes.

When at last he reappeared, she felt the familiar tingling fear, and controlled it as usual with an imperious tilt of her jaw. Abner never did that to her, made her ache at the bottom of her belly. But Dixie did, half in anticipation, half in dread, half in expectation of wild giggling fun. Abner was skinny and homely as a potato with too many eyes, but Dixie always looked grand, big and lean except for a potbelly he tried to hide in black britches.

He slid at last up the broad steps.

"You made me wait," she accused.

"I'm worth waiting for."

"What took you so long?"

"Temptation."

She didn't fathom what he was talking about, and thought better than to ask, but she smiled.

"Are you ready for me?"

"Oh, Dixie. You have such conceits."

He laughed, muffled and soft, with a sound that scarcely slid into the yard. Off on a distant swell, a coyote echoed him.

He lifted her bodily from her chair — she would let him, she thought — and hugged her, and she felt his disciplined body tight against her. So strong. Dixie had been a Confederate sergeant once. From Tyler, Texas, he'd said. He always made Abner seem like a yokel. She kissed him back, feeling herself melt into beeswax, and then struggled loose.

He lifted her again, intending to carry her upstairs, but she squirmed free.

"I'm not ready yet," she breathed in his ear.

"Since when has that stopped us?"

"You were late, so I'll make you wait."

He laughed and caught her wrist, tugging her toward the open front door.

"You didn't bring me anything."

"It's not visible."

"You have to bring me things. You promised."

"I'm all I ever bring."

25

"Then go away."

He laughed happily.

"Abner won't let me buy things anymore. He says he's in trouble," she added hastily.

He stared.

"What are you going to buy for me then, when he's gone?"

"Later," he said, tugging her.

She felt that thrill of terror again. She loved that feeling, like swooping down the arc on a child's swing and feeling like she needed to go, the spasm all up and down her legs.

"I know you're taking his cattle. Maybe I should tell on you."

That stopped him. He stared, clamped his hands around her neck and tightened. She screamed and pummeled him and felt iron fingers clamp her windpipe and cut off breath. She snatched at the black Colt nestled in his black holster, but he kneed her. Then those fingers released her and she tumbled to the porch deck, gasping.

"You don't know anything," he said gently.

She peered up at him, trembling, dizzy, and saw him leering at her. He pulled a pouch of Dixie Cut Plug from his shirt and placed a pinch under his tongue. She hated that, hated the smell of it when they were upstairs. Abner didn't chew or snort. But Dixie did, and always left an aroma behind him, so strong it sometimes alarmed her. Dixie spat juices, too, in the bedroom, in the barn. And always left the hayfork in a different place, as a calling card. Like a big male cat, marking his territory.

But that was the fun of Dixie. She'd never exerted the slightest control over him, never knew what he'd do to her. That made him a terror and joy inside of her. All her life she'd plucked men as if they were grapevines. She knew exactly what they wanted, and simply promised it, and had gotten everything she ever wanted by promising it. She'd learned some of it from her daddy, back in those camps along the Union Pacific tracks where Agamemnon Bills huckstered town lots while his only daughter Eve Bills studied him. Her daddy knew what to do, and somehow so did she, but she had all the advantage because she was female. All she had to do was dance and promise, not even do anything bad, and soon she got everything. First in a Denver City hurdygurdy, and then at Maiden, up in the Judith Mountains, where she sold miners and cowboys watered whiskey, dances and promises, and coined money all the while.

Until she'd met Abner Dent. She had liked the skinny galoot and had grown weary of fifty dances a night, getting stepped on, getting herself mussed and her clothing torn, and soothing men with smelly armpits who'd been

27

promised things she wouldn't do. She'd never crossed the line and never intended to. Not that some hurdygurdy girls didn't cross it. And not that lots of people, wives especially, thought there was no difference between dancehall girls and the other kind. She'd grown weary of defending her virtue up there in that gold and silver camp, and decided to change her life. So she'd made Abner build her a big new house with shiplap and gingerbread and every convenience for a wedding present, to make up for his homeliness, and then said yes. She had never dreamed a ranch in new country would be so dull. Or that Abner would look dumber and dumber to her every day.

"I'm Abner's wife," she said obstinately.

He didn't reply, but fondled her for an answer. She giggled.

"He's going broke anyway," she added. "He can't afford me."

"He can't afford the Judith Basin," Dixie said. "Too soft. It takes men."

"Like you and Marvin Trump."

"Like me."

"Abner says it'll be a fast trip. It's cool and the beeves are in good flesh."

"Does that worry you?"

"Well —"

"Maybe he'll catch us — before he dies."

28

"Oh, Dixie." She did fear it. She dreaded what Dixie might do to Abner. She didn't like Abner much, but she didn't want him to be hurt. He was a lumpy scarecrow of a man, but not someone she hated. And she didn't want her secrets known, either. Respectable women could have anything, but tarnished ones couldn't. She didn't want gossip. Didn't want Hungry to start talking. Of course, Dixie would do something to Hungry, too. Dixie would stop at nothing.

"I don't want you ever to be here when he comes home, Dixie," she said seriously. "I really don't. I'll break off with you if you get careless. I know what you do for a living. And other people know, too, even if they don't say anything. If I'm caught, I'll tell them you forced me. I'll tell them you violated me. I'll tell them, and they'll believe me. They'll come and get you and lead you to a cottonwood tree in the night. You think you own me but you don't. Nothing stolen is ever really owned. It's just possessed. I'll not let you —"

Dixie Lacy sighed, lifted her bodily with his massive arms and carried her past the parlor with the sheets over the horsehair furniture, up the grimy stairs with the oriental runner pinned by brass carpet rods, across a creaking upstairs hall and into her bedroom — their bedroom. She struggled at first,

29

feeling fear in her throat and fire in her loins and not really wanting him to stop, and then she began unbuttoning the white sateen bodice even before he dropped her unceremoniously on the fourposter.

"Damn you, Dixie!" she cried. "You've torn my dress."

Abner had started as soon as enough light lay over the Judith to permit trailing. But he'd been up for two hours putting grub and camp gear together. He and Hungry would each take soogans, and he'd pack enough sowbelly and beans to sustain them for three days. He boiled up some oatmeal for them before they took off — plain fare but he couldn't afford anything else, and besides, it made a fast meal. He left the dishes at the drainboard, knowing they'd be there when he got back, along with every other one in the place. He saddled Boots, his odd-colored orange gelding with black below the knees and hocks, and slid his old cowboy carbine, a battered Winchester, into a scuffed boot. He never bothered with a sidearm these days, when the only problem was a wolf or two.

At the last, with blue light boiling over the eastern mountains, he leapt up the broad stairs, two at a time, and sat down beside Eve. She slept, or feigned it.

"Back maybe in three days, honey. This one should be fast. Please —" He checked himself. Day by day he'd waited for something good to happen, for her to ease the life at the ranch, pitch in, mend, hoe, feed, cook, clean, wash, make economies, get along without luxuries, find pride in honest labor, add something rather than subtracting — and day after day nothing happened. His admonitions, gentle and not so gentle, had melted none of her ice. All that was left to him was hope, but he was not a quitter and not vindictive either, and so he'd waited for whatever time would bring. But what time had brought was a deepening sense of being caught in a brutal trap.

"Eve," he said, and took her hand. She opened her eyes and smiled at him, her thin face framed by loose jet hair. He didn't know what to say. Tenderness would win a cold stare. Anger would close her eyes. He sighed, gathered courage, and kissed her.

"I want you, Eve," he whispered, doubting that he did.

He and Hungry trailed the nine steers and the aged bull northeastward in chill haze, seeing nothing but gray grass and gray mountains. The longhorn beeves walked easily, wide horns swinging, in the freshets of cold air. His passage took him straight toward Warm Spring Creek which led up to Maiden.

He always drove his beeves that way if he could, but sometimes he'd been forced into roundabout routes, when creeks flooded, or herds massed on the open range. With a drover or two who were more skilled than Hungry, he might have pushed his beeves right through without losing any of them into the range herd, or picking up any either. But not Hungry. The awkward Creole-Cree lad never quite turned himself into a savvy cowboy and was scarcely worth his twenty and found.

He didn't want to be caught, even for a minute, seeming to drive beeves with other brands to the butcher in Maiden. Marvin Trump complained endlessly about these trips, and that often set off Leo Pelz and Ben Hruska, too. They all seemed to think no cattle should be taken to market except at roundup time, or at least as a joint project.

The drive proceeded routinely until mid-afternoon, when Abner spotted three riders waiting on an easterly roll of the tall-grass prairie. A while later he made them out to be Marvin Trump and his segundo, Rooster — a banty cock of a man — and one of Trump's drovers, Lucius Marcullus Washburn, the only fat cowboy Abner had ever known or heard of. They would examine his beeves this time, he thought. Good enough.

He nodded to Hungry, and they turned the ten beeves slightly in the direction of his neighbors.

Trump, a purple-faced man, sat his claybank as if he were a commanding general of an army rather than a bachelor cattleman living in a log cabin twelve miles north of Abner. He'd arrived only two years earlier, and in months had thrown awesome numbers of beeves onto Judith grass, and had been pressuring Abner in ways that begged for retaliation. But Abner had refused to take the bait. He had too much to do to indulge in such foolishness.

"We just thought we'd have us a look, Dent," he said in his river-gravel voice.

"I've always said you were welcome. I'd prefer that you send a rep each month."

"Never had time to waste on that."

"Go ahead and look."

"We don't like it a bit that you pull beeves off open range without us saying so."

"They're my beeves."

"Not the way I'm thinking. You and the Missus live almighty high down there for five hundred beeves. Maybe they're not all yours."

Abner had been through this several times before, and said nothing. Hungry looked nervous under the glare of the florid cattleman.

"You ain't answering because you got no

answer. You make a man wonder, you and that half-assed breed cowboy."

"If you're making accusations, Trump, come right out with them."

Trump grinned. For a reply he nodded at Washburn and Rooster, who touched heels to their cowponies and rode downslope to Abner's beeves, elaborately examining their rumps for Abner's mark, a Bar D, and then circling each animal, as if examining contraband. Abner watched them, seething, but said nothing. The fastest way to get past the harassment would be silence.

"This here's a bull, Marvin," yelled Rooster.

"A bull? By gawd, driving a bull to the butcher. You can't do that, Dent."

Abner sighed, saying nothing.

"A bull, is it?" Trump yanked his claybank around and pushed downslope to examine the gaunt brindle longhorn. "By gawd, it's a bull. Better cut him out, Rooster."

"What's this all about?" Abner demanded.

"The range needs bulls. I hardly got any, and neither has nobody else. We all depend on you for bulls, Dent."

It startled Abner. Using his bulls. All the open range ranchers had agreed to maintain adequate numbers of bulls for their tally. But it seems they'd been using him. At least Trump had. Anger rose through him now.

"He's got my brand and he's going to the butcher."

Trump smirked. "Naw. That ain't neighborly. I figure you owe us bulls, long as our cows and calves keep disappearing in your direction."

"What's that supposed to mean?"

"Just like I say. We got lots of cows with sore bags and no calves. We got critters with blotched brands. Someone's messed up the brands. We got tracks leading south toward your outfit. You sneak beeves out from us, the least you can do is provide bulls."

"Maybe you'd better take that back, Trump."

"I'll let it ride, Dent."

Abner sighed, and unbuckled the coiled lariat that hung from his centerfire saddle. He reined his horse toward the bull, building a loop. If that bull went anywhere, it would be to Maiden on the other end of his rope.

"We're thinking maybe you and Lacy's partners, Dent. You both got a lot of female to pay for."

Abner didn't like the sound of that, either. "I'll settle this at the next district meeting," he said, keeping his response civil, against the rage clawing at his throat.

He watched Rooster and Washburn haze the bull out of the bunch, skillfully thwarting its efforts to return. That suited him fine. He whipped the loop into a fine roll and let it sail delicately over the bull's horns. He dallied the rope around his horn.

"That bull's mine and he's going to market," he said wearily, as he felt his horse edge back, keeping the line taut.

"Try it," bawled Trump. He sat there leering and purple-faced, the bore of his big Colt Peacemaker aimed at Abner's chest.

Abner froze, astonished. Would the man murder him for a bull?

Trump's revolver exploded. Abner felt his orange horse shudder, sigh, and buckle under him. Abner swore, kicked his boots free, and slid out of the saddle just as the gelding caved into the grass, gouting blood from a dollar-sized hole in his chest.

Trump's revolver never wavered.

"No bull, Dent."

"That's my horse!"

"Funniest-looking horse that ever died, Dent. Now lift your arms."

"You shot my horse!"

Trump leered.

"You owe me a horse! A good horse!"

"Maybe you'd better cancel the contract with that butcher in Maiden and ship beeves proper with the rest of us, Dent."

Abner said nothing. He glanced around at Hungry, and found the lad staring into space, his hands carefully clutching the pommel. Off a hundred yards, Trump's men shoved the bull westward and then out of sight beyond a roll of prairie, the lariat still dangling from its neck.

"Like I say, Dent. It's time to cancel that contract. If Zimmerman wants beeves, maybe the boys in the district will do it jointly."

Realization swept through Abner. The district cattlemen were stealing his market from him. Along with anything else they could take. These roosters would peck him to death. Unless he did something about it.

"You have a revolver pointed at me," Abner said softly. "But it's not over, Trump. It's just begun. I'm easy to get along with — up to a point. Up to a *point*. *Up to a point*."

Trump hoorawed, but Abner was rewarded by the sight of a certain wariness creeping into Trump's florid face. But that wasn't much of a payment for a shot horse and the use of his bulls.

Chapter Three

Abner Dent boiled. He'd lost a damned good horse, a fine honest friend of a horse. Murdered by a neighbor who'd turned mean and greedy. He'd had his own bull hazed out from under him, at gunpoint. His own beef! And he'd learned his neighbors ruthlessly used his bulls instead of providing their own. And there he sat, a dozen miles from home, without a horse, and with a contract obligation to deliver ten beeves in Maiden two days hence.

He thought of going to the law, but whatever law there was — a sheriff and a deputy in White Sulphur Springs — slumbered a hundred miles and a mountain range to the west. He thought of snatching the nearest Trump steer and taking it along in partial payment for a good horse — and knew that'd get him into worse trouble fast. Anyway, it'd take five or six fat beeves to pay for that good gelding. He rubbed his eyes, and then pushed his anger aside, knowing it wouldn't help him get out of this fix. At least he'd learned something about Marvin Trump and the rest, he thought.

He stood restlessly, watching Hungry circle the nine steers. He was going to have to borrow Hungry's horse and trust the boy could herd these critters on foot for a time. He squinted up at the heavens and found no sign of thunderheads. A storm could scatter the steers in moments. On foot, Hungry would be helpless to collect them. Satisfied, he tugged at the offside cinch buckle on the cooling mountain of cinnamon hair, hoping he could pull the saddle off. The girth sprang free at last, and fell into the grass. He tugged at his saddle, pulling it from the back of the animal, but a skirt, stirrup, latigo and cinch were pinned under the dead gelding. He yanked again, working up a greasy sweat, and then summoned Hungry with a yell. Between them, they sawed and tugged the saddle loose, and moments later Abner had anchored it to Hungry's pony.

"I'll be back late this evening, Hungry. You watch them. I'm leaving everything. Soogans, slickers, chow. My Winchester, too. I'll fetch another horse and another steer if I can find one, and get back fast as I can."

"What if they get thirsty and go for water, Mister Dent?"

"Follow them." But he considered the matter further. The next water would be Beaver Creek, several miles east. "No, Hungry. Just get their direction fixed in your head and let them go. You'd best stay with your saddle and gear, right here."

There wasn't a tree or bush in sight. Nothing but foot-high wheatgrass and bluestem, leaping into the May skies. Nothing to protect Hungry from the sun, but this time of year the sun would not torment him.

Hungry grinned, his soft brown eyes saying he'd manage. Abner didn't feel much like smiling, but he nodded and turned the pony westward, kicking it into a reluctant mile-eating jog. At five miles an hour, minus a rest or two for the pony, he'd be back at the big white ranchhouse in three hours at the outside. Still daylight. In fact, he'd get back to his steers and Hungry again before darkness overtook him. He rode through drifting shoals of longhorns, mottled every earthen shade known to the eye, some solid-colored and some speckled, and some even brindled. His brand was scarce among them. By suppertime he'd raised his ranchhouse, a white apparition on the western horizon, just across the Judith River.

As he splashed across, he saw her on the veranda in that pink calico she'd just gotten, her jet hair loose over her shoulders. She saw him at the same moment and leapt upward oddly as he kicked the pony up the bank and onto the trail to his yard. Then he saw someone else, a large man, sitting up alertly on the white wicker. Lacy. Dixie Lacy on his veranda. It startled him, but they seemed even more astonished to see him trot the pony toward them. Slowly Dixie Lacy unfolded from his squeaking chair and stood, poised catamount. One thing struck Abner at once: Lacy wasn't wearing his gunbelt with its bullet loops and heavy dark holster. He'd never seen Dixie Lacy unarmed before.

The man had been sipping amber spirits of some sort, and slowly he set the tumbler on the veranda rail, as if he needed both his hands for whatever would come. Eve gaped uneasily. The whole tableau made Abner feel bad somehow, though he could see nothing much wrong with it. Neighbors visited. In that lonesome land, any visit would be welcome.

"You!" exclaimed Eve.

"Eve? We've got company?"

She looked flustered, but gradually she composed herself and plucked at her hair. Abner slid off the pony, feeling something dark crab at him, feeling some menace rise from the mocking face of this neighbor he scarcely knew or saw, this man who was the subject of dark whispers and angry suspicions. Lacy watched alertly.

"Didn't expect you," said Lacy. "You got trouble or something?" He studied Abner, his clothes, his belt, looking for what was not there.

41

"You didn't expect me?" Abner muttered.

Eve stared at Lacy, caution pinning her expression.

"Thought I'd pay a visit to the little lady whilst you delivered yoah steers to the butcher," Lacy continued.

"Oh, Abner, he just stopped a minute ago and I mentioned you were gone . . ."

Dixie Lacy, sniffing around his wife. Abner didn't like it one bit. Dixie Lacy didn't know what was his and what wasn't. Or maybe he did.

"Been more than a minute, Eve. We've been whooping plumb through the afternoon." Lacy seemed to be enjoying himself hugely. "What brings you back to the white house, the palace, the heart of the empire, Dent?"

"What brings you here, Lacy?"

"I'm an opportunity man. If I can't find no opportunity for me to turn to my use, I just invent it."

"So it seems. You're not welcome here, Lacy. You're especially not welcome when I'm gone, but you're not welcome anytime." Abner surprised himself by saying that. He wondered what he might have said if Lacy had been armed.

Lacy laughed easily. "Hard to pass by a pretty thing in white setting on her veranda."

"Pink," said Eve.

"White earlier. She wears white real saucy, Dent."

"Pink," Eve insisted.

"Well get on your horse now and leave. There are things a man does, and things a man doesn't do, and you've — where's your horse, Lacy?"

"In the barn. I gave him a bait of oats." Lacy's eyes danced again, some mad joy streaming from them.

"I have hitching posts here," Abner said, feeling more and more irritable.

"How come you to be here unexpected?" Lacy asked, as if nothing else mattered.

"I lost a horse." Abner felt like saying no more. And he felt like booting this uninvited lion off his place. He led his pony to the pens, trying to make sense of it, trying to deal with jabbing suspicions that rose up in him like lava. But he wrestled them down. They were simply sitting outside having something liquid. He couldn't fault Lacy for that, or Eve either. But that didn't console him any. He damned well didn't want that hulking bandit — no, that wasn't proper. No one had anything definite against Lacy tomcatting around this place.

He found Lacy's stallion in the barn aisle, saddled, loose-cinched, munching from a feedbag. Light blistered through the rear door, whiting the aisle. He never used the rear door. Beyond, the rear pen lay blue-shadowed in the low sun, its pasture gate wide open. Irritably, Abner stalked out to the pen, swung the creaking gate shut, and then closed the rear door. Why couldn't visitors leave things as they found them?

He unsaddled Hungry's pony and put it in the front corral where it would find a hay rick and river water. He was stripped of horses, like everything else on the place, but he had Eve's two blooded Morgans she'd begged him for and then never rode. They'd be rank, and knew nothing about cutting cattle or herding, but that was his only choice. He brushed and saddled one and haltered the other, aware that Lacy lounged behind him, watching.

"Ladies' mares," said Lacy.

"Your horse is in the aisle waiting for you."

"Thanks for the oats, Dent."

Abner said nothing, and led the Morgans toward the veranda where Eve sat bolt upright, a slender woman surrounded by pink skirts.

"Those are my horses!"

"I need them." He tied them to the hitching posts and mounted the veranda steps.

"Where are you going?"

"I want my belt and Remington." He kept

the sidearm in his bedroom and he intended to have it on when he expelled unsavory guests or dealt with predators out on the high grasses of the Judith.

"I'll get it!" she cried, exploding to life so fast it astonished him. "Just wait. I'll do it." She raced inside and up the stairs, taking them like a girl, while he gaped. He stared at the porch, at two cigar butts, a half-empty bottle of Crab Orchard Whiskey, and then at his dining table, obliquely visible inside, with dirty dishes scattered over it. Eve swept down the stairs, his worn brown belt and holster banging against her frothy pink skirts, and handed it to him.

"Here! Now you've got it." Her gaze seemed expectant.

He swung it around his waist and buckled it, feeling a weight on his hip heavier than he ever wanted to bear. Most cowboys and cattlemen hated that weight, the burden of the least and most valuable tool on a ranch.

Behind him Lacy grinned, sitting his sleek blood bay.

Abner turned to him. "You'll be leaving now. You should know better than to visit when — you should know better."

Lacy grinned and tipped his white sombrero. The blood horse quartered and danced, and then jogged toward the Judith.

"Eve — you shouldn't let a man like that —" His words faded. She was engrossed in Lacy's passage. Something crawled in Abner's stomach. He mounted the mare and swung away, suddenly puzzled by Eve's strange dance up the stairs to fetch his gun. Had she feared Lacy so much? Did she want Abner armed and ready for trouble with the man? It made no sense to Abner, and he didn't want to think about it.

Eve waited for Dixie on the shadowed veranda, not sure she wanted him to come back. An apricot dusk settled over the basin, turning grasses orange and mountains tangerine. Abner had been gone two hours, but Dixie was biding his time. They still had two days to enjoy each other, she thought. She wondered crossly whether Dixie would return at all. It'd be unlike him to let a brush with Abner stop him.

That puzzled her. Dixie had all but boasted of his conquest. She'd feared it would all spill out in the midst of Dixie's taunts. How strange that Abner hadn't picked up on it; acted as if he had been deaf to Dixie's hints. She settled sulkily into her wicker chair, an afghan wrapped around her against the high country chill, unable to plumb her own twisted emotions and needs. The whole thing annoyed, frightened, amused, and angered her. Too many feelings to cut through or make sense of. But mostly she felt angry. At Abner for coming, at Dixie for — she didn't know why he angered her, except that he always frightened her, made her belly squeamish with unnamed terrors.

They'd spent their lust upstairs through the late afternoon. Dixie was as frightening and uncontrolled upstairs as he was on the veranda, maybe more so because he mesmerized her, made their union a spasm of terror followed by liquid laughter. Then she'd cooked him supper — she hated that part of it — and they'd come out to the veranda for the cool, and were there when Abner returned unexpectedly. That had never happened, and she still felt that earthquake tremble her.

Dixie emerged like a stalking puma just when the night grew so thick she couldn't see more than fifty yards. He steered the blood bay quietly to the veranda and slid off silently.

"Dixie! You made me wait!"

He said nothing, but bounded up the steps, catlike, and into the darkened house. She heard nothing, but a minute later he reappeared, so silently she felt rather than heard his presence, and he sat down across from her, wearing the black gunbelt he'd left in the bedroom.

She sensed anger.

"Next time you take me to bed, I'll leave my gunbelt on," he muttered.

She giggled, a retort in mind, and then thought better of it.

"First time," he added.

She wasn't sure what he alluded to. But some sort of heat effused from that catamount of a man, and she froze in her seat. She felt funny quivers lace her loins.

"Yoah vamp," he said, deliberately.

"Dixie —"

"Cheating on your man."

Toying with her now, seeing what would drive her into a snit. Her pulse quickened.

"Cheap hurdygurdy woman. Look at this rotten house. Dent's a fool."

This wasn't toying, and she thought to spring at him and scratch that square, pocked, weathered face. Scrape his eyes out.

"Dixie, stop that."

"Lazy whining worthless thing."

Now her pulse raced. Something in this excited her. "Dixie, kiss me."

He grunted and pulled a cheroot from a vest pocket. The scratch of his match yellowed the night, revealing crazy eyes that sent chills racing through her. The match blued out and he studied the night, listening to its rhythms. The bay at the hitching post lifted its head.

48

"You bleed the man white, make him build this dump, make him buy you blooded horses, make him pay for a hundred dresses and shoes and crap, make him wash his dishes and cook his chow and feed the hens and wash the windows. Yoah some Delilah."

"He promised me help."

"Yoah too lazy to enjoy what you got."

Some wild thing stirred her body. "Let's have fun, Dixie," she replied huskily. She'd never been with a man she could control less.

He beamed suddenly, his face showing orange amusement as he sucked his cheroot. "I'm going to reform you," he said. "Yoah going to enjoy all that you got."

The cheroot sailed out into the yard, spinning sparks and then glowing on the ground like a luminescent slug.

He rose swiftly, and pulled her out of her chair, his grasp incalculably strong and frightening. He led her to the parlor and lit every coal oil lamp in it, the four in the chandelier, and three others on sidetables.

"Clean it."

"Clean it?"

"Get them sheets off the furniture and keep them off. Heat scrubbin' water. Get the mop and broom. Get the furniture wax. Get the window washin' rags. You sunk a man getting this stuff and this house, and now you'll enjoy it."

She gaped at him, rage building, and then settled it down in her throat. "Let's go sit on the divan," she said huskily.

"Get to work or I'll pain you good."

"I won't. I've never had to do that in my life and I won't start now."

He slapped her so hard the crack of it exploded in her face, and she spun to the floor. She sat there, dumbfounded. Dixie meant it. What had come over him? She had to stop it.

"Get busy," he said, drawing his boot back to smack her.

"Dixie! You can't —"

She felt the jolt thump her ribs, stinging outward like a wave, knowing she'd be marked there for days.

She giggled, feeling the terror of it, and stood up slowly. He watched, cat-eyed, while she tugged dusty sheets from the horsehair sofa and chairs, watched while she reluctantly fetched a broom and water and mop and soap and began to work, getting grime on her pink skirts.

She featherdusted thick silt off tables and lamps, broomed dustballs from corners, swept the carpets until she thought the roses in them would come off, too, washed the greasy film off the wavery glass of the windows, pulled the antimacassars and doilies off the furniture and beat the dust from them, wiped grime from gilt-framed paintings, and all the while he stood in the middle, watching her like the big cat he was.

"Let's go have fun now, Dixie," she said provocatively, playing with bodice hooks.

For an answer he dragged her to the dining room and pointed, and suddenly she knew. Before the night ended, he'd make her do every room, even the summer kitchen and pantry. Sullenly, she cleared dirty dishes, started water heating in the stove reservoir, began dealing with a grease-coated gummy kitchen, and all the while he sat watching her, puffing cheroots.

By midnight weariness stabbed her, and every unused muscle in her howled, but whenever she slowed he reacted viciously, the back of his hand driving her to work again. He never even let her get her breath, except once when she defiantly slipped into the water closet and hid there as long as she dared — indeed, until she heard his footfall.

"Why, Dixie?" she asked once.

"Lazy bedbug."

"Let me go. I need coffee. I need rest. I'll — do the rest tomorrow."

He looked amused. "Dent didn't know how to treat you."

"And you do," she flared. "Well this is my house. You can just leave now."

He laughed softly.

She felt too scared for tears, and as she worked under his watchful eye she began to get another idea: the derringer she'd kept on hand when she'd been a dancehall girl. She'd needed it several times to control big galoots who'd followed her home after the hall closed. She had a dandy that used brass cartridges rather than powder and ball. Up in her room. She'd go there and get it and make him leave, and if he didn't, she'd — shoot him.

She finished the dining room and kitchen, scouring bitterly through years of neglect, all the while daring herself to do it, get the deadly little weapon, point it at that cat watching her and pull the trigger. She ached and he watched unblinking.

She supposed it was three when she nerved herself to try it, and when she did, he seemed to know. He turned down wicks and padded upstairs beside her, grinning crazily.

"Now you'll get your wifely reward," he said.

Chapter Four

Abner seethed as he rode through the long spring dusk. Dixie Lacy on his porch. At his table. Sniffing around Eve while he was away. Mocking him, daring Abner to do something about it. Dixie Lacy, who had some sort of camp far up the Judith River, in the mountains, guarded by hard men who formed an impenetrable wall, turning away anyone who strayed into that country.

They all suspected Lacy of stealing cattle, but no one had proved it. Someone was stealing. The tallies always ended up short of what they should be. Calves vanished before they could be branded at the communal roundup. And oddest of all, cattle were showing up with blotched brands and altered earmarks, making them ownerless. There were maybe a hundred of them running the range now, beeves that no one could claim and sell. But their numbers weren't large enough to excite the basin ranchers into concerted action.

Dixie Lacy. Abner knew the type and despised it. Lacy had been one of the multitudes uprooted by the war. But that was long ago. Most Texans had rebuilt their lives, as Abner had done, but some, like Lacy, lived adrift and would die adrift, cynical, anchored only by the existence of prey. The building instinct, that thing that led a man to create a farm or a ranch, to sweat and save and scrape by, to defer to tomorrow, and let his herd multiply — that instinct had died in people like Lacy, murdered by the war and after it the flood of Yankee carpetbaggers who took whatever hadn't been destroyed by a ruined economy. Abner was sure that Lacy fit that mold, along with the men he had gathered around him.

And yet it was all speculation. No one in the Judith knew anything concrete about Lacy, other than what Lacy himself let be known in Maiden saloons and occasional encounters. All anyone really knew was that the Little Belt mountains around the Judith River drainage were effectively sealed off by silent men who didn't act like cowboys; and that Lacy never let his beeves run in the basin or bothered to come to the communal round-ups. In Maiden he was a popular visitor, spending generously, making bar friends easily, quick with jokes, and bubbling with humor. But the town shied away from the vacant-eyed men who came with him.

Eve. What was she doing, entertaining Lacy? Maybe she didn't have a choice, Abner thought. Lacy would get whatever he wanted.

The thought troubled him. Maybe Eve enjoyed the company. That thought pained Abner, too. Maybe — Abner didn't want to think about it. He had little hope of making a good marriage now. If only she'd take hold . . . If only she could plunge into wifehood the way she plunged into — the dancing at the hurdygurdy. Lacy. Did she . . . He wouldn't think about it. Maybe Lacy should take her. They were two of a kind, predators feasting on those who worked and saved and built.

He felt a moment's pang, a welling thrust-back hurt that bled through him from a thousand old wounds that Eve had cut and poked in him until he wondered why he just didn't send her packing, and start over before his bitterly won little outfit collapsed.

The Morgan mare felt fat between his legs and jogged eagerly eastward, followed by the other Morgan which jogged at the same pace and didn't need to be dragged. A good breed, he thought. Not much used for ranchwork, but he thought that would change. Too expensive, but maybe just right for working cattle. These would be almost useless if it came to cutting out beeves, but he and Hungry could herd with them, drive the nine steers to market well enough.

Daylight folded into a thin blue line at his back, and then faded altogether, and he found himself in a moonless void, with only low stars perched on the high-country air to steer him. He rode east, feeling the magic of a surefooted horse in pitch dark. He'd ridden in darkness often on the cattle drives up from Texas. Some horses had night-sense, some didn't. This one did, and he experienced a floating sensation, scarcely broken by the rhythm of the animal beneath him. Some horses got spooky at night, shying from every coyote bark and breeze-waved branch. Others exploded at lightning, or stopped and quivered at imagined terrors. But not this good mare. He steered lightly, hoping to wind up at the place he'd abandoned Hungry, and wondering if they'd connect in the indigo dark.

The grasslands had a sameness to them, and Abner steered his horse by dead reckoning rather than any landmark. It'd be hard enough to find Hungry by day. At night it'd be sheer luck. But eventually he'd hit Beaver Creek, and there he could wait for dawn, find his beeves and backtrack to Hungry's camp. All along, the thought of Eve and Lacy nagged at him like a wasp-bite that needed scratching. One way or another he'd have to resolve it. And it might kill him. He needed facts and he needed to act. He couldn't escape it. Not for Eve's sake, but his own. He didn't want to think about it, but his mind still worried it around, and he could hardly steer his thoughts away.

Some while later he sensed he was in the country where he'd left Hungry, and he steered his horse to the top of a swell to look around. He'd acquired some night vision now, and a sky alive with stars gave him some penetration. Off to the east, the black bulk of the Judith Mountains loomed, radiating pine scents like a giant sachet, and far to the south, the Snowies. He saw no fire, but didn't expect any. Hungry would be miles from firewood.

"Hungry!" he yelled, cupping his hands into a megaphone.

The night answered.

He tried a few more times, and then reined the mare toward the creek, knowing he would pass Hungry by. But then, after half a mile of travel, he heard a chant on the air and turned toward it.

"Mister Dent," it said, and a minute later Abner found his young hand.

"Didn't know as I'd find you, Hungry. Are the beeves —"

"They drifted to water, just like you thought, Mister Dent. I followed a mile and then came back here to wait."

The creek, then. "All right, Hungry. I'm glad all's well. We'll saddle up and load the gear and ride to the creek and spend the night there. The beeves should be around in the morning."

In less than an hour they unrolled their soogans on a grassy bench above the creek. A few hours later, feeling half-rested in a frosty dawn, they wiped heavy dew off their centerfire rigs and hunted their stock, which they found only half a mile away in a shallow coulee. Abner paused long enough to mash some roasted Arbuckle's beans with the butt of his revolver and boil some coffee, and then they were off. He intended to make Maiden that night, pushing the beeves almost thirty miles to do it. But he wanted to get home — if he could call that white house home — and try to deal with the thing that was tearing him to shreds.

"Not even breakfast?" asked Hungry.

"We'll feed tonight. Some all-night chow places for late-shift miners up there."

"You in a rush all the sudden?"

"Yes," Abner replied tartly.

The lad caught the tone. "I rightly'd be mad too, after getting that bull took."

Abner didn't reply. Let Hungry think what he would.

"That was something, Mister Trump taking your bull like that — and fessing up that they all use your bulls instead of keeping their own around. You been being took."

"Get your roll tied down and line out those steers."

Hungry stared. "Don't know what's in your craw," he muttered. "Starving me, too."

Abner pushed the silent beeves into a trot and kept them at it ruthlessly, knowing it'd run off good flesh. But this time by God he'd do the trip in two legs rather than three and get back and by God ask Eve some questions and by God maybe ride into that nest of toughs up in the Belts and have it out.

"Zimmerman ain't gonna like getting a sweated-up bunch," Hungry muttered, as they pushed the unhappy animals through chill air, swinging northward a bit toward the foothills of the Moccasins to strike Warm Spring Creek and the trail into the mountains. Often they stopped at Reed's Fort and the little log sprawl of Lewistown for a break and gossip, but this time Abner cut that corner and jammed his steers as fast as they'd walk.

If Lacy was hanging around his place, he'd by God surprise him again. Surprise them, he corrected himself. By noon he and Hungry had hit the Warm Spring and turned up the wagon road beside it. He rested the stock an hour later, letting Hungry nap for a few minutes under a jackpine on an emerald slope. A Diamond R freight outfit out of Fort Benton, twenty mules on a jerkline, pulling a three-hitch load, lumbered by as they dozed.

"Beef for them miners," said a teamster.

"For Zimmerman's shop," Abner replied.

"I could eat one of them critters whole," said the teamster, pausing as the train rolled by. "We got tomatoes in airtights, lots of stuff, off Cow Island."

Abner watched them go, smelling the acrid odor of the sweated mules. Maiden was quite a camp now, with twelve hundred people, some said. That many people kept the freighters plenty busy, and added to the prosperity of the big shipping outfits headquartered at Fort Benton, the head of Missouri River navigation, although more and more freight was coming up from the Northern Pacific tracks to the south.

He pushed his beeves ruthlessly through the cool afternoon, along the creek bottom which ran between dark slopes into a narrowing gorge. His stomach rattled, and Hungry stared angrily at him, but he didn't relent. The bawling, footsore cattle rebelled, halted to drink at every opportunity, and forced Abner to slow the pace. He could go only as fast as the laggards would move.

Late in the afternoon they entered the mining district, and spotted tailings and shacks and tan gloryholes pimpling the hillsides. Everywhere, the ponderosa had been hacked away to feed fires, supply boards, and muscle up steam at the mines and mills above. The naked bones of the Judith Mountains jabbed starkly above them. And still Abner pressed on, ignoring the plaintive bawling and the slobbering of weary steers. Woodsmoke hung in the narrow gulches and side-canyons, blueing the air. They passed miners on the road, men in scuffed hightops trudging from town to their claims. These were hardrock men, not placer miners, and many of them worked for someone else. And they all ate beef, Abner thought. His ten steers a month supplied only one of three butcher shops, and some of the restaurant-operators bought and slaughtered beeves as well.

At last, as lavender dusk settled, and purple shadows crossed the bottoms while the peaks still blazed orange, they rounded the last bend into Maiden, which lay wedged in a narrow valley dominated relentlessly by naked gray slopes, once verdant with trees. It always amazed him that so many men — and a few women — could cram themselves into so small a flat. Two streets, Main and Montana, traversed either side of the creek, and were sectioned by several short cross streets with small log cabins lining them. Above, the thundering Maginnis Mill dominated the head of the gulch like a giant cathedral. There, the ore-rich quartz was stamped into bits, concentrated, roasted, and treated with dilute sodium cyanide, which resulted in a precipitate of silver and gold and lead. Much of the highgrade ore from the Maginnis Mine just above, and the Spotted Horse, War Eagle, Black Bull, Alpine, and Collar mines nearby, was treated there.

Zimmerman's butcher shop lay at the lower end of Main, saving Abner the ordeal of driving range cattle through town and past the numerous saloons above. The narrow log building, weathered gray by alpine moisture and sun, hulked dark as Abner expected, but the corrals at the rear would not be chained, he thought. He and Hungry drove the muttering beeves in, bucketed water up from the creek into a trough, and stared at the drooping longhorns, which slumped wearily into the muck.

"I'll have to find Zimmerman," he said. "Here — go eat."

He pulled a silver dollar, his only cash, from his britches and gave it to the starved lad. Hungry took it eagerly. Abner knew where to find him: only one hash house in town served breeds, Allen's, over next to the hurdy-gurdy joints. Later, Abner would take Hungry to one of the saloons for a beer or two. Hungry would have no trouble there as long as Abner stayed with him.

His bones ached. Not a lifetime in the saddle saved him from that after a hard drive. He creaked up into his battered hull again and steered uptown, and then right on an obscure cross street whose name he'd never learned, and stopped at Zimmerman's white frame cottage. The man was clearly one of substance in Maiden. A lamp glowed faintly within, which gladdened Abner. Most men didn't waste precious lamp oil by staying up long after dark.

"It's you," said the massive butcher.

Zimmerman stood in the door in a tattered robe and slippers, holding his kerosene lamp.

"I've the beeves."

"Awful damned late. You could deliver during business hours."

"We could do it in the morning, Conrad."

"No. I'm plumb out, except for some elk a hunter brought in. I'll slaughter one right now and hang it. Save work in the morning. Let me throw some duds on and I'll be along. I want to talk with you anyway, Dent."

"I could eat while you dress. I'd need four bits."

"Naw, I'll be along, dammit."

Abner nodded, turned back to his tired mare, and slid into the hard saddle again. Her sweat had dried into a white rime over her withers and around the blanket. He turned her downhill toward Main, weary but excited. Maiden always did that to him, lifted him up with its raw vitality. Lamplight glowed orangely from small windows of wavery bubbled glass, casting faint light onto the street. Night-chill rolled down the slopes, bringing on it the aching scent of the high country, pine and juniper and sagebrush. He enjoyed the place, and had he been someone else, instead of a cowboy bred to the range, he might have prospered here.

Someone had written a ditty about Maiden a couple of years earlier, one he'd memorized. It amused him to recite it as he walked the mare down to the shop:

Oh, Maiden, beautifully fair,
　　Couched between those mountain hollows,
Charming thy form and golden hair
　　And eyes bright as silver dollars.
Maiden of wealth on paper told,
　　Breast of pearls ribbed with silver,
Awaiting ready to unfold
　　And give up her rarest treasure.

Maiden whom many anxiously sought,
　　Fondly courted and strived to woo;
Who to empty words heeded not,
　　Smiled when heartbroken they withdrew.

That was it about mining camps, he thought. They smiled when the heartbroken withdrew. That had appeared in the Rocky Mountain Husbandman, and whoever wrote it had a wise eye.

It seemed only a minute before Conrad Zimmerman loomed through the dusk at the corral, and they walked in. The butcher lit a lamp and scowled.

"I count nine. Where's the tenth? And these have been pushed. You know what that does to beef."

"I started with ten — ran into some trouble," Abner replied dourly.

"That don't help me none. Sweated up animals, too. Look at them."

Zimmerman muttered, wandered through the steers, examining each. "Good flesh," he said at last. "Come inside. I have to talk with you, Dent."

The butcher unlocked a padlock and steered Abner inside, where the rank smell of an abattoir smacked him. The bobbing beams of the lamp revealed almost nothing hanging except an elk quarter. Zimmerman pushed ahead to his begrimed office, where the smell abated slightly. He set the lamp down on his raw plank desk and motioned Abner to sit on the bench opposite.

"Nine beeves ain't enough. Ten beeves ain't enough."

"That's all I can average. I could bring more one time, less another time."

"It ain't enough. I get a few from other outfits — mostly from Granville Stuart over on the other side. The DHS outfit. But they don't like to drive three-four-five animals up here — takes two men two days. I got more market, much more market. I keep running out by the third week of the month, even when I scrounge the other beeves. We got twelve hundred people now. I'm thinking maybe to get twenty in, maybe twenty-five, one a day except Sundays. I could sell it all and not piss around with deer meat."

"I could maybe drive up a few for my neighbors — they're always growling at me anyway and if they added part of it —"

"Dent. No. This is the last from you. I talked with Stuart and they'll bring twenty-five and make two trips, every two weeks, so I don't have to buy so much hay and feed out so much. They'll bring up the prairie hay, too, few extra dollars, wagonload each trip. Sorry, Dent. I like you and all, but you're too small. Your outfit can't fill my needs."

Abner sat numbly, listening to his doom. "Mister Zimmerman, I can get the beeves. I'll put together some Judith ranchers and we'll pool and I'll get these up — cheaper; I'll make sure it's cheaper — more profit for you . . ."

Zimmerman said nothing.

"I'll be back with something, back with a good offer," Abner said.

The butcher sighed. "It's done, Dent. You did the best you could, only we're growing here, and the DHS is a sight closer and all. Glad I done business with you. Here — I'll get these paid for. Beef's still four dollars and forty a hunnert on the Chicago market, and I'm still paying thirty a head if they arrive in good shape, and these didn't — but, hell, I'll give twenty-nine. Times nine . . ." He worked the figures with a greasy pencil on brown butcher paper. "Two hunnert and sixty-one. Agreed?"

Abner nodded.

The butcher turned to an iron strongbox bolted to the puncheon floor and inserted a key as long and mean as a green river knife. The box clanged. He licked his thick thumb and began counting off greenbacks.

"Prefer specie," Abner said.

"Take what circulates here. You want it in notes or you want a draft on the Miner's Bank?"

"Notes. I'll be back in the morning. I still want Francis Matz to give me an inspection letter."

"Your neighbors still don't trust you?"

"They trust me. They're just looking for excuses."

Zimmerman slammed the box shut and handed the notes to Abner. He whetted a throat-cutter and trudged into the rear corral while Abner stuffed the cash into a moneybelt he wore on these trips. He saved out some notes, and hunted for Hungry.

Doomed, he thought. No markets close at hand. Ship east now twice a year and scrimp in between. Doomed because of that big house that cost him over half a herd; doomed because Eve devoured his increase. Without Eve, he'd have seventeen hundred beeves and could have supplied twenty-five a month easily.

He stepped into a bitter night, not knowing any kind way to lay off Hungry.

Chapter Five

Abner found Hungry nursing coffee at Allen's Eats, the log joint sandwiched between Maiden's two hurdygurdies. Abner slid onto the bench opposite, and waited for Allen, the quaking albino who would soon appear with the house's four-bit repast, a plate of boiled potatoes, cabbage, and whatever meat the man could lay in, also boiled gray. Abner thought some of it might be wolf or dog. There were no choices other than salt and pepper.

Abner didn't know how to do it; didn't know what to say, so he stared quietly, trying out words.

"You mad at me?" Hungry asked.

"No. I got bad news. Zimmerman's through with me. I couldn't deliver enough beef and now he's got the DHS. Over at Gilt Edge."

"You're mad at me."

"No I'm not."

"I yam twenty a month you don' got."

Hungry was guessing right, Abner thought. Allen appeared and trembled a battered white plate down. Its boiled-white contents didn't smell so bad at all after a hard day's drive. Allen's silverware amounted to one large spoon, but nothing else was needed to down the mound.

Abner sighed, studied the place — he never drew cash from his poke or belt in the presence of others — and pulled out some greenbacks. He gave Hungry his month's pay, paused in anguish, and added another ten dollars.

"What's the extra for?"

"Help tide you over till you get something."

"I can get work."

"Take it."

Hungry pocketed the money in his britches. "You mind if I ride back with you in the morning? I got a few things there."

"I expected you to."

"Mind if I buy the lineback dun with the ten?"

"Take him. Take the old hull. You'll need the pony and the hull to get work on the ranches. I got the Morgans and I'm going to work them both."

"Thanks, Mister Dent."

"It's not half what I wish I could do. You're a good man, Hungry, worked hard, learned fast, coming good."

"You think the other outfits will take me?"

"Why shouldn't they?"

Hungry lowered his brown eyes and said nothing.

"They need good men. Never enough men out here."

"I'll see," said Hungry. "I'll see."

"Hungry — I'm sorry."

Hungry smiled. Abner spooned up the boiled stuff, feeling it fill the hollow in his gut. The sound of a scraping violin drifted in from one of the hurdygurdies. The other had an out-of-tune piano that got hammered all night by a wire-haired musician, Professor Bardenwerper. Sometimes the violin and piano clashed, sending wolf-sounds shivering through the walls.

Abner had found Eve at The Star, the one to the east with the piano, which was a nickel a dance higher than the Maiden Hall, to the west, perhaps because the girls were slightly younger and prettier. He'd ticketed her up every time he came to Maiden, spent an extravagant five dollars some evenings just to monopolize her and keep the other dudes out of her arms. She'd tried to peddle booze, but learned soon enough he hardly drank. Actually, he didn't drink so he could invest every dime in her. At two-bits a whirl — of which she got twelve and a half cents — an evening ate up five dollars fast.

She hadn't minded his plainness; he could tell that. He liked whirling the girl with the flying jet hair round and round, until they seemed like one person and all awkwardness vanished. That had been a good sign, that they

71

had become a unity with themselves and the rattling piano. So he had talked. Told her about his place, his growing herd, his future. She'd listened, weighing him. He didn't know much about her because she rarely replied, and never about herself. But she'd smiled a lot and listened and complimented him, and took his money, and it all seemed grand. Eve Bills, she finally had told him. Until then, she'd used her dancehall name, Maiden Mary.

Now Abner listened quietly, hearing the same tunes, the same rattling piano, the same waltzes and polkas and schottisches, the same thunder of miners' brogans. Back then he'd come to dance with Maiden Mary whenever he could, braving forty miles of winter and summer and slopes and rivers to do it. Every couple of weeks for five months, he'd come to whirl Maiden Mary. She had smiled, and begun to talk about herself a bit; about her weariness, sore feet, ripped dresses. The time she had a phrenologist read her head and tell her she'd be a perfect little wife. Her dreams of a happier life. Of the men and the propositions she'd turned down. She'd asked him for new dancing slippers — told him he'd worn out three pairs — and he'd bought them. He'd never proposed, really; just talked more and more about teaming up. He'd found out good things: she never took men to her rooms.

She could read and do figures. Her daddy had been a townlot seller.

And after a couple of months, she'd danced closer and closer in his arms, and had started talking about a house — a big house with lots of nice things in it. He'd felt her hard animal heat, thought it felt like love, and had agreed, scarcely thinking about anything but the time when he could rescue her from her miserable life. He could barely remember whatall he'd promised, but it all shone bright, like moonlight . . .

"Let's have a goodbye beer, Mister Dent."

"Okay, fine, on me, Hungry."

They burst into a cool night, leaving the smell of boiled cabbage and unnameable odors behind. Muted music and weary lamplight crisscrossed the rutted road, making soft the sights and sounds of Maiden. The only problem with saloons was picking one. Six lay at hand, mostly empty until a shift ended, and then swollen with miners for an hour or two. Some never closed. But Abner steered them toward The Highgrade, a place where they'd never had trouble, and Hungry seemed welcome.

It was a log place, carelessly chinked so air boiled through it. Sullivan, the keep, stuffed a mix of mud and grass into the cracks in the winter, and then fired up the potbelly,

73

but the rest of the year one could well wear a jacket in the grogshop. Sullivan saved on lamp oil, too, and kept only one lit, and that on the split-log backbar next to his cashbox. But it didn't matter. Men drank to the sound of voices, not the sight of faces. And The Highgrade always served the breed, Hungry.

Sullivan drew two mugs the color and taste of varnish, and Abner threw down some wooden nickels, Allen's change. The coin of the realm hadn't reached Maiden, so the bank had carved and stamped its own. Both mugs ran to foam, which was Sullivan's way of high-grading his barrels, which came all the way from Fort Benton and God knows where else. Abner sipped, and thought maybe a dog had gotten there first.

"I yam sorry, Mister Dent."

"Things might have been different . . ."

"I know. It's not your fault."

Eve's, actually. That hung there starkly, even if they delicately avoided it. "You got plans, Hungry?"

The boy shrugged.

"I'm leaving early. No need to get Francis Matz to look at the stuff this time. Trump and his men saw every animal. And I'm done here now. No more trips."

"Maybe you should anyway," Hungry said, eyes averted.

"Maybe you're right, Hungry. You read people well."

"I got to," he replied, his lips puckering at the taste of the swill.

The boy knew the realities. His father, Pierre Billedeaux, had died of typhoid. His mother lived with the Crees in Canada.

"Have another. We'll celebrate the beginning of nothing tonight."

Hungry did. They guzzled six mugs of the fetid brew silently and solemnly, until at last Abner felt compelled to impart the world's wisdom to Hungry.

"Young man," he said, wanting to convey something important. "I don't understand women. No man can. My advice to you is, don't try."

Hungry snickered. That seemed odd to Abner. The polite young métis had never snickered before.

"You should take me seriously," Abner said.

Hungry sipped and laughed, a grin splitting his face in two.

"You're fired, Hungry," Abner muttered, getting mad.

Hungry chortled. "You sure don' understand her."

"I didn't ask your advice!"

Abner felt huffy and drained the last of his

varnish. He slapped the mug down on the plank and stood, waiting for that villainous breed to follow. Out on the dark street, Hungry howled like a lobo wolf, and Abner eyed him narrowly, and couldn't decide whether to suffer a fit of laughing or hold it all in and stay mad.

In the morning Abner paid some of the rankest bills at the mercantiles, kept a hundred in cash, and hunted down Francis Matz after all, not trusting Trump one bit.

He nabbed Francis gumming steak and eggs at Ambassador Estleman's Chow Palace.

"You always fetch me in the middle of a sitting," the town marshal muttered, dabbing at his lips with his sleeve. "You ought to bring me a quarter of beef some time."

But he followed Abner out, and wandered through the pen, muttering. A moment later, in Zimmerman's office, he scratched a letter on butcher paper, saying he'd inspected the brands of eight steers and one hide, all Bar D.

"Thanks, Francis," Abner said.

"I don't get paid enough," the marshal replied. "Not like you rich cattlemen."

After that Abner and Hungry rode west, down the long twisting canyon, under an overcast which would go away when they hit the Judith Basin. The mountains made their own weather, Abner thought.

"You mind if I stay on?" Hungry asked.

"In the cabin? Stay as long as you want. Maybe I can feed you."

"I mean keep on working."

"I can't pay you and I'm no slaver, Hungry."

"I'll work. Maybe you can pay me when you ship your steers in the fall."

"I may not have the place by then, Hungry. I've got — debts that can't wait."

"I'll work anyway."

"No. Hungry, you're risking too much. If creditors attach me, you'd be least and last on their list."

"Well, I could stay a month and work for the lineback dun and the old hull."

"You already have those — least I can do."

"I don' want to work for no others, Mister Dent."

The boy looked troubled, and Abner let it ride. He could sure use the labor.

She saw Abner ride in with Hungry a day early and was not glad. Only an hour earlier, Dixie had suddenly gotten restless and left. They'd been sitting on the veranda like a lord and lady when he began acting itchy, stood, and announced he would ride out. She'd begged him to stay. He'd said he would heed his sixth sense; he didn't want to face Abner. Not yet. Later. She'd called him a coward. He'd laughed and patted her behind and rode the blood bay up the river.

She frowned, watching Abner unsaddle from her station on the veranda, feeling faintly annoyed and superior. She had secrets he was too dense to figure out. Whenever she'd been with Dixie a while, she knew of manhood, and felt it as iron filings feel a magnet. Dixie made her vibrate, and made her heart leap in ways that were beyond Abner. She'd married a rube who didn't know how to treat a woman, and acted like she was stained glass. Dixie always hurt her a lot and was never polite, and love felt like going over a waterfall in a barrel.

It made her cross to think she was stuck with Abner. Well, she wouldn't be. Dixie would rescue her soon. He hadn't said it, but he would. They made a pair, she and Dixie. Not like her husband. Hungry was a boy, too. She didn't like Hungry. Too polite and shy. Why couldn't she have real men around her? Now she'd have to wait another endless month.

Out at the pens, they finished with the horses — her horses — and separated, Hungry to his old log cabin and Abner to the house, to her. She toyed with the idea of telling everything, a gigantic taunting confession, just to see his face.

"You're early," she said.

"I pushed hard. You can guess why."

She guessed Dixie, and smiled. "He's not here."

"I don't want him around here."

"He does what he chooses."

"Not anymore. That was my last trip. Zimmerman canceled."

It hit her. "You mean you won't be going —"

"I mean I'm going broke."

"You — won't be taking steers there? To Maiden? Not ever?"

"I couldn't supply enough." He looked like he wanted to say more, his gaze snapping and boring into her.

"If you ranched better you could —"

"Cut it out."

"You didn't even look for another butcher to deliver to."

She had him. He blinked and looked funny.

She pressed him. "You didn't look. You didn't try the restaurants. You didn't try."

She felt triumphant.

He muttered to himself. "I had things on my mind, reasons to get back."

"Now what?"

"Now we ship once a year in the fall, when

the rest do, after the fall roundup. Maybe a few in the spring. And I'll get less. Pay to drive beeves down to the rails at Big Timber because me and Hungry can't leave . . . The freight to Omaha takes away a lot. And we have to borrow in between. Pay interest."

"You better go back to Maiden and find a market."

"If there is any."

"I ruined my pink dress."

He stared, his lips compressed, choking back something. She wondered if she would ever see him roar instead of choking back. Dixie roared. She wished he'd do something, even hit her. How dull life was in the middle of the Judith.

He stared at her, and she felt his gaze running like fingers through her hair, touching her eyelids and strong-lined white face, and slide past her too tight gray bodice. He sighed and walked in, and she settled back, making the wicker squeak. Sometimes she had nothing to do but squeak the wicker.

"What's this?" he yelled from within. "Eve!"

She settled back. It would be funny.

She heard him creeping around in there, like some old coyote examining a fresh buffalo carcass that came down from heaven.

"Eve. Tell me about this."

She would. Not about Dixie making her do it, though. Not about Dixie hitting her, twisting an arm when she wouldn't. But about the rest. It'd be fun. She stood, feeling a surge of anticipation, and entered.

"This!" he said, waving wildly at the immaculate house, at a parlor with furniture uncovered and the rug brushed and floor polished and lamps cleaned and windows bright, and dustballs gone. At a kitchen that shone, scrubbed free of scum. At dishes shelved and pots on hooks and an empty zinc sink. At a kitchen floor that didn't stick to shoes, and kitchen windows one could see out of. And the water closet, the vitreous china bowls shining, the seat wiped clean, the rank odor gone, the floor gleaming.

"You did this?" he asked, his eyes wild with something she could only guess at. "Is it your time — you know — of month?"

"Why shouldn't I?"

He looked nonplussed. "I didn't expect — I didn't ever think — Eve. Eve . . . You — I'm glad you did."

"For you, Abner. You always wanted me to."

"For me? What? For me?"

"I thought it would be nice."

"It is nice. The nicest thing that's happened. Eve, this is a beginning, isn't it? A beginning of a home, of being together, working together, isn't it? Are you sure it's not your —"

She laughed. He rubbed a hand over a counter, touching its cleanness as if it were an infant's skin.

"I never had time," he muttered. "Say, are you expecting?"

He peered at her, assessing her. She met his gaze.

"I did it for you," she said, encouraging him.

His face turned grave, and a longing filled him, so strong in his eyes she wanted to look away. Love was terrible to behold. But she held his gaze.

He slid his arms around her gently and drew her into him, as if she were a porcelain doll, and she wished he'd do more.

He hugged her, groaning, hugged her with big work-hardened hands that swarmed tenderly up and down her back. He wrapped his whole large frame about her until she felt penned inside. He groaned and kissed her ear and neck and pushed her coal hair off her forehead to kiss there, too.

"Eve," he said, "I knew if I just waited, if I just waited, everything would turn out fine."

"Yes."

Something grave lit his lumpy face. He

tugged her toward the parlor and the horse-hair sofa where they'd never sat, and where she and Dixie had sat and doodled with each other a few hours earlier. Abner tugged her there and sat her down as gently as a minister presses baptismal water on the head of an infant.

He took her hand and held it, his eyes searching her, peering down into her, the spark in them glowing.

"Eve," he began in a grave sweet voice she'd never heard in him before. "This is the most important moment of our lives. This is the beginning of everything. Your work, this place, this making a home of a house — I can't tell you what it means."

She smiled, feeling his rough hands cup hers.

"Eve, I despaired. I didn't know if I could continue much longer. I was losing my courage, feeling burdens I couldn't bear anymore. I — feared we'd lose everything, and you wouldn't care if we did . . ."

She squeezed his hands, and encouraged him.

"Eve, I had this dream for so long. This place and you. The ranch, growing, solid as the earth under us, our cattle on distant fields, and always you at the center, here, making a home, starting a family."

She sighed, thinking of the pennyroyal she used. She'd learned about pennyroyal from the hurdygurdy girls who used it regularly. The ones who made extra money after the dancing. If you drank pennyroyal tea at a certain time, it would start the flow and there'd be no babies. She'd never wanted babies. Never. Abner never knew. Neither did Dixie know. They only knew she liked a strange herb tea she made by steeping the leaves without boiling them.

"Now our life's beginning. I almost lost my courage, and I got impatient. I'm sorry I got impatient, Eve. I always knew it'd work out, that you'd take hold and put your good roots down. I always knew. I love you. I'd forgotten how much."

"Kiss me."

"Now? But Hungry's waiting for supper."

"He can wait. And afterward, you can fix him something, can't you, Abner?"

Chapter Six

Relentless showers from gunmetal clouds harassed the spring roundup, slanting ice-water into them all, dousing branding fires, making newly castrated calves shiver and suckle their mothers. Heavy drafts lowering from the vaulting thunderclouds chilled the drovers and reps who'd gathered for the annual spring event, forcing them to break out slickers and woolies, and sleep under wagon boxes to keep the rain off. The Judith was unfenced and unsurveyed, and cattle from all seven ranches ran where they would, bred as they chose, and wandered in and out of the basin when the spirit moved them.

The drovers had started, as usual, at Leo Pelz's place on the north side of the basin, and worked clockwise, day by day, around the valley. Before each dawn they rode out into frigid blackness until they reached ridges, and then drove wild longhorns, as crafty as cougars, out of coulees and brush and bottoms of tiny creeks, back toward the day's camp. By the nooning they had the day's gather compressed into a bawling mass of angry beeves, as varicolored as Joseph's coat. Twice, sharp cracks of lightning had set them all running, an explosion of cattle in all directions that cost the drovers hours of labor not to mention injured horses and broken gear. Once, men and stock had been hammered viciously by hailstones the size of quarters. It had not been an easy gathering at all.

On the dryer days when things went well, they built several branding fires early in the afternoon, and set irons from the several ranches to glowing in them, plus some running irons for the use of the reps from the spreads to the east and south. The afternoons were filled with sweaty, stinking work as drovers lassoed calves, fought off their bellowing mothers, castrated the bull calves, notched ears, and jammed the red-hot irons into young hides, making living flesh sizzle and the air foul with smell of burnt hair and flesh. Some of the owners, like Abner Dent, slaved along-side the drovers in the brutal work, but others sat their horses or stood watching, keeping tally books. Dent, who could contribute only his own labor and Hungry's to the roundup, asked Ben Hruska to keep tally for him.

There were never enough men. Never enough to scour every coulee, peer under every juniper bush or box elder, drive every beeve in the country to the branding camp. Never enough to cook, fetch wood, keep irons hot, circle a bawling herd that could explode like a plugged cannon barrel at any moment, cut out pairs and then rope calves, noting the brand on the mother cow. Never enough to wrestle a bawling slippery calf to earth and pin him in his own green manure, cut him carefully, slice the proper earmarks, and then go for the next. To make matters more complex, there was a growing bunch of culls and shipping beeves that would be driven to the rails, and that herd had to be kept separate from the rest, though only two drovers could be spared to do it. Most shipping was done after the fall roundup, but money-starved ranchers always sent a few down the pike in the spring to tide them over. The reps from other ranches might have helped, but they were privileged characters whose task was to watch and make sure the stray pairs from their outfits were properly branded.

Marvin Trump watched the reps grimly, resenting their leisure while the rest of the shorthanded roundup made do and fought crises that would not have exploded upon them if they'd had a few more drovers. On this day the shipping herd had flown apart twice for no reason at all, other than some notions buried deep in the skulls of the longhorns. Trump thought maybe rattlers had done it, but he didn't know. And then the remuda had exploded, half-broke broncs snorting and bucking off toward the hills, shrieking and whinnying like scared children. And only one half-baked fifteen-year-old bucktoothed wrangler holding them. That took another hour and every man who could be yanked from anything else. Even the gimpy cook.

They worked down at the south end of the valley now, near Dent's homestead. In fact Trump could see it, a macabre white ghost two miles or so to the east. The palace that Dent built. Or that tramp of his. No one with more brains than an ant would have built that killer house, he thought. Not even patent land under it, just hazy squatter's rights. A rube trying to be a man, that was Abner Dent. And not succeeding. A peculiar irritation rose through Trump, and he recognized it and knew where it came from inside of himself. Long ago, Trump had been forced to learn about himself, and now he made do with the character he owned. He spat, and eyed Dent angrily. The fellow was at the branding fires, dirt-grimed from pinning down calves.

Dent was the trouble, he thought. He'd brought just himself and that useless breed boy instead of the five or six men he should have come with. The world was full of parasites, not contributing a fair share to the task at hand. Not that the situation would last much longer, he thought. Dent was finished. Still, it irked him that Dent wasn't holding up his end. Two more men on the shipping herd, and one more at the branding fires, and another wrangling the broncs, would have made all the difference.

They'd gotten even though, by God. Two years ago, before the spring roundup, Trump and a few of the ranahans who could be trusted to keep their yaps shut, had driven a score of Dent's paired up cows that had big bull-calves on them into a box canyon way over in the Highwoods. They'd put Dent's Bar D brand on the bullcalves, and cut Dent's ear-mark into their left ears, and hid them there through the roundup, releasing them when it was over. So Abner Dent had twenty more bulls than he supposed, and Trump and Pelz had carved more steers from their own bullcalves than usual. In fact, that year he and Pelz each had fifteen fewer bulls coming along — and fifteen more market steers. Last year they did it again. But the thought didn't amuse Trump.

They'd started that morning probing south into the foothills of the Little Belts, the mountains massed along the south flank of the basin. Most of that country lay angled, like tilted tables, with anonymous slopes of dense yellow pine where the beeves wouldn't go. But there were long grassy valleys piercing into the high country, and these had to be scoured for the critters. In particular, the Judith River and its bright tributaries offered water, lush grass, and a cooler climate than the basin, and the longhorns always headed into it. And so did certain humans, Trump thought dourly. No one really wanted to go in there, yet it had to be done. That morning, in the gloomy smoked light of wet-wood campfires, the basin's drovers had strapped on sidearms. Usually those who had them simply left them in their soogans and bedrolls because they were a nuisance and a weight on their hips. They'd still be a nuisance this morning, but a comfort, too.

They didn't talk about Dixie Lacy and those unblinking men he had around him, but Lacy was on their minds. No one had ever accused Lacy of stealing beeves, at least beyond an occasional butchered steer to feed on, but that didn't mean anything either. Anyone wandering up into that country would be chased out with bullets that came from nowhere and spanged up dirt inches from an invading horse and rider. So they'd all let their suspicions eat at them like maggots in a wound, afraid to tackle that problem head-on. Trump supposed that this roundup, and this tally, would force the issue. If enough beeves had vanished, they'd have to act.

Actually, they had acted: they'd alerted railroad dicks and responsible people at every shipping town along the rails. They'd described Dixie Lacy, described his men, set the thin corps of territorial lawmen looking for altered brands. But nothing had ever come of it. Not one stolen beeve had been traced to Dixie Lacy, and he remained a mystery to them all, living by no known means, showing up at Maiden now and then with plenty of cash in his jeans and a mocking humor that dared the world to do anything about it all. The new Montana Stockgrowers Association had drawn a line under Lacy's name and put him on their blacklist. And over in Helena, officials studied the brand books, looking for any mark claimed by Dixie Lacy, and finding none. That man Lacy was as slippery as a newborn calf, no doubt about it.

By the time dawn grayed the night, drovers had ridden deep into those mountains, far up the Judith drainage, the Ross Fork country, as well as Louse Creek and Sage Creek — and had come out with nothing. Not a beeve. They found fresh cowflops back in there, bedgrounds here and there, signs of grazing, but not an animal. And no sign of Dixie Lacy or his men. They finally turned around where the grass thinned into brown pine needles and the creeks rose out of rock, and walked their broncs out, feeling itchy-backed and imagining buckhorn gunsights following them out. But there'd been beeves out in the basin itself, and these few had been gathered at the branding camp. They'd be done with them by early afternoon.

So far, Trump's tally looked normal to him. But one never knew. He couldn't come to any conclusions until the end of the gather, when he could compare his gain against the fall tally. There'd been plenty of pairs around, including some cows with a blotched brand and altered earmarks, and a mysterious Lazy Questionmark brand recently burned into them. Whoever claimed that brand would be in for a hanging, he thought. Quite probably it would turn out to be some ranny on one of the ranches, trying to maverick a herd for himself.

He spotted old potbellied Hruska standing near the branding fires, two tally books in hand. The man's sunblasted face reminded him of an ancient buffalo. He peered at the angry mother cows and bleating offspring from rheumy eyes bleached of all their color by a life lived outside.

"How's your tally look, Ben?"

Hruska spat, snuff juice adding to the mud. "Can't say as yet. Don't see a thing wrong, but there's funny business. The count's about what I'd expect, except for all these blotched animals. Who the hell owns them? What do we do with the calves? Give them to the Association, like we're supposed to? We're about half done with this, and I got about a thousand steers and heifers showing, six hundred pairs, and my bulls. If it holds for the rest, I'm showing a good gain."

"So'm I. How about Dent?"

"Now that's a thing and a half. He's showing seventy-five, eighty animals, bulls, heifers and steers, and hardly no pairs. Maybe he's been selling off pairs without us knowing."

It puzzled Trump. "That all? You sure?"

"Sure as I'm chewing Dixie Plug."

"Does he know it?"

"Course he does. He checks my tally every night. He says maybe they all drifted west this time, and we'll get to them."

"He's not worrying? Acting like maybe he shipped some off?"

"Worrying plenty. Acting like he's got so much on his mind he don't hardly know what to do next."

"You mention rustling to him, maybe? Lacy?"

"I did. Last night. He stared at me, and stomped off, like I'd been a rattler biting him."

Trump grunted and watched a DHS rep put

a running iron brand on one of that outfit's strays, a scour-stained brindle, while the boys kept the furious cow at bay. After the round-up, the rep — this one was named Mert — would drive his strays back to his home range the other side of the Judiths, if he could manage them all alone.

"Ya blotched it, Mert. Maybe we should make supper with it," yelled a red-headed kid.

Mert smiled, and set the running iron back in the coals.

It had to be Dixie Lacy, Trump thought. Just had to be. He could almost crawl inside Lacy's mind and taste the thoughts in it. Lacy was picking off the weakest, deliberately picking off Abner Dent, swallowing the mouse. Plucking Dent's cattle out of the basin and selling them somewhere, maybe branding the calves with some unregistered mark and peddling the cows to the Injuns — damned Blackfeet were half starved and the Crows not much better. Nightriding the cows out for whatever price he could get — Injuns were damned poor these days, and had nothing but a few skins or half-broke mustangs to trade with. Hiding calves up there somewhere, up in those dull empty mountains, so featureless they grew tiresome to the eye and confused travelers. If ever there were mountains that didn't impress him, didn't inspire him, the

Little Belts filled the bill.

Had to be. Trump let his thoughts roam into the veiled area, the part of him he hid from the world as best he could. He knew what Dixie Lacy was up to because his own mind ran the way Dixie's did, with one slender but important difference. Marvin Trump knew where the line was and tried not to cross it. There had to be a line or the world would go to hell.

He'd grown up in Sioux City, almost frontier then, but it had civilized by the time he'd reached twenty and gotten married. He and Alma had had a boy a year after that, and the boy, Eddie, had gotten poliomyelitis which had withered up his left leg. Trump was still married, but no one here knew it, or knew what had driven him west. The truth of it was that Marvin Trump couldn't stand civilization. He'd tried to harness himself to a job and pull, day by day, but something hot and big in him kept breaking out, too big for quiet places. He'd tried all sorts of jobs and gotten along with no one. He'd bull into everything, take it over, drive others out. He'd gotten into brawls and flattened salesmen and beer wagon drivers and butchers and a lawyer, until the sheriff warned him that one more time and he'd be in serious trouble. He'd smacked Alma a few times when she'd annoyed him, and immediately felt bad about it. He'd once slapped the kid, and then got drunk trying to forget he'd tossed the crippled boy clear across a room.

He'd worked on it. Tried religion. Meek and mild Jesus, turn the other cheek, blessed are the peacemakers, do unto others . . . until he punched the preacher who'd called him a sinner, an unrepenting sinner. Maybe he was, he thought, but there was more to it. He lived through his days full of strange heat, half crazed, holding himself in check, feeling webs and bonds and strings and an itch to pull down the temple, like Samson, because living in a town full of churches and weaklings and children drove him crazy. He didn't think of himself as evil, but as someone almost out of control. He dreaded the day the last shreds of his self-control might snap.

Bad blood, he called it. Bad blood drove him mad with pushiness, made him a bull in all the world's china shops. After one last scrape he'd told Alma he had to get out, go someplace where people didn't crowd him. She'd agreed, relief in her eyes, which usually reflected terror when he was around. And so he'd come west, to the Judith, where nothing stopped him and no law checked him. And yet, he was no Dixie Lacy, breaking the law at will. That's what separated them, he knew.

Trump respected civilization and its necessary rules, but couldn't live in it because civilization ate him alive. Once he got out to the Judith, he knew, with terrible relief, how narrowly he'd escaped: if he'd stayed back there in Iowa, he'd be busting rock in a penitentiary now. Not because he was criminal, but because some hot need drove him beyond the limits.

He saw it in Lacy, and saw the difference, too. Trump could live with limits out here, where there were few. Stay inside the law and enjoy the respect of his neighbors. The wilderness did that for him. But Lacy couldn't ever live with limits. Trump knew himself to be all bull and no cow, knew he'd drive weaklings like Dent out — some hot bull-testicle force inside of him needing to maul anything that didn't resist him. But it was impersonal, a need rather than a hatred. He sometimes hoped Dent would make his way to some mining camp and clerk there. But Lacy was different. Lacy crossed lines and loved it. And Lacy, like Trump, spotted a weakling in Abner Dent, and was circling in like an eagle who'd found a rabbit.

That Eve, out of the hurdygurdy, had done it, he thought. Showed Dent's soft side to the world and turned him into prey. Trump mostly stayed away from women, except now and then when his juices betrayed him. Alma had taught him all about women, and living in houses with women, and holding it all in because a woman was there; holding things so tight inside that he sometimes burst a gut and stalked to the corner saloon, Wiggins' place, and sucked beer until the tension bladdered out of him. He knew about morals and ethics and manners and delicate women and streets with glass-windowed houses and baby carriages on the brick sidewalks. That was civilization and he wanted none of it. If civilization ever arrived in the Judith, or the Territory for that matter, Trump planned to get the hell out before it killed him. He was running out of enough wilderness for his private wild, and it scared him. Canada, maybe. Alaska. If they settled the Yukon, he'd just shoot himself rather than run again. That was his nightmare, that march of the women and children and schools and churches.

He watched Dent work, and knew the man was exhausted. Not a man, really. In his thirties somewhere, but not really a hairy-bellied male. They used to count him a man, until he showed his soft side. Abner Dent had worked harder than anyone, but that fool breed hand of his had been so helpless they'd made him a cook's helper, toting water and washing pots. When Dent folded — maybe right now, maybe at the end of this roundup with all the chips down — Eve'd go back to the hurdygurdy, hooting at poor homely Abner Dent. That's how it'd be, Trump thought. Life went to the strong.

It was still mid-afternoon, but the branding was winding down because the morning's gather had been small. The crew had let two of the fires die, sparing only one for the cussing bald cook, who spat chew juice into the pots whenever anyone riled him, which was constantly.

"What's Dent's tally now, Ben?" asked Trump.

"He's got scarcely a hunnert tallied, and those are bulls and steers, a few heifers. Damned if I know where his pairs got to."

"He's being rustled blind. Too help-shy to do anything."

Hruska eyed Trump somberly.

"You're saying a lot, Marvin. You know something I don't? All I know is that he's got one hell of an expensive female on her featherbed over yonder. Strange house, ain't it? Poking up there like a lord's castle? Craziest thing I ever seen."

They watched Dent unwind the last piggin string and loose the last calf, a burly little black devil that belonged to Law Perce, who ranched under Square Butte. Dent wiped sweat from his face, spreading the grime over his burnt cheeks, and trudged over to Hruska and Trump, eyeing them wearily with no warmth in his face.

"What am I now?" he asked.

"Ninety-seven. Forty-two bulls. Danged if I know why you got so many bulls. You collect 'em or something?"

Dent stared, then glared at Trump.

"You got only two pairs on the books so far, Abner. You been out fetching your pairs to market?"

"I knew it. I hardly saw a calf of mine get burnt."

"You still thinking they all drifted west, and we'll fetch them tomorrah, Abner?"

Dent shook his head for a reply, his lips compressed.

"You ain't got the hands to keep an eye on them, Dent," Trump said, needling. "Maybe you've been too busy playing house."

Abner Dent stood quietly, his face expressionless.

"You play house, and someone like Dixie Lacy comes along and steals the silverware, Dent."

Dent licked parched lips, lifted his tally-book from Hruska's hands, and studied it silently.

"Boy," said Trump, "I think you're done.

I think you should sell your hunnert bulls and beef critters and git into Maiden with the lady."

Abner Dent set his tallybook in the trampled grass and cocked a fist, which delighted Marvin Trump. The burly rancher crouched and waited, ready for anything. A few moments later Abner Dent sprawled in the grass clutching his belly, with blood gouting from his pulped nose and leaking from his battered gums. And all around him stockmen and drovers grinned.

Chapter Seven

Abner decided to go home. He wiped the blood from his nostrils, feeling sicker than he could ever remember, and stood shakily. He'd gotten exactly what he might have expected, taking on a proddy man made of cast iron. Under Trump's snide bullying, he'd lost control. He hadn't done that since he was a boy. He had a flash point, like fulminate.

His home — if he could call it that — lay only two miles away, and a hot soak in the clawfoot tub seemed good to him after this, and after days of wrestling calves covered with green manure. And he had other reasons, suddenly. He wanted to find out things, find out if she was worth it. He wobbled on his feet, feeling nauseous and shaky, close to losing whatever was in his belly because of Trump's massive gut-punch. They were smirking, all of them, not just about this, but about Eve and the whole thing. If he rode home, they'd think he was running. But suddenly he didn't care what they thought.

He spotted Hungry, who alone eyed him solemnly.

"Hungry, saddle up your pony and move all my bulls over into the sale herd. I don't need fifty bulls."

The boy nodded, fearfully, and started toward the remuda, but Trump's massive hand caught him.

"No," said Trump. "Them bulls stay."

"They're my bulls, Trump. I am shipping them out."

"Naw," said Trump grinning. He clamped Hungry so tightly the lad winced.

Abner stared at the other cattlemen, Hruska, Pelz, and Perce, and found no sympathy in their eyes. "Are you backing him?" he asked.

None answered.

"Are they your property?"

Pelz hawked up some brown juices and spat, nailing a grasshopper.

"You've been using my bulls, hiding them from me, and shorting on your own," Abner said. "Maybe there's not much of a line between you and Dixie Lacy."

Hruska didn't like that, but seemed afraid to say anything. Trump intimidated them, somehow.

"You're in front of a lot of witnesses, Marvin. You let the lad do what I ask now."

Trump smirked, but the rest were unable to meet Abner's stare.

"Takes a man to ranch in the Judith," said Trump.

There it was again, Abner thought. He walked toward the remuda while they watched him, and saddled the Morgan mare.

"Going home to mother," said Trump, and one or two laughed uneasily. But Abner felt something else, too. A lot of the drovers and some of the stockmen were more sympathetic than they let on. Beneath all this, he had good friends there.

He kicked the mare into an easy jog eastward, wondering if he could have done better. Maybe he should have tackled Trump again and taken more punishment. Maybe he should have threatened to bring in the law. But all of it would have been empty posturing, he knew. This was a pecking order thing, and the chief rooster was pecking him out of the country.

He didn't know where all his bulls had come from — but he suspected Trump was behind it. They'd sell for canner prices, maybe two dollars a hundredweight, and end up stew meat for state prisons, or cheap beef for immigrant grocers. Nothing like the price they'd fetch as good fleshy steers. So they'd done that to him too, used him and got more steers of their own out of it. And these were the ones who called themselves builders and founders and pioneers, and organized the Montana Stockgrowers Association, and hunted down rustlers with range detectives, and kept blacklists. And if he tried to do anything about it, with the association, with territorial officials, they'd laugh and slap their knees, but never call it a form of theft. At least it lay uneasy on their souls, and he suspected that some — Ben Hruska especially — would come to him privately, full of embarrassment.

As his white house rose larger out of the prairie, he wondered if he'd find Lacy there, sniffing around in his absence, smoking fat Havanas on his veranda. Or inside. He didn't want to think about that. He wanted to talk with Eve now, test her, test himself because he didn't know what to do. Most of his remaining herd had vanished. The closer he got, the taller his house loomed, like one of those new skyscrapers in the East, poking upward and white as heaven. He could hardly imagine it was his, that white thing.

It depended on Eve, and he had to find out. After that burst of cleaning that had given him such hope, she'd slid back to her usual ways, doing nothing, complaining, hating her life. What had inspired her? Why had the big house sparkled and glowed, just that once? He had to know now, had to set her down across from him and ask things, and put it all on the table. If he really meant something to her, that would give him a clue. If she thought she could try, that would be a clue also. If he found the house shining again when he stepped in — maybe she could only do it when he was off somewhere — that would tell him a lot.

She was glued to the wicker on the veranda again as he rode in. Pasted there. What a way to spin out a life, pasted to white wicker. He slid from the wet mare and pulled his saddle off and ran his fingers through the slicked down sorrel hair, roughing it up and helping it dry. Then he led her into the pen and watched her roll, legs pawing at God, caking dust and manure into a fine flyproof coating over her back and withers. Then she stood and shook, deranging horseflies.

He limped slowly toward the house, dreading everything and feeling every insult to his muscles and flesh he'd experienced since the beginning of the spring gather. He wanted it to be fine, wanted her to leap up from her glue and rush down the chipped stairs and hug him and laugh.

But she didn't come running.

"You're back early."

"We're half done. Branding not far from here."

"There's nothing to do. I might as well be in a prison."

"That's what I want to talk about, Eve."

"If you start nagging again, I won't listen."

He peered wearily at her. "No. I'm going to heat up some water and bathe. Then I'll ask you some questions: do you want to go on? Would you like a divorce? Do you want to start over, try it out here? Go back to Maiden? Think about it because I'm making my decisions right now."

"No," she said.

He didn't know what the *no* meant, and it didn't matter. He trudged inside, bone-weary.

"You're wrecking my mare," she yelled. "Look at her."

He stared at the parlor. Dust skimmed it again, and puffballs lay under tables. He walked into the kitchen and found the usual litter of dishes, fly-specked food, and a piece of something crawling with white maggots. The Majestic range lay sinister and cold, disapproving of him. He kicked it. The hot water reservoir held only an inch, and that tepid. He drew water from the faucet — that worked, at least — and poured a bucketful into the reservoir, and then three more.

He could find no paper or kindling or stove wood out in the summer kitchen. Irritably he stalked through the weedy yard, intending to steal some from Hungry. But she'd gotten there first. His place lay a mile from a grove of cottonwoods along the Judith and getting wood had always been an annoyance. He thought of smashing up some fence posts with a maul, but his weariness stalked him. He clambered up the rise to the holding tank below the windmill, and found the water in it sun-warmed and bearable. It was a long walk back to the clawfooted tub.

He opened the valve and let it splash in, but didn't drop the rubber plug into the drain until the cold pipe-water had cleared and the sun-warmed water flooded in. Then he tugged at his clothes, with scarcely the energy to yank his worn boots off, and clambered in. The valve chattered as if some sinister snake banged at it from within. Colder than he thought. Uncomfortable. Like his life. It raised goosebumps all over his body and didn't relax his abused muscles at all. He scrubbed vigorously with a used cloth, finding no fresh ones, and soaped his hair. It didn't feel clean, and he didn't much care. He dug a tick out of his white calf.

She appeared in the doorway. "Now you see what it's like to live here without help," she said. "No one to get wood."

Awkwardly he ducked his head under the valve and turned it on, to rinse the soap out. The cold bit him. The water in his ears rumbled like her.

"You see?" she said.

"You have answers to my questions, Eve?"

"I can't make up my mind."

"Are we married?"

"What do you think?"

"Eve — don't fence. For once, level with me. We married for better, for worse, for richer, for poorer. I'm broke now. What does that mean to you?"

She shrugged. "You promised me a lot more than —"

"Let's not go through this again. You couldn't wait. I sold down the herd to pay for —"

"There you go again — it's all my fault. My fault that you bought the house, my fault that I'm lonely and stuck in the godforsaken place and you're gone all day and I go crazy staring at grass. I buy a few things and you just rant at me."

He sighed, wearily. They weren't covering any new ground at all. He itched to tell her that if she'd worked these past years and built up the place and not bought luxuries, they could afford a few frills now — trips to Helena and Fort Benton, a little fun. But she'd been a dead weight on him, a stone pulling him under. Still, he might hang on if one thing remained.

"Do you love me, Eve?"

"Did I ever say I didn't?"

He didn't like that sharp answer. "I've loved you. I thought you were wonderful. I wanted to give you a better life than you had, dancing for a living. I wanted to give you a home, and share each day, the good and the bad. I tried to give you everything in me, all I had. I wanted your happiness. I hoped we'd have a family." His eyes darkened. "I don't know why we haven't started one. Sons and daughters, our pride and joy."

She laughed unpleasantly. "I'd be a slave. I never wanted children. I don't want your children. I use something. I always used something."

Used something. He didn't know. He'd been too busy to guess. But it helped him decide what he'd do. He pressed water out of his hair, thinking.

"I'll take you back to Maiden. And when I can find time, I'll get to White Sulphur and file the papers."

"You can't do that. You don't have grounds."

There was only one ground, and he had no proof. But he could separate and he could protect himself from her squandering.

He stood, letting water river down him. She stared at his lean body, curiosity in her face.

"I've made up my mind. You're going back to Maiden. As soon as the gather is over. And

110

I'll tell the merchants they won't get a cent from me for any purchase of yours. And publish notices about that."

"You can't do that."

He toweled himself with a grimy cotton thing, and walked downstairs, still naked, letting the spring air eat at the drops of water beaded on his red-bruised flesh. He lowered himself into the chair at his rolltop desk, feeling clammy leather on his buttocks, and began adding the pile of bills, oblivious of her.

His remaining hundred beeves might, if he was lucky, pay current bills. Almost all of them hers, he noted. And for the damndest things, such as the Power and Company bill for a gross of Dailey's Magical Pain Extractor, and another gross of Dr. Williams' Pink Pills for Pale People, plus a dozen bottles of Nuxated Iron and six of Vegetine Blood Purifier. That plus new highbutton shoes, a parasol, and a silver-mounted bridle for her mare. One invoice in a stack of thirty-odd.

"You're doing your bills naked," she said at the door.

Abner rode back to the roundup that evening, dressed in the same grimy duds he'd started with because nothing had been laundered. It was a long ride, because the crew had moved west eighteen miles to Wolf Creek. But it gave him time to think in the quiet dark, as the sure-footed Morgan mare poked steadily through the cloudless night. Wolf Creek lay in a steep prairie valley in a pregnant corner of the shouldering mountains, and he might miss the camp unless he spotted its fires. But he'd unroll his soogan somewhere close and find it in the morning.

It felt good to have a plan, to act, to take measures. He'd floundered for months, sty-mied by his own hopes and a dogged belief it'd work out, she'd change, settle down, start building a life with him. He'd blinded himself, perhaps because of the rare good moments. But even those — he bitterly admitted — had been loveless. He surveyed the ruin of his life and knew he'd been foolish about a lot of things. He'd be a fool to blame her for it all. He also knew he had a lot of fight in him and he was far from finished. He would surprise them. He'd surprise Marvin Trump most of all. The man pushed and pushed, and anything weak in his vicinity he destroyed because he had to. A strange man, Abner thought. But Trump was in for some surprises. Abner had been on his own since the age of twelve; he'd been through times tougher than Marvin Trump could imagine.

Around midnight he heard the bawling of

the sale herd soft on the breeze and veered left down a long grassy slope. The fires were out, but he made out the wagons and clutter of the camp in a gray smear of light from a quarter moon. He unsaddled and slid into his roll without stirring anyone, and he doubted that even the night herders had seen him come in.

Abner awoke before dawn, when the camp started to stir and the cookfires flared, and rolled up his soogan silently, dropping it in a wagon along with others. He expected trouble; smirks, heckling, whatever these knotheads could invent. But it didn't turn out that way. A few of the drovers stared, grinned and headed into the dust-blurred cavvy with a rope to catch their first bronc of the day before they chowed down. He spotted Hungry, mixing flapjack dough while the cookie growled.

Out in the skittery horse herd freckled old Red Wainwright ghosted up to him.

"Hey, Abner. Glad you're back," he said. "The boys are glad you're here."

That pleased Abner.

"None of us cottoned much to Trump's talk. You ain't the first man to have woman trouble, you know. Half of us wish we got woman trouble instead of no-woman trouble."

Abner grunted sourly. "I'm ending the

trouble," he said, not wanting to spell out details.

"I figured," Wainwright said. "That's what you strung back to your outfit for. Whiles you was gone, me and the boys got ourselves busy. We had to wait until old Trump was setting on his bedroll licking his pencil and adding up figgers, and then we got to work. We figger a man's got a right to sell his bulls if he's of a mind to do it. So about twilight, just before they let loose the day's catch, me and others, most of us Hruska boys, we got Hungry and we saddled up and quietly cut out them bulls slick as beargrease and shoved them over into the sale herd. Thirty in that gather. Trump don't know it, but Pelz and Hruska saw us. They didn't say nothing."

"You did? You did that?"

"All of it. The boys loved it." Wainwright's plaited rawhide loop suddenly slithered into the haze, and settled on a walleyed black monster that pulled the line taut and quit.

"Red, you know where those bulls come from?"

"I heard Trump done it last two years. He's been laughing at you ever since. But it don't sit so good with some."

Abner grinned. "I owe you, Red. I owe you lots. And I want you to know I'm not quitting. I'm starting over. I took a big loss, but I'm

114

staying right in the basin."

"We figgered that," Red said. He clapped Abner on the back, and dragged his ebony devil toward camp, while Abner drifted through the milling broncs, looking for his morning ride.

Ben Hruska caught him as he saddled the Morgan.

"Seen you talking to Red. Steadiest man I got. Say, Abner, I don't know how to say this. I get — I get around Trump and I turn to tallow. I'm all tallow anyway but hate to be reminded of it. He's so proddy I turn yeller and then hate myself for standing there being yeller. I just want you to know what a lily-livered coward I get to be sometimes."

Abner gaped. "Ben — you're one of the strongest I've ever met. You shouldn't say that or think it."

"It's a streak in me," Ben muttered. "Like Marvin's got holt of my tongue or something. Or got a twitch on my lip. At least I know what a man's supposed to be."

Abner couldn't think of a thing to say. No cattleman in the basin had ever admitted being anything but a mossyhorned giant taming the wilderness. Including himself.

"Ben — I got into foolish trouble, and I'm fixing it."

"Figured you would."

The drovers rode out before the sun pried up the eastern night, and the Morgan felt good beneath Abner. She was learning fast, and had a stamina that kept her stepping lively for hours after the mustang broncs under the other cowhands had faded.

They'd probably be at this camp two days, he thought. The cattle liked this southwestern corner of the basin where the grass grew thickest and the mountains churned up blessed showers all summer long. The Little Belts poked higher here, green timber-clad slopes to the south, while the Highwoods loomed azure in the northwest. The country had so many hollows and eye-trumping dips in it that they'd have to cover it twice to catch all the beeves hunkered under every cutbank and juniper thicket.

He rode with Red Wainwright, who'd amiably paired up with him for the day, and they poked along Wolf Creek deep into the mountains, enjoying each other and saying not a blessed word. With a savvy hand like Red scouring around, not a beeve would escape. He could head for a cottonwood thicket knowing a dozen pairs hid in it, and not a one visible.

Up as high as good grass ran, Abner and Red rode opposite sides of the creek, and then Red steered into an aspen grove and vanished from sight, heading toward a meadow visible above the aspens. Abner couldn't see him but knew he was back in there.

Moments later Red appeared, waving his sweat-stained hat, and Abner turned his mare in that direction. They plowed through the aspens into the park beyond, and Abner saw pairs, forty, fifty pairs of mother cows and calves. They rode on through, letting the big old longhorns scramble up, rear-end first, and trot to their calves.

It couldn't be, but there it was. All the cows were branded Flying D. Abner's own.

"It ain't natural," said Red. "I think these got away from somewhere up yonder where they got took by someone. Let's look at them calves over to the nursery."

They headed for the calves, which naturally collected together while their mothers grazed.

"Be damned," Red muttered, staring at the fresh Lazy Questionmarks on their young hides. "They'd be a Spoon brand should someone finish a line across the top. You know anyone that owns the Spoon?"

Chapter Eight

No wood. She needed firewood and not a scrap of it lay about. Irritably she wandered through the weeds, looking for some. Not a bit in the summer kitchen. Nothing at the woodpile. Not a stick at Hungry's cabin.

She'd gotten so filthy she needed a hot bath. Worse, she had nothing to eat. There was meat in the icehouse she couldn't cook without wood; potatoes and beans she couldn't boil. Eggs she couldn't fry or boil. She couldn't even have her Corona coffee. The plates were all used up and she could hardly wash the scum off one. The house mocked her. At least she had some airtights of tomatoes left on the pantry shelf, and she could pry one open and eat from the can, and have some Empire soda crackers. But she'd done that three meals in a row, and couldn't bear the thought of another.

In the summers Abner or Hungry drove the wagon upstream to the cottonwoods every little while and filled it with limbs they hacked from the big trees. In the fall, they made repeated trips a little farther to the foothills and brought back dead pine from a grove of standing burnt ponderosa. He hadn't done a thing about wood before he left for the spring gather, and it angered her. In fact she hated him for it more than anything else, more than all his broken promises that he would see to her comfort and supply help. She hated him with a cold steady contempt now that simply rooted right there in her mind.

She wandered about looking for wood, and headed down along the streambank, finding occasional bits of dead brush, and despising Abner. But a half hour of that didn't supply her with enough wood for ten minutes of flame in the Majestic range. She needed wood for an hour or more to heat water for a bath and cook a meal. She'd kill him. She'd kill him and Hungry, too, for leaving her in this mess.

She remembered what the homesteaders did in Nebraska when she was a girl, and it excited her. There wasn't a tree in sight of the townsites where her father hawked lots along the railroad, and the homesteaders burned dried buffalo chips or cowflops in their stoves. They made a grudging, smoky fire, but at least it was hot enough to cook with and heat their soddies. She found a frayed canvas in the barn and headed out upon the wet fields, hunting for the flops. She found them everywhere, rain-soaked, dripping when she lifted them. She tossed some onto her canvas anyway, and brought in a wet load that she would start drying in the barn.

The wagon stood in the aisle, and for a moment she yearned to harness up a horse and drive it down to the cottonwoods and chop wood. But she couldn't. She didn't know how to harness. She didn't know how to drive it. And the horse Abner used for it had been shot by Marvin Trump because Abner had done something or other dumb, the way he always did.

She felt filthy and she could smell herself. Her ebony hair felt so greasy she feared she'd be picking lice out of it soon unless she could wash it. She wandered up to the holding tank at the windmill and found the water cold, with bugs and a drowned mouse in it, and despaired. In the kitchen she downed her fourth meal of cold Blue Hen canned tomato, and tried to plan her future. First she wanted to get even with him, and then escape. She wondered how she could hurt him most.

He said he would take her to Maiden after the spring gather and just dump her there without money or anything. That infuriated her, too. Treating her like that. Making her go back to the hurdygurdy after she'd become a wife of a rich rancher with the biggest house in the county. She hated the house. It had become a jail, mocking her. It wasn't even very snug when the wind blew. But she didn't want to go to Maiden, either. She didn't want to stay here. She didn't want to spend another minute with Abner. She didn't want to see a ranch ever again. She didn't want a divorce because of the accusations. If it came out about Dixie, she couldn't marry again. Abner didn't know and she wasn't going to tell him.

She didn't know what she wanted except money, and Abner wouldn't give her any. He could sell the ranch and give her some, but he wouldn't. If she could just get enough out of him to buy a ticket to somewhere, she could start over. But he was so dumb he couldn't even give her that. She wondered how she'd ever been so stupid as to marry him.

Two or three more days, she thought, and he'd come back. She didn't even have enough tomatoes to last that long. She had to have wood to cook with or she'd starve. She was going to have to walk all the way to the cottonwoods with the canvas and throw some limbs on it and drag it all the way back, just for one or two little fires. She'd never met such an inconsiderate weakling.

A coy sun that peered now and then from between billowing clouds with bottoms as black and smooth as a flatiron warmed the veranda a little and she thought of sitting there with a comforter. But she knew her own greasiness would make her squirm. She had to wash, and it would be painful. Angrily she headed for the bathroom and turned the valve, letting chill water fill the tub.

She threw her filthy dress and chemise and drawers into a corner. At least the clothing would be no problem: she had a whole chifforobe full of it. Then she crouched in the tub, squatting on her heels, hating the feel of that living water eddying around her toes. She found a ball of good English soap she'd gotten from Benton, and eased down on her hands and knees. The sting of cold pouring over her black hair was frightful, but grimly she held her head under the flow, and then began soaping it, angrily, shivering, wanting to leap out. But she endured, washing the hair and rinsing it, knowing it'd be dull from soap film.

"Yoah a sight," said Dixie.

She startled, banged her head on the faucet, dabbed water from her eyes and turned back to stare. He filled the door, leaning on the jamb, leering.

"Dixie! How dare — oh. You caught me!"

He laughed.

"Go away. You aren't nice."

"That's right."

She eased down into the icy water, seeking any position more dignified than the way he'd found her. "I will be out in a minute," she said primly. "I'm not done."

"You've hardly begun."

He lowered the seat on the oak commode and sat on it, feasting on her with his eyes. She turned off the valve and stared back, crazily enjoying it, feeling goosebumps all over.

"I don't have any wood. He didn't leave me any."

"So I see. Why did he come here yesterday?"

"You were watching?"

"I see everything in the basin."

"He came for a bath — and nag at me again."

"About what?"

She didn't want to tell him. And she wanted to finish. And he wasn't going to budge. She began soaping her goosebumped arms and breasts and shoulders, hating the cold. He grinned, his alert eyes missing nothing, and she felt helpless. He always made her feel helpless, but especially now.

"He's quitting me. Taking me back to Maiden when the gather is over. He says I can work in the dancehall again. He wants a divorce and I told him he doesn't have grounds. He said he'll separate anyway and not pay any bills."

Dixie stared. "Took him long enough."

"What do you mean by that?" she asked, indignantly.

"Yoah not going."

"Maybe I want to. I hate this place. I'm always alone. You can visit me there."

"Did he talk about the gather?"

"He's missing cows."

Dixie grinned. "I think now's the time."

"I'm not following you."

"You will," he said cheerfully. "I'll get wood. You put on old clothes."

He stood, enjoying the white sight of her, and wandered out.

"Dixie!"

But he ignored her.

She dressed in her bustled lemon sateen, just to spite him, wiped behind her ears with her lilac perfume, and made her way to the veranda, where a chill wind bit at her damp black hair. She didn't feel any better, and hardly even felt clean after that icy blast. But the cold had leached the anger out of her until all that remained was a deepening sadness. Everything had gone wrong with her life, and she felt helpless to do anything about it. Why had she ever married the homely fool?

At last she saw Dixie riding back with a big canvas-wrapped bundle perched behind him somehow, and she knew he'd gotten wood. Enough for tonight, anyway. He dismounted, undid the load of sticks, and let the blood bay into the barn, just as he always did, keeping his horse out of sight. But then he brought it out again, unsaddled it, and shooed it into the corral with the hay rick. He'd never done that before. It was as if he no longer cared who saw him. No longer worried about a quick departure. It puzzled her.

He carried the canvas bundle up the wide stairs to the veranda, mocked her with his eyes, missing nothing about her best dress and whited shoes and damp strings of hair, and disappeared inside. She heard him in the kitchen and knew the sounds. He yanked on the grate handle to shake the ashes into a long removable pan. Then he pulled the sheet-iron pan out and walked somewhere outside, behind the house. Then she heard the whack of an ax, crumpling paper, and finally the chatter of a warming oven. She heard the valve running too, chattering at her, and the sounds of bucketed water and she knew he was filling the stove reservoir. It annoyed her.

He appeared at the front door, staring out upon the grand vista of the Judith Basin. She watched him from her wicker chair, seeing him enjoy the sight, acting as if he owned it.

"You shouldn't have to do that," she said.

"That's right."

"You don't care who sees your horse."

"That's right."

"You don't care if Abner comes. Yesterday

you stayed away when he came. But now you don't care."

He studied her, wildfires flaring in his eyes.

"You're a man. Abner isn't."

He laughed. "Do you want to clean in that yellow thing, or take it off?"

A horrible sense of the immediate future filled her. "You — you can't make me."

"I'm a man, remember?"

"You wouldn't!"

"Want to fight me?"

"You don't know how to respect a lady."

"Never learned."

"Dixie? I'm all fresh. Let's go sit —"

"When I'm restin'." Catlike he grabbed her arm and pulled her up, some giant force lifting her bodily. His eyes gleamed.

"On or off?" he said, undoing the little hooks of her bodice.

"But Dixie! This is out —"

He laughed and hauled her inside and stripped the yellow gown off her. She wore silky white things.

"Now. While we wait for the water to heat, do the parlor. Dustballs again. And look at that rug. Get the Bissell."

"I'll kill you. I'll tell Abner!"

"That's fine."

He sat on the settee while she worked, blowing Hilt's Best cigar smoke at her and having a fine time. She ran the carpet sweeper and dusted and wiped the wainscotting and took lamp chimneys into the kitchen. She thought of ways to shoot him, ways to get even, ways to embarrass him. She'd tell on him. She'd tell everyone Dixie Lacy stole cattle.

She worked up a fine sweat and felt oily again. She mopped the vestibule and washed windows. When the water felt warm she did dishes. He lounged at the kitchen table, enjoying her. She collected the garbage and food scraps and took them outside for the cats. Her fresh chemise, one she'd never worn, blotted up dirt. She tossed more wood into the firebox and added more water to the reservoir.

Dixie Lacy didn't say a word, at least not until the house had been thoroughly cleaned.

"Cook," he said. "For, let's see. Nine."

"Nine?"

"Me and my friends. Here." He tugged her toward the south window and pointed.

At Hungry's cabin strange men lounged. Another stood at the barn, looking at a dozen or so horses she'd never seen before. Some of the men were toting bedrolls and gear from the corrals to Hungry's cabin. She'd never seen any of them before, but they looked old, and wore gunbelts and revolvers. Far up the slope where the windmill and water tank sat, she spotted another man, crosslegged in the grass, with a rifle across his lap.

"You can't do this."

"Land doesn't belong to anyone. Squatting is all. No title. A place goes to who can hold it."

"It's mine, not yours."

"Cook."

"I'm going to Maiden."

"Cook."

"Abner wouldn't do this to me."

"I'm a man — remember?"

He meant it. Bleakly she surveyed her future. Dixie meant to keep her here and use her like a galley slave. He always took whatever he wanted, and now he took this place — and her. Her chance of escaping, with those men guarding the place, was almost nil. Suddenly Dixie Lacy wasn't fun anymore. Her life wasn't hers anymore. She would obey his beck and call or — be hurt. She could see that in him, his invitation to test him. She suddenly hated him, hated with a rush that poured through the fibers of her soul. Some moment she'd catch him unawares, and she'd escape — or kill him. She knew it would come to that.

"I don't die easy," he said.

So he'd read her every thought. It terrified her. For once she longed for Abner, who'd been patient and never imprisoned her, and had indulged her until recently. But they'd kill him, or drive him off. This thing — this moving into Abner's homestead — was a death sentence for Abner. Maybe a death sentence for the other ranchers in the basin, too, if they objected.

She turned woodenly to her work, ignoring them. She'd never cooked a meal for nine. She'd never been a servant, but now she would serve. At table. In bed. Hate flowered in her, but not hate for Dixie. She hated Abner, who'd gotten her into this with his weakness. She set the spider on the hot stove and started some lard melting in it. She filled a kettle with water and started it heating. She ran Corona roasted beans through the Elgin National coffee mill. She walked through the summer kitchen and then outside, to the icehouse cut into the hill, and there sawed away slabs of a hanging beef and dug up some of last year's withered potatoes. She scarcely knew what else to feed them, unless beans, and those would take some soaking first. Heavily she carried her burdens back to the kitchen, wondering how she could survive, doing this twice or three times each and every day, into the endless stretching future, as imprisoned as a canary in a cage. Only when she saw strange men staring did she realize she'd come outside in her begrimed chemise and petticoat.

An hour and a half later, and back in her lemon sateen, she banged the steel triangle with the rod. Six men emerged from Hungry's cabin. The seventh stayed up on the knoll at the windmill. She watched them troop in and settle into the creaking highbacked chairs and survey the table set with her good china and silver. She had settings for eight, and had used them all.

Middle-aged men, she thought. Not a young one among them. No one like herself or Abner. None had shaved. Apparently none had bathed either because the air in the dining room was redolent with the odor of unwashed bodies. They'd lived out of doors and were stained by sun and wind. They didn't look like cowboys, not a bit like the drovers who had come to see Abner now and then. They gazed furtively at her from jaded eyes but said nothing, jabbing at meat on the platter and heaping potatoes onto their plates. Few of them handled silver properly, but one vacant-eyed one ate elegantly. Odd men, saying nothing! Mad, some of them quite mad! It dawned on her that she sat at a table of lunatics. Except for Dixie, who had settled into the chair at the head of the table, grinning and chewing beef as if it had been prepared in a French restaurant instead of a ranch kitchen by a helpless cook.

In minutes they'd devoured everything

she'd prepared, and she wondered about the one remaining up on the knoll. Dixie watched them amiably, and at the instant they'd put away the last, he nodded. They scraped back chairs and filed out, leaving a table full of dishes before her.

"Good men," said Dixie. "You'll have to cook some more for the one up yonder."

"You might have introduced me," she said acidly.

"They know yoah name."

"I don't know theirs."

"Maybe I'll share you with them later."

Something as disturbing as moth wings fluttered across the back of her mind. She watched him pull an Eventual cigar from his shirtpocket and light it with a sulfur match. He owned the place and filled it better than Abner ever did. By his mere presence he possessed it all, and possessed her.

"Had my eye on this a long time," he said, reading her again. What uncanny, mad thing in him allowed him to plumb her very thoughts? It disturbed her.

"Just a matter of timing," he added. "When yoah late husband comes back, he'll sign a paper. Not that I need a paper for a building on government land. But it'll be something to show around."

He drew smoke, brightening the embers in

the cigar, and exhaled. The heavy smoke smelled better than his unwashed men, she thought. Maybe — maybe she could like this. This was Dixie, after all. He'd be king; she queen. They'd have lots of help. She saw the wild mockery in his eyes, but she smiled.

"Dixie. I like you."

"Cook some more for the one up yonder," he said. "Take it up on a tin plate. Then do up the dishes."

"Alone? All these? I've already done them once!"

He blew smoke at her. "Yoah learning," he said.

"I won't! You can't treat me like this!"

"Set the table for breakfast," he said. "They've got a lot to do. Firewood tomorrow. Get used to it."

She raged at him, already weary from an afternoon's toil.

"And when yoah done, I'll be waiting."

Chapter Nine

Abner had the prickling feeling that he'd feel a bullet pierce through him momentarily. He squinted uneasily at the surrounding uplands, looking for the glint of metal or the bright color of a shirt.

Wainwright studied the rising slopes, too. "A fella could get himself killed just by seeing what we're seeing."

Abner nodded. "I think there's more of mine, and maybe others, up higher somewhere. Back in a gulch." He eyed the old cowboy. "You up to driving these down to the basin?"

"You heeled? I ain't."

"I didn't see the need, just gathering beeves."

Red spat. "I figure this bunch broke loose from others being herded up there. Someone'll be along, soon enough. Their trail's plain as fresh cowflops. We got a long drive, Abner, pushing the mess of bawling cattle down the creek. We could get ourselves shot to bits."

"I'd like to get my stock back, Red."

"All right. All right. At least you got brains enough not to go after the rest up there." He stared at Abner with watery eyes. "Shooting starts, I ain't hanging around to herd beeves."

Abner nodded. He didn't intend to either.

They worked their ponies around the fugitive herd, until the mothers wheeled into action, bawling and spurting away, with their calves at their sides. Abner watched them, full of foreboding, his squint ruthlessly probing the high country. But nothing happened. They pushed the cows through the aspens and into the narrow creek valley, and started them at a brisk trot. It might cost a few pounds of flesh, but Abner and Red had wordlessly agreed to get out just as fast as they could run the beeves. When the valley widened a bit and the brush wasn't so thick, Abner pushed even faster, feeling his back itch. The cows slavered and foamed even in the morning cool, and bawled angrily. Their butt ends turned green and wet as they emptied their bellies.

Two hours later they left the Little Belts behind them and pushed the beeves out upon the verdant basin. But Abner didn't feel much safer, unarmed and miles from the roundup camp. Still, they slowed the critters down and finally let them rest and pair up at a freshet.

Red pulled a tin of plug, and placed a pinch under his tongue. "I don't know if them calves are properly yours, with that ear notch I ain't ever seen. And that question mark burnt in.

I suppose you'll have to get the sheriff over from White Sulphur and show him how they're paired up," he said. "Now why'd some jasper do that?"

"They're mine."

"Sure they're yours. All you got to do is prove it."

"I'll prove it." He kicked the sweatcaked Morgan to life, hoorawed the cows and suckling calves, and slowly the protesting cattle began their weary walk northward, the outraged calves blatting.

"What do you tally, Red?"

"Forty-seven pairs."

"That's my count, too." Almost a hundred of his animals recovered. And probably more up there somewhere, if they hadn't been weaned, sold off or run to some buyer a few hundred miles and one or two territorial boundaries away. It puzzled him. Why were all these cows his own? The beeves in the Judith Basin wore five major brands, and some of the drovers had a few cattle under their own brands. But every one of these bawling cows they pushed along wore the Bar D. Coincidence? It didn't seem likely. Someone wanted his cows and calves, and not those of others.

He felt the weary mare slow under him, saw her head droop. She'd had a week of hard riding and hadn't been muscled up for it first.

But in the week she'd turned into a fair cow pony, and she had heart. The steep grassy bluffs kept the cows from straying out of the creek bottom, so he and Red could ride close together. He steered the mare over to him, wanting to ask a few questions.

"You got any notion why these are all my pairs, Red?"

"Not the slightest. Someone don't like you."

"You think it's Marvin Trump?"

"He don't like you, but I don't think so. I don't take him for a cow thief."

"He shot my good cow horse a while ago."

"So I heard. And you done nothing about it."

"What's an unarmed man supposed to do against Trump and his two yahoos, him pointing a sixgun with a cannon bore at me?"

Red grinned. "Holler a little."

Abner felt irked. "Red, tell me something. If Trump'd shot someone else's horse — someone who was unarmed like me — let's say Ben, or Law Perce — would you be saying the same thing?"

"I don't follow you."

"You said, *and you done nothing about it.* Would you have said that about them? How come it's said of me?"

Red shrugged, uneasily. "Different men got different handles, Abner."

136

"Trump calls me a rube. Is that it, Red?"

Red shrugged again, stared at the green-stained rumps of cows.

"Will you level with me, Red? Is that just Trump talk, or do you all believe it?"

Red scratched his belly, spat at a sagebrush, and squeezed his boots to his pony. "Let her ride, Abner," he muttered. "Everyone likes you well enough."

Abner watched the old cowboy veer off to the left, evading the whole matter. So that's the way it is, he thought. He didn't do anything about the horse because there was nothing to do. Complain? Sue? Go weep to the sheriff in White Sulphur? No. He had better things to do. Retaliate? Shoot a few Trump broncs? That didn't make sense either. But that wasn't getting to the real heart of it. They'd got it in their heads that there were real cattlemen like Pelz and Hruska and Perce, and there was Abner Dent. It didn't used to be that way. Before he married Eve, he'd simply been one of the cattlemen, honored for being first and weathering the worst of everything, including renegades, thieves, and wolves.

It riled him, this thing that snaked beneath the surface of things. Not a man. Abner Dent wasn't a man. He decided it didn't matter. He knew what he was. He'd fought Indians and floods and Jayhawkers and rattlers clear from Texas. He'd started here when buffalo still roamed and Blackfeet hunters circled his cabin, stared, popped arrows into the plank door and killed his dogs. He'd bought a few calves and nursed them; plowed every penny into bred cows; ridden alone month upon month, his carbine in his lap, nursing his little herd. He'd cut prairie hay with a scythe and stacked it with a pitchfork to cut down winter loss while the others just let their cattle live or die through the Montana winters. Once he'd found two tramp drovers with a quarter of beef hanging from a cottonwood, and chased them off, shooting one's horse and injuring both. He'd worked a deal with Zimmerman up in Maiden, a deal that gave him cash money and a local market, while the others in the basin suffered through seven-percent livestock loans and drove their herds a hundred twenty miles to the rails. By God, no one had called him a kid for doing all that. Not until later. Not until Eve. Not until he began cooking the meals and washing the dishes. He'd never said anything, but that sort of thing got around, and everyone in the Judith Basin knew it, knew he'd turned the joker over when he came home with Eve.

Even Red, he thought, glaring at the old man on his flank. They'd all judged him, with

Trump egging them on and twisting the knife in that brutal way of his. Even Red. It made him wonder suddenly if those rannies were right after all, and he slid into a funk the rest of the way to camp. Not a man.

A layer of blue dust and smoke lay ahead, penned in by the grassy bluffs, and he knew that just around the bend they'd encounter bedlam. He and Red would probably be the last in, and the branding would be well along. That suited him just fine. He had something important to show them all.

When they rounded the shoulder a wall of noise smacked him. Roundups sometimes sounded like that, like an angry roar. He smelled scorched hair and burnt flesh and fresh manure and human sweat. He saw a churning mass of beeves, red, black, white, brindle, yellow, and everything in between, under a dome of tan haze, and here and there above the horns, horsemen bobbing, shouting, and tossing rawhide lariats.

Abner and Red steered their gather not into the holding herd, but straight toward the branding fires, where drovers scrambled out of the way, let calves loose, set irons in the fire, and prepared to jump aside.

"What the hell are you doing, Dent?" roared Trump.

Abner said nothing, and continued to push

the pairs toward the camp with Red's help. Red wanted to show this little herd to the assembled crew just as badly as Abner did.

Ben Hruska jumped onto the nearest pony and began shooing the cows off. "Red, what's the matter with you?" he yelled. "Git these into the herd."

"Take a look at them pairs, Ben," Red yelled back.

But his voice was lost in the roar. Every drover who had a saddled horse leapt for it, intending to drive this outlaw bunch away from the fires. Pelz stood his ground, swearing, and Law Perce sounded like a rattler rattling, but then Hruska reined up and stared, and hollered at the rest, pointing at Bar D cows, paired to otherwise slick calves with a left-ear notch, and some others with a Lazy Questionmark brand. One by one drovers stopped their ponies and gaped.

Marvin Trump smirked. "They sure knew who to pick on. I don't see no other brands on them cows."

A few drovers laughed uncertainly. Rustling was a felonious thing, a hanging offense.

Abner ignored Trump's predictable sallies, and began chowsing the milling cows toward the main herd. He didn't want to disrupt the business of branding longer than necessary.

Other mounted drovers helped, and in moments the forty-seven pairs had been pushed into the herd, bawling unhappily.

He and Red had missed the nooning, but the blue-speckled coffee pot still sat over some coals. He eased off the tired mare, feeling hard clay jolt his leg muscles, and took a few tentative steps toward the cookfire, where Hruska and others waited. The drovers had drifted back to their work.

"You're lucky," said Ben. "Where were they?"

Abner found a tin cup and poured some bitter black juice into it. "Head of Wolf Creek. Unguarded. I guess they got away from a herd up on top. There must be more above."

"It proves what we've been thinking," Ben said. "Funny they're all yours."

"We don't know what's back in there," Abner said, carefully.

Marvin Trump couldn't let that pass. "None of mine back there. They know who's safe to pick on. All yours Dent. None of the rest of us got losses, except those blotched ones."

"I'm not sure of that," muttered Pelz. "We'd better go up there after the roundup and clean 'em all out."

"They ain't bothering me none. Just this family man here," Marvin said.

"You don't know that for a fact," Abner replied.

"Sure I do."

"I suppose this was Lacy's work. We should do something about him," said Law Perce.

"I intend to," Abner said.

Marvin Trump's pig eyes gleamed.

Abner pitched cookie's caustic dregs to earth, and headed for the branding fires, Trump's mockery hard in his ears. He couldn't do it now, although he wanted to. He had to finish up the spring gather, tally his beeves, decide which to ship. But as soon as he was free, he intended to ride up into the mountains. He'd send Hungry back to the ranch to look after things. He didn't want to endanger that boy anyway. And he'd put off doing anything about Eve. If there were beeves of his up on the Little Belts, he intended to find them and drive them down if he could. If they were guarded — he'd deal with that when he got there.

He didn't want anyone along, either. Gangs of cowboys and cattlemen, out hunting rustlers, would never find any and never see a stolen beeve. No, this would be a trip to ride alone, a stalking ghost up there. His beeves were the ones being rustled, and it was his war, not anyone else's.

As usual, Pony Gargan was doing the branding. Pelz's half-Pawnee foreman had a knack for it, pulling the iron off before it burnt into muscle under the skin. Ben's boy, Mike Hruska, usually did the castrating, while Abner cut ear notches and held down the critter when Pony asked him to.

A Pelz calf lay before him, so Abner cut an inside notch on the right ear.

"You got some notion how you want those rustled calves branded, Dent?" asked Pony.

"On the other hip. I want my mark somewhere, even if that's not the right hip."

"You suppose that's the way to do it?"

"I don't know. But they're mine and they're going to wear my mark."

"They won't wear your ear notch, Dent."

Abner nodded. "Leave that. Something to show the sheriff when I fetch him."

They finished with the Pelz calf, which lay bugeyed, its thick pink tongue lolling out, squirming now and then, too shocked to bawl. Off in the dust, a drover hazed its mother off. Abner unwrapped the piggin string and the calf scrambled up, stood tentatively, blood dripping from its nether parts, and then spurted off bellowing. But by then drovers were dragging a tan heifer to the fires.

"That one's Trump's," yelled the drover.

"Well look at this," Abner muttered. The heifer's muzzle looked like a pin cushion, with so many porcupine quills projecting from it she couldn't eat or suck. "Little lady's half starved."

Pony grunted. "She ain't gonna like this. Hold her down, Dent."

Abner threw himself over the writhing, bleating, defecating little gal while Gargan yanked. Each tug sent a spasm through the calf. Gargan cursed, and the calf heaved under Abner. "Get me some pliers. I broke off about half," the foreman muttered.

Abner found a pliers in the wagon, and Gargan completed his surgery.

"I figure it was Dixie Lacy took your beeves, Dent. He's got an eye for that house."

"He can have it," Abner muttered.

"I hear he's got some pretty tough old boys working for him. Not the kind that wrestles cows."

The stink of burnt flesh and hair rose from the squirming heifer, and then they were done. Abner untied her legs but nothing happened. She lay there, bugeyed.

"You suppose we done her?" Gargan asked. He poked, and the calf trembled. "Drag her over there. She'll come around, I think." He nodded toward a pile of dead calves. "As I was saying, Dent, Lacy's got men as would shoot you if they feel mean."

"I've heard it."

"It wouldn't be good to take a notion to go hunting stolen stock alone. Specially a fella like you."

Abner felt heat boil through him, and said nothing.

The tan heifer decided she'd live, and clambered to her feet. A drover dragged the next critter toward the fires, and Abner bulldogged the blocky bull calf and whipped his string around its front legs, while the calf leaked green manure.

"That one's yours, Dent," yelled the horseman. Gargan reached for the Bar D iron, while Hruska's boy swiftly castrated.

"Here's one they don't got that question-mark on," Gargan muttered, holding the hot iron steady. "Like I was saying, Dent. There's sensible ways, and fool ways. Me and the boys here, we know what Trump's always saying. And we know it sticks in your craw. What Trump says ain't the way it is. You came up the trail like the rest, and you scratched out a outfit while we drew wages and drank them up. You're one to ride the river with. Don't you let Trump push you none — you know, to prove something."

Abner lay over the writhing animal while cutting his own notch in its ear, half in a rage at Gargan, even though the man was making friendly noises. "You got a point,

145

Pony, and I'm obliged."

"Red Wainwright says you're a man to partner with," Gargan added, as they loosed the castrated, branded, and ear-notched new-made steer.

Abner stopped feeling mad.

For three more days the combined crews of the Judith Basin ranches gathered and branded. The next camp sat on Brown Creek, beneath the Highwoods, and the final camp on Arrow Creek, at the foot of Square Butte, in strange whipsawed country where cattle hid in canyons and whole herds could be overlooked. But at last they finished up, reasonably sure they'd put an iron to nearly all the beeves in that country. The reps rode off, most of them pushing a few head. Others simply consigned their strays to the sale herd. The dozen or so cowboys driving beeves down to the NP rails at Big Timber would have a week of work, and then a wild blowout at The Mint in Livingston, or maybe Bozeman City over in the Gallatin Valley. Some of the others drifted up to Maiden, and a few simply headed back to their outfits to while away a long sunny summer.

Abner's tally expanded to three hundred thirty-seven before the roundup ended. He should have tallied around five hundred fifty, even after running beeves up to Maiden all year. Short two hundred, and most of them cow-calf pairs. He would have been three hundred short but for his sheer luck at the head of Wolf Creek. Enough to destroy him, if he wasn't destroyed already.

He found Hungry cleaning up the last of the black pots at the chuckwagon under the sour eye of the cook. The cookie would drive the battered wagon to Hruska's place, where it would remain unused until the fall gathering.

"You about set, Hungry?"

The boy nodded.

"I'm not going straight home. But I thought you might mosey back there and keep an eye on things while I do a little poking around."

"You're going to look for stolen stock."

"Maybe."

"I'll come with you. You'll likely get into a jackpot, all alone."

"No, Hungry. I want to do this alone. You go on back to the place and look after it. I'll be along."

"I yam coming with you. I got Injun eyes and see things you don'."

"Hungry! I'm not asking, I'm telling."

Hungry cocked an eyebrow. "Seems to me I yam not working for you, Mister Dent. You couldn't pay me, and I said I'd stick around. Long as you don't employ me, I think I'll come along."

"Hungry, dammit."

"I got that old six-gun and you got that old carbine, and maybe we'll need both, Mister Dent."

"No. I'm going alone, Hungry."

Abner saddled the mare and started south. But shadowing behind a half mile or so, in plain sight, rode Hungry.

Chapter Ten

Abner chose a ridge between creeks to climb into the Little Belt Mountains. He feared ambush in the creek bottoms more than he feared being seen running the ridges. He steered his Morgan mare up grassy slopes with increasing wariness, and a mounting terror deep within him. He'd been a cattleman all his young life, and knew little of weapons. He'd used the battered carbine in the saddle boot to hunt deer and antelope when he lacked meat. He'd shot at wolves. He'd hardly ever aimed it at humans, and wondered whether he could even pull the trigger if he had to. All his life he'd done what he had to to defend against predators, but he had never felt comfortable with these engines of pain and death.

The Judith Basin fell away behind him, and as he climbed he could see northward farther and farther, clear to that awesome ditch where the Missouri River ran. Each time he turned to peer back, he spotted Hungry a quarter mile behind, urging that crowbait pony upward. It annoyed Abner. That boy would get himself killed. Whenever Abner halted to let the mare blow, so did the boy, who never closed the gap but never let it widen, either.

Above, a mile or so, he'd strike timber. Scattered copses of ponderosa first, surrounded by grassy parks, and then, where enough moisture fell, dense lodgepole forest. Off to his right the vast gully of Wolf Creek lay hazy in the morning light.

Abner nooned at the edge of the lodgepole forest, eating cold beans he'd conned from the cook when the spring camp broke up. He sat on a giant shoulder carpeted with thick grass, and waited for Hungry. Better to have the boy with him than to leave him to his fate below. Abner had been a hardened drover trailing herds up from Texas at the same age, and as he sat there he remembered how he wanted to prove himself to the older men, the risks he took, his recklessness crossing rivers. He grinned. To older, wiser eyes, he had been demonstrating his youth, not his maturity. But he didn't know that then. Hungry didn't show up, and Abner decided the lad was nooning under some ponderosa below.

He tied his mare and slid down the right side of the shoulder a hundred yards, until he was well below the ridge, and then walked softly toward Hungry's location, planning a little surprise. A quarter of a mile down, he cut back to the ridge, knowing Hungry would be around there somewhere — and found nothing. He studied each tree and shadow, looking for the boy hunkered against it, and that pony, and saw only a jackrabbit and magpies. Annoyed, he trudged back up to his camp, puffing on the sharp grade, and found Hungry sitting in his own camp, watching.

"You need me," said Hungry. "I yam half Injun."

"I don't," said Abner. "You'll get us both in trouble."

"You took the ridge. That's good."

Abner gazed at the boy. It was the first time Hungry had ever judged him, at least out loud. "Up here you'll do as I say."

Hungry smiled lazily. "No, you don' see nothing. Up here you let me show you."

"You know this country?"

"No, but I see things you don'. How many trails did we cut so far?"

Abner stared blankly.

"We cut three horse trails. All old. Nobody been around here last few days."

That afternoon they pushed through patches of dense forest, open parks, and rocky shoulders, climbing all the while. Hungry had taken the lead, steering his ribby pony ever upward until at last they stood on a high ridge with a view down toward the head of Wolf Creek, and the hidden slope where Abner and Red had found the rustled cows and calves. A summer wind cut sharply through the bending grasses, creating a faint mountain roar. In the far meadow two elk grazed, peering about them every few moments.

"My pairs were down there. Red Wainwright and I thought they'd come over that saddle ahead."

Hungry steered his pony down a gravelly slope and out upon the gentle saddle, which was dotted with brown cowflops. The boy seemed unconcerned about ambush or trouble, and scarcely bothered to scan the surrounding country. It puzzled Abner, and he resolved to redouble his efforts to see before they were seen. Down the other side of the saddle a clear trail of bent grass showed them the way the cattle had come. Below, in a blue haze, lay a giant gulch, Yogo Creek, Abner believed. It drained into the Judith, which ran past his house many miles away.

Down in the blue-shadowed bottoms miles below, the earth had fissured and broken in strange ways, with rock dikes piercing out of dense forest now and then, fencing shadowed parks, turning them into great corrals. Hungry led the way again, as nonchalantly as before, which made Abner squirm. He touched heels to his mare and caught up with the boy.

"You're not watching."

"No one here, Mister Dent."

"We've got to watch."

"Oh, I see good. I don' see no crows upset or magpies squawking or deer running or nothing."

Abner halted the mare and gazed down the steep slope into the gloom. "Do you think they're down there, Hungry? Shouldn't we be careful now? They'd be guarded."

Hungry shrugged. "You'll see."

They approached a long rock dike that rose like a crenellated wall before them, fortress-like. The cattle trail narrowed there but still pierced straight toward that sinister rampart.

"Hungry — a man could get himself killed there. One sniper with a rifle in that . . ."

The boy shrugged. Abner didn't like it a bit, and pulled the carbine from his boot. He peered at the dark rock wall and felt dread in him, the dread of cracking rifles and whining bullets. But nothing happened. The late sun blazoned the wall, turning it orange on one side. At the base of the wall the cattle trail wheeled sharply at right angles and pierced through an angling crack only a few yards wide. Abner and Hungry rode through it, feeling a chill in the gloomy light, and then suddenly found themselves peering down into a shadowy valley with a tiny silver creek threading through. Even from their height, they could see the flats had held stock. The grass had been eaten down. The country formed a natural corral, except for the crack they'd just ridden through, which could be reached only by climbing a treacherous gravelly slope so steep Abner steered the mare at a shallow angle rather than straight down.

"That's how the cows got away. Lacy didn't know," Hungry said. "But no one's here. Gone away. Otherwise they come looking for the cows and find this crack."

Abner wasn't so sure. His body had tensed with its instinct for trouble. Abner studied the long slender valley, deep in late-day gloom now, and thought it might hold a couple hundred beeves through a summer, with the help of a little rain. This was where the cow thieves had penned their herd. A few men with rifles could easily keep any stray drover from coming near, and not until an outsider gazed over a ridge and into the hidden valley would a herd be discovered. Along the thin creek two mule deer stared up at them, and then bounced away, not really alarmed.

In the twisting floor a stunning chill smacked them, and Abner wondered at it, cutting into them on a June day. Hungry followed the creek downslope, oblivious of danger, but Abner peered red-eyed at every rock. They passed an odd dike of bluish gray clay, and pressed around a bend. There, before them, lay a thick brush barrier eight or ten feet high, a man-made wall. The creek ran right through it, or under it. At the left side they found passage against a vertical rock cliff, and in that narrow gate lay evidence of heavy use by cattle and horses. On the far side of the brush wall they found a log hut built against a gray cliff, with a heavy earthen roof. Abner swung his carbine around, but Hungry simply shrugged. It was empty, its door ajar, no sign of smoke from its tilted black stovepipe.

"We got a place to stay tonight, Mister Dent."

"I'm not so sure. What if they come back?"

"No cows," said Hungry. He slid off his pony and peered in.

Nothing. A moment later he emerged. "Maybe bedbugs. Not very clean."

"I think I'll bed down outside. And back away from there. But we can cook on that stove, and that way we won't have a fire for anyone up there to see."

Not a blade of grass grew around the cabin, and finally Abner released his mare in the holding pasture beyond the brush wall, and watched her uneasily as she rolled and then drank at the wandering creek. He smelled cattle here, smelled his own cattle in some mystical way, as if the pungence of his own beeves was somehow identifiable. He wondered if other cowmen could smell their own herds, or whether he was thinking nonsense. In the blue twilight he found the charred remains of branding fires near scarred earth. Someone had used this place to hold large numbers of cattle and rebrand them. Someone had also known it would be discovered eventually — even back here, loners wandered through undetected and saw things. Whoever that someone was, he'd abandoned it recently, and driven his entire herd elsewhere. Tomorrow he and Hungry would follow it out and find it — and possibly die in the process, he thought. It had to be Lacy, who lived on down the Judith ten miles or so. Lacy controlled the traffic up the river, and had let no man through.

He walked through the chill indigo night. Hungry waited for him at the passage through the brush wall, a dark wraith. Together they piled brush in the gap.

"I think you got the story, Mister Dent."

"Part of it."

"I know the rest of it."

"How could you?"

"I know what I know. Maybe it's the Cree half of me. We got ways of seeing things you don' got. I get medicine talk in my head, and I listen. I make medicine sometimes when I

156

think of my mother. My pa, he don' like that. Heathen stuff."

"What do you see then, Hungry?"

"I see this here trail going straight back to the big white house, Mister Dent."

Abner didn't like that. Hungry irked him. His outfit would be the last place rustlers would take these stolen beeves. He worried it around in his head all night, missing sleep because of it, and by blue dawn he'd turned owl-eyed and angry. He sat up in the still air, knowing it was not far from frost, and peered around. The abandoned cabin grinned evilly at him a few yards away. Hungry slept the sleep of the innocent, which irked Abner even more.

The whole place smelled of cow, the way an overgrazed pasture did on a windless day. His cows. He stretched, pulled his boots on, felt the brown stubble of his unscraped face, and stood stiffly. In all his years of ranching, twenty or so miles away, he'd never seen this place. He wondered if this was the whole of Dixie Lacy's outfit, this crude cabin and brush fence that enclosed a natural boxed pasture. He pulled brush out of the pasture gate, grabbed the two bridles, and walked in, seeing nothing. A half a mile and several twists later, he found the Morgan mare and the ribby bronc down in cattails and caked with mud

157

against the flies. He bridled them and led them back. Hungry was up and waiting.

"You could have made breakfast," Abner said.

"I don' work for you."

"You could have anyway."

"You have more practice," Hungry said, his face mocking.

It irked Abner. The kid was rubbing it in. "You could have made some coffee," he muttered.

"Me, if I get married, she's going to cook. What you should do is put her truck out the door. That's what the Cree do. A man gets rid of a woman by putting her junk outside the lodge."

"I didn't ask your advice."

"I don' work for you, remember?"

Abner remembered.

"Me, I think you got to get rid of her. She's a pain in your butt. Mebbe too late. Mebbe she took up with Dixie Lacy."

"Why would she do that? He's crazy."

Hungry grinned and wiggled a pair of upthrust digits.

"I don't know what's got into you, Hungry."

"I'm fixing you for what you'll see today. Anyone can see what's coming, except you. You don' see. So I give you eyes."

"What are you talking about?"

"This here is your cabin now and Mrs. Dent and Dixie Lacy, they got your outfit now."

"That's crazy talk!" But Abner knew it might not be. That very possibility had snaked through him all night, souring sleep.

"You should have got rid of her. I think long ago, she's killing you. Now it's too late. You just kept delaying and acting dumb, like you got too much pride to admit you got big trouble."

"Just shut up."

Hungry smirked.

The day had started badly and was going to get worse. Abner started a fire in the dugout stove and smashed some Arbuckle's beans for the blackened pot. At least he'd have coffee soon.

"You're a good cook, Mister Dent," Hungry said.

"Go to hell."

"You'd make somebody a good wife, Dent."

"You're fired. Get out of here."

"You fired me in Maiden." Hungry leaned against the doorjamb, enjoying himself.

"I don't know what's gotten into you, Hungry. You know how I tried. I waited. I forgave. I loved. I treated her good. You know what she was? A miracle. Look at me, one eye green and the other brown. I'm not even fit to scare crows out of cornfields, but she didn't mind. Look at these ears, big enough to be a cabbage. She never noticed. She, so pretty and all, and she didn't notice that. She hugged me, and no girl ever done that before. I gave her all I could, more than I could. I thought, well, she'd grow. I was patient — wait it out, that's what I thought. She needed to get used to it. Living out here alone, miles from another woman. She needed time to make a life like that." Abner glared at the lad. "Don't you know what love is, Hungry? I loved her — does that mean anything to you?"

"She's no damn good, Dent."

"How do you know that! She's got lots of good things."

"Like what?"

"None of your business. Git out of here."

"Like what? Nobody sees what. They come and they don't see nothing about her. They say you're crazy. Lovestruck, like some half-baked kid. Blind as a bat."

"I was never blind — I knew better than anyone —"

Hungry laughed, and Abner felt like throwing something at him. "She wrecked you good. Too late now. She and Lacy, they're some pair."

The boy was hurting him, deliberately.

160

Abner clammed up, seething inside.

"Every time we get back from Maiden, I eat in the big white house and smell cigars all over. I think, not only is Mrs. Dent no good when you're around, she's worse when you ain't. But you don' smell the cigars. You don' see fresh green horse apples in the barn aisle. You don' see how she looks at you when you get back from our trips, like you've interrupted her."

Abner turned his back on the boy, feeling something sag in him. He'd known, somehow. He'd known for a long time. And the boy was right: he'd lost his place, his wife, and the esteem of his neighbors. Everything.

"Hungry, I need to be alone a while. You watch the coffee."

Abner slid outside, looking for a hole like a wounded animal. The sun blazoned the high ridges now, turning them lemon while the valley remained lavender. And above, June thunderheads were building in great black pillars. It would be a violent day.

He crossed into the pasture and walked toward the silvered creek, needing to move but not needing to go anywhere. Of course Hungry could be wrong. Probably was — at least about the place. They'd ride in and everything would be just as it always was. No, not as it always was. In minutes this morning

161

the boy had torn away everything Abner had clung to, rotted dreams and feeble hopes. The great white house had become the decayed corpse of a man's life. If it was true — all these things that damned boy had taunted him with — he didn't have much left. He'd become some kind of laughing stock, whittled down from man to a kid, from strong to weak. Maybe he was. He didn't know. He did know he didn't used to be, before Eve.

Off to the west, a white flicker caught his eye, and then the distant boom of thunder rolled sullenly down the valley. That's the kind of day it would be, he thought. He wondered if he'd see tomorrow, and he wondered whether he cared. He'd felt this thing for a year or so now, felt something at the roundups that he couldn't put a handle on, felt that the ranchers at the roundups were thinking unspoken things, somehow faintly condescending. He thought they'd been envious, pretty young wife and all that. Married cattleman instead of one of the vagabond cowboys who lived alone and squandered their dimes in wild towns.

The western sky had blackened, and sunlit ridges facing east glowed. He would have enjoyed a sight like that, but not now. He didn't know what to do other than let the thread lead where it would. The boy might be wrong. But right or wrong, he'd never set foot on Dent property again.

Abner walked back to the cabin, calmer but no happier. He didn't wait for coffee, and didn't speak to the boy. He rolled his soogan and tied it behind his cantle, and tied down his possibles sack over that. He knew Hungry watched him, leaning against the doorframe with a tin cup in his hand, but he ignored him. He checked his cinch and then wheeled up on the mare, feeling the familiar comfort of a good horse between his thighs, and then turned her downstream, following the plain browning spoor of a lot of cattle on the move.

All morning he rode down the Yogo, his mind elsewhere. He watched no ridges and never studied copses of alder or aspen or ponderosa, not caring what lay behind them. Lightning danced on ridges and cold rain burst down in gusts, soaking his shirt and then surrendering suddenly to hot gold sun. White-tail deer burst from a brushy swale, and he scarcely observed their flight. He saw, instead, the face of Eve, sharp-lined and alive with life, framed by jet hair with a hint of blue, her eyes meeting his and enjoying him, dance after dance after dance, two-bits after two-bits, and she never minded his cauliflower ears or his squinty eyes or Roman nose or mouse-colored hair.

He didn't know or care whether Hungry rode behind. Around noon he had pierced well into the Judith River valley, working north toward the great basin and his home, such as it was. The spoor of a lot of cattle had become his highway, and he followed the swath of bent grass beside the river, the trail galvanizing all his thoughts. He concentrated on that alone, shutting out the world, and all the while the trail led north, never leaving the river. It plunged out into the lush basin, and never wandered. He left the mountain showers behind, rumbling ominously in a purple afternoon sky, hiding the late sun in a shroud of gray and amber. He hadn't eaten all day, and was barely aware of hunger.

Then, just before sunset, the long rays of the sun slid under the overcast and blazoned his white house a mile or so ahead, making it bloom like a clipper in full sail, yards of canvas straining from every arm and mast, against a purple heaven and a golden land. Black cattle dotted the unfenced rolls of prairie around his place, held there by some unknown power. And he made out horses in his corrals, none of them his own.

Chapter Eleven

Abner Dent sat his mare, staring at that malign house, and knowing failure. He'd experienced setbacks, defeats, losses before, but not this. This was something different. A man tries, slaves, gambles, does his best always. A man calculates and plans and dreams. And if it all works out, some small part of his hopes come to pass. He'd weathered all that more times than he could count. He'd had a sweetheart once in Oglalla, along with a half a dozen other drovers, and lost her. Once a bolt of lightning had hit a prairie nursery, killing seventeen calves grouped together while their mothers grazed. He'd weathered all that and worse. But he didn't know if he could weather this.

The low light lit the summer-slick flanks of horses in the corrals, until they glinted gold and wine. More horses than he'd ever owned at once. He stared at the windmill knoll, and thought he saw a small figure sitting in the grass there, near the tank. No guest of his. There'd be others in Hungry's bunkhouse, men he didn't know. The dying sun blazoned it all with eerie beauty, like rouge and powder on a corpse. This sense of utter failure drained through him, like hemorrhaging blood collecting in his boots. This defeat. Never before had his soul and body been transfixed by defeat and yet he could not deny the thing that lurked just behind his conscious thoughts. More than defeat. Utter rout. By stronger men.

He had to do something. He could turn tail and turn it over to Dixie Lacy and Eve and the hard men he knew would be there. He could leave the country and never be seen again in these parts. Or he could go on, walk into some trap vice that might twist life from him. Beneath him the mare sidled irritably, eager to go home and be freed of his weight. Her lashing tail caught his boots. He had, at that point, nothing in him but a sense of destiny: he would let Fate, which had used him so badly, finish the story. Once, in his occasional readings, he'd learned that the ancient Greeks thought that character is Fate. His own had brought him to this, and he'd let Fate spin out the rest.

He kicked the mare and she lurched ahead crossly. He rode alone, totally alone with no help in all the universe beside him, toward his own ranch. He ceased to feel anything beyond a vague curiosity about what had happened. Had Eve and Dixie planned this? Did she know? What would they do with all the cattle they'd stolen? Curiosity, then. Nothing else lay in him. He felt no anger or self-pity, or harbored any fool dreams of getting this back. If they shot him, and well they might, he'd simply die, and that too would be his Fate. And yet — he would not run from Dixie Lacy. He'd confront the man and his shadowy crew this one last time. He owed that to himself.

They watched his fated progress, vacant-eyed men lounging on corral rails or hunkering against the bunkhouse. Their faces were as blank as his own thoughts, and he felt no hostility or danger emanating from them. Only impersonal Fate, playing out a solitaire hand. He rode around the corrals and down the slight dusty grade to the lawn, and along the riverside lawn to the house and the veranda, lost in velvety lavender as another day died. No lamp gleamed from within. A peace lay upon the Bar D.

"I was expecting you, Dent."

The voice rose softly from a wicker chair, and Abner followed the gravelly baritone to a glowing point of a cigar. He made out Eve in the chair beside, and heard a slight squeal of enameled wickerwork.

Abner slid down, flexed his imprisoned legs a minute, driving pain away, and tied the mare's reins to the hitching post there.

"I seem to have visitors," Abner said.

Lacy chuckled softly. "You're welcome to stay, Dent."

"Eve's been entertaining you."

"For a long time, Dent."

"I know."

"Go wander around in there, Dent. Tell me what you see."

Abner thought he knew. "I will, after you and your men leave."

"They're not leaving, can't you see that?" Eve said.

"They're leaving. They don't own this. I do."

Lacy chuckled, and drew on his cigar until the glow lit his mocking face. "She's some woman, Dent. Just needed a man, is all. Take a look around."

"Eve?" said Abner.

"He's going to get me a servant — won't you, Dixie."

"No, and don't ask again or I'll bust your arm. . . . See, Dent. It takes a man."

Abner thought of killing him. Cold-blooded murder. After which the others lounging around would kill him.

Lacy watched. "Don't," he whispered in a voice so low it scarcely carried off the porch. "If you want to leave."

The man read his thoughts.

"Eve? Do you want this?"

She didn't answer.

"The cattle have my brand."

"Used to, Dent. To make a brand, a man has to hold the iron. Same with women and land. They take a man."

"My brand's in the book at Helena."

"It's my brand, Dent. The Bar D is mine in Texas. The Lazy Questionmark is nobody's brand. You've done me a favor, Dent, putting my brand on calves. Proves I drove them all up the trail. That's what I did."

"Mine have my earmark."

"Now they have mine. A slight alteration."

"I have neighbors."

Lacy enjoyed that. "They'll like my brand," he said. "Nice place here, comforts a man can enjoy."

It was spinning out the way Abner expected. He stared at white walls not his own, at dim windows full of blackness, at a moonless June night oppressed by stars. There remained the last card, the ultimate Fate.

"Both of you leave now," he said. "And take your men."

Off on the corner of the veranda a shadowed man stood, with a long gun, probably a shotgun, cradled in his arm. Abner hadn't noticed him before, or maybe the man had quietly slid around that corner.

"Goodbye, Dent," Lacy said, tossing his

cigar in an orange arc to a spot near Abner's boots. "It's healthier down south. Colorado's fine, I hear."

"If I don't?"

"It's healthier if you do. You're not foolish."

"Why?" Abner asked.

"The other is messy. Offends the neighbors."

"I have a few things inside." His voice faltered. "A tintype."

"Send me your address, Dent."

"I have clothing up there."

"It fit some of the boys. They needed it."

A great hollowness filled Abner.

"That's my mare," Eve said.

"You riding that Morgan, Dent? Better return it, don't you think?"

Abner ignored him. He turned in the soft dusk and started to untie the mare. A shot slapped violently past him. The horse careened sideways, staggering him. And then she danced, wildly.

"Go," said the baritone voice on the porch.

"How about another horse, Lacy?"

"Horses require a man's hand, Dent."

"I'll take the mare."

"Walk."

A darkness soft as milkweed down had settled upon his ranch. Something in Abner had gone hollow, so that nothing mattered. Let them. What difference did it make now? He

170

climbed aboard the mare and turned her. Nothing happened. He didn't care if anything happened. He touched heels to her and she broke into a brisk walk.

Then a rope tightened around him and yanked him off. He admired that, even as he felt himself plunging out of the saddle and the mare skittering sideways. Roping in that kind of dark. He hit hard, hurting a shoulder and forearm and banging his head because he couldn't protect it with his arms pinioned by the braided rawhide. A good Texas vaquero reata. The blow knocked the breath out of him, and he lay gasping,his lungs refusing to function.

"It's her mare," said Lacy.

Abner wondered why he hadn't been shot, and then he knew: Lacy didn't want that kind of trouble with neighbors and law. Not that it mattered. Nothing mattered to him.

He felt clever hands, roper's hands, loosen the reata and dig at his holster, extracting his battered six-gun. Then he sat alone, his head ringing and his shoulder screaming at him, and his ribs protesting every bellow of his lungs.

"Walk," said Dixie Lacy.

"Go to hell."

"Drag him."

Steely hands of two shadowy men lifted him

by the shoulders and slid the reata over him again.

"Across the river a way."

Abner thought about being dragged, and stood. "I'll walk," he muttered.

"Too late," said Lacy. A man on a horse broke into a trot, and the lariat yanked violently, spinning Abner off balance. He ran, wanting slack so he could pull the rope off. But he found no slack.

They plunged down the bank and into the Judith, and he lost his balance, feeling icy water wash over him. He gulped air and caught water and coughed, while his body bounced over slick boulders and splashed like a fish on a line. He felt himself skidding up the east bank, felt cactus and sharp rock tug at his shirt and abrade his back, felt the rawhide reata burn cruelly into his chest and arms, on and on. Then motion stopped. His skin stung. The line went slack at last, but he lacked the strength to free himself.

A rider did it for him.

"Goodbye, Dent. Don't be here when I come back," the rider said.

Abner lay quietly, smarting, gaining strength, feeling water drip from his britches and boots. He stood at last, staring into the unclouded dome of heaven and finding no solace there. Off to the west, a lamp still glowed in the starwashed house — in an up-stairs window. He stared at it, the orange glow from his bedroom.

He hurt. He walked a few steps. Every muscle howled at him. The eddying evening air cut through his dripping shirt and chilled him, but he'd survive that on a warm June night. He had to walk somewhere, wearing high-heeled boots meant for riding. He couldn't imagine where to go, but finally headed east, away from the white house, toward Maiden. Now it all mattered.

Abner walked. He didn't know why he walked. He didn't know where he could go. He could just as well sit where the horseman had left him and let tomorrow take care of itself. But he walked, forcing feet forward, feeling ache protest his every step. Whatever impulse to walk that he had didn't arise from his will, because he had no will. He couldn't imagine a future. Even tomorrow seemed a mirage. It wasn't just failure that gripped him, but something more profound. Everything within his mortal frame had collapsed.

He walked for an hour until his feet swelled and then he rested. He'd swung north but had no reason for it, walking toward the north star as the dipper swung around it. Maiden lay northeast; the little hamlet of Lewistown due east. But he pointed north, like a magnetized needle, and it made no difference to him that he did. He stumbled through one of those living nights with crystalline air and a sky that ascended rather than lowered upon him. He rested at random, feeling hunger — his last meal had been high in the Little Belts, with Hungry — and ignoring it. Thus he continued through the night, walking and resting, oblivious and empty, his aimless journey mimicking life itself. Once or twice things of the night rushed and crashed and whispered past. Although the starlight made contours plain, he made out nothing and cared nothing. He always knew precisely where he was: he'd roamed this land, herded across it, countless times. But it didn't matter, any more than his life mattered.

Dawn came while he rested on a grassy rise. First it cut gray teeth into the Judith Mountains, northeast, and then stained the world milky white, and finally tinted it. He sat four or five miles from Marvin Trump's rough headquarters, which consisted of two mud-chinked log buildings with sod roofs, and corrals, set in a protected dish of good grass on Big Spring Creek, south of the Moccasins. He couldn't imagine why his feet had taken him in that direction, toward the home of a man who'd ridiculed him, belittled him, and cheated him of wealth. A man, moreover, he had despised as a natural blowhard.

He walked in that direction, not knowing why unless to fill his complaining stomach. But he doubted that. He didn't care if his stomach growled, and wouldn't care until he weakened from hunger. He walked north anyway, noting dew on the high Judith bunchgrasses and hearing the first tentative trills of meadowlarks. Two pronghorns watched him, and then trotted lazily over a crest. The sun behind the Judith mountains turned them into blue toothworks. An hour or so later he trudged into Trump's place, and found the day's labor well underway. Breaking broncs. The spring gather was done, and the hay wasn't ready to cut, so they were breaking broncs. Abner spotted the burly man at the corral, watching, a bunioned foot cocked on the lower rail.

They saw him coming on foot, horseless, a stubble of brown beard smeared across his face, hatless, his clothes indescribably muddied and bloodied, and they stared uneasily.

"Dent," said Trump warily, surveying his guest with faint amusement. "The boy wonder. You've had a wreck. Eve threw you."

Abner nodded, not caring. He'd never cared so little about anything. "You owe me a horse.

A good horse, as good as the one you shot. And I'll take an outfit. And some chow. And I'm going to take more for the bulls someday."

Trump smirked. "Our boy's in trouble, seems like, ain't he?"

Some of Trump's hands watched unhappily, not liking this treatment of a man in need.

Abner didn't care. "I'll take one. You owe it."

Something in his tone caught Trump's attention, and he peered into Abner's eyes. Abner stared back from eyes flat and lifeless as a rattler's. He wheeled off to the bunkhouse, which had a kitchen and dining tables at one end, and slammed inside. The palsied cook, who was scrubbing tin pots, peered sourly at him. Abner found a kettle of oatmeal gruel, and ate from it.

"What the hell you doing?" the cook demanded.

Abner ignored him, hunted down some bread and sampled some half-done pinto beans boiling slowly on the black wood range. He commandeered the bread and wandered outside toward the corrals. Trump stared but said little. Abner found a manilla lariat coiled over a post, plucked it up, and let himself into the corral. One of the drovers was up on a rank bronc that wheeled and crowhopped while the drover whooped and dug his spurs deep,

176

infuriating the crazed bay horse. All the broncs in this pen were rank, he decided. He didn't want a rank horse. He wandered into the next pen, where a dozen horses bore the stains of saddles on their backs.

"What the hell you doing?" Trump had followed.

"You owe me a horse and I'm taking an outfit."

"The hell you are."

"Stop me," Abner said, some bristle in his tone.

Marvin Trump squinted warily, and only then did Abner understand the rasp in his own voice had somehow slowed this beefy man who could pulverize him at will.

Abner ignored him, settled on a good yellow gelding with a wide chest and alert eyes, maybe fifteen hands, and dropped the loop easily over him.

"That's Bo's bronc."

"It's got your brand. Give him another," Abner said. This one led easily, didn't pull back or tighten the noose around its neck. A fair trade, he thought. Trump muttered something, and Abner understood right then and there that he had the man licked, at least for the moment. Maybe Trump's men thought Abner had a horse coming to him.

He led the gelding out of the pen to a

hitchrail, and went hunting for a saddle. All of Trump's had his brand on the skirts, which was all Abner needed to know. He found a new Miles City centerfire hull with a high cantle, and pulled it off its peg, along with a blanket and snaffle-bit bridle. A few minutes later he had a saddled yellow gelding in hand.

"Fetch the bronc that threw you and bring this one back," said Trump.

"No, I'm keeping this outfit. You owe it."

"Sure, Dent. Go find your mare."

Abner rode out, not caring what Trump thought. It felt liberating, not giving a damn what anyone thought. Maybe he'd been in a prison of his own making, caring about the esteem of others.

A yellow horse under him, and a good one. He ran it through the gaits: jog, trot, lope, and then settled into a fast walk that preserved his tailbone but still made time. A yellow dapple, he thought. Faint white spots all over it. But he wasn't even with Trump yet; not until he squared accounts for the bulls. He rode south, looking for cattle, feeling better. Suddenly he gave a damn. The yellow sky was dappled with puffballs, like the coat of his horse, and he felt glad to be alive. He rode to a long grassy ridge, a divide actually between a couple of nameless creeks that checkered the Judith country, and stood on the roll of the hill, feeling June zephyrs toy with him, sluice the last moisture from his damp shirt and britches and boots. He looked like a wreck, he knew, bloody, muddy, and with a patch of stubble surrounding his droopy mustache. But it wouldn't make much difference in Maiden.

He spotted a bunch a mile east, in grasses with blue shadows sweeping across them, as clouds chased each other. He'd lost his hat, and felt the fierce sun on his forehead and the half-bald crown of his head where his hair had thinned.

He angled toward the beeves, and then walked gently through them. They edged away, but not in a hurry, and he had time to study brands. He wanted his own. He spotted Trump's and Pelz's in this bunch, and one of Ben Hruska's heifers, but none of his. One of them humped her back and hung her head, looking sick. He topped a roll of land and saw other beeves just beyond, and there in a grassy dish he found two of his heifers, Bar D, and no sign of a Lazy Questionmark.

Now he'd see what sort of horse he'd commandeered, he thought. He pushed between steers and heifers, severing his own from the rest. They ducked and dodged, trying to return, but his yellow bronc had spent time at this, and it spun on its hind feet one way and another until at last Abner was able to turn the ladies toward Maiden. He ran his hand over the animal's wet withers, pleased with what he'd grabbed. The heifers settled into a docile walk that would put him in Maiden tomorrow. He could always peddle two somewhere.

Chapter Twelve

Eve hurt. Every muscle and bone in her complained. She had sat in her wicker chair on the veranda, Dixie half-mad beside her, watching Abner come. Dixie's hand clamped a revolver she could barely see in the brown twilight, and she feared he'd shoot Abner. She'd never seen murder before and the thought turned her witless. An explosion, gore, a man dying, life seeping away. Her husband. She had turned to Dixie, saw the contained wildness in him, and dreaded what was to come.

But it hadn't gone that way. Dixie toyed with Abner, lion and lamb, and Abner stood out in the dusk blotting it up, like some sheep being shorn, pinioned to the ground by Dixie's will. Some small tendrils of sympathy built in her as she listened. Abner wasn't much, but at least he didn't slam her around, work her like a slave, pound on her when she resisted, and then do things to her that hurt — upstairs. Dixie made her laugh, though, and Abner never did. Crazy Dixie, twisting her arm, roaring, slapping her behind, shoving her into the kitchen, making her cook nonstop, cook, cook, cook for all those lunatics, and then making her wash until her hands turned red and her arms ached. That's all she knew, Dixie's maniac laughter, his blows and a hundred times more toil than if she'd stayed married to Abner.

Fleetingly, she regretted it all, inviting Dixie in when Abner rode off to Maiden. But Abner had been such a — a frog. Still . . . a yearning built in her for poor Abner as he stood out there on the lawn listening to Dixie toy with him. She watched in terror, wondering if Dixie would lift that blued revolver in the dark and end Abner forever. Dixie and Abner, the only two men she'd taken to her bed. She hated Abner, hated him for not standing up to Dixie. Why didn't Abner pull that old revolver and shoot?

"He's got my Morgan mare," she whispered to Dixie, and a few minutes later it was hers again and Abner Dent lay out in the dark somewhere, stripped of everything but his wet clothes. The last blue light had vanished, and nothing of day remained but a warmth off the earth.

"You married a dilly," he said.

"Better than you."

A massive blow ripped her wicker chair off its legs, and she tumbled to the enameled deck. "Fetch me a drink. With ice."

"Get it yourself," she muttered, clambering to her feet.

He was on her like a cat, a cruel hand clamping her arm, adding to bruises there. He dragged her toward the icehouse while she stumbled and careened, unbalanced by the force of him.

"Never say you won't. When I ask, you do."

The terror of him slid through her like a charge of lightning, tickling muscles in her belly and making her feel odd. She liked the terror. Solemn, safe Abner never terrorized her. In the blackness of the icehouse she felt for the pick, pushed sawdust aside, and hacked a piece.

He slammed the heavy door shut, pinning her inside the chill dank dugout. "Never say you won't," he muttered, and she could barely hear him through the foot-thick door. She pounded on it but it wouldn't budge.

"Abner wouldn't do that," she yelled.

Maybe he'd let her freeze to death here. It wouldn't take long for the chill to slice through to her bones. A hundred times in the last few days, she'd thought of escaping from this monster. But she knew she couldn't. He had a man posted up on the knoll beside the windmill, and by night he had a man up in the cupola. She could usually hear the man moving around up there. It had been odd in the bedroom, with that man up there hearing them, hearing Dixie grunt and making her laugh and cry and swear. A man listening up there, listening to them rather than watching the night, and it felt like spice, like salt and pepper on what they did. Sometimes in the middle of the night she heard the man come down the tiny stairs to relieve himself and go back up again, like some ghost in the big house.

But she had to escape. Everything inside her hurt from his beatings. She sat on sawdust, knowing the cold would soon pierce through, waiting in the dark, choking back panic. Then, just when she'd concluded he would make her spend the night inside that cold prison, he opened the creaking door.

"Never say no to Dixie Lacy," he whispered.

She made him his drink: good Crab Orchard bourbon, with ice and a bit of water. Then she waited, afraid. Whenever he drank, he turned mad — he had bilious humors — and she'd come to dread that above all else. She had to get away. Go to Maiden, anywhere. Dance for two-bits. Anything. Find Abner. She pushed that out of her mind fast. He'd gotten her into this with his weakness. If he'd been strong, she'd never have let Dixie through the door.

"I got your mare. You should thank me," he said.

"I don't know how to ride."

"That's good. Stay that way."

"Abner was going to teach me."

Dixie laughed.

"All you do is use me."

"That's something you recognize."

"Can't you think of anything nicer? For a man and woman?"

"Don't take notions."

"I want something nicer. I could get a divorce and we could get married and then you'd treat me good."

"I treat you good. You should see me treat you bad."

"Dixie, let's be happy."

"Like you and Dent."

She wanted to say things, but didn't. He'd hit her again. "We could be happy, Dixie. You could get a cook for these men. I don't even know their names. You could get a cook for them and a servant for me. And then we could be happy. I like to read and improve my mind, but you don't let me."

"You don't have a mind."

"Dixie, just once be nice to me."

At the bunkhouse the door opened, throwing amber light across the yard. A man emerged, and disappeared into black shadow. She heard the faint music of spilling liquid, and knew what he was doing. They all did,

185

right there, making the yard smell. Sometimes it reached the veranda. Hungry never did that and Abner would have stopped him instantly.

"I wish you'd make me happy," she said sullenly.

"In a few minutes, baby."

"I don't mean that."

"I do."

She dreaded it. At least with Abner she'd had fun, but Dixie made her scream. Maybe if she fed him enough drinks . . . he'd leave her alone. But he sat beside her radiating heat, grinning at the blackness, his body rank with dried sweat. Abner had always washed, and had sometimes stropped his straightedge in the evening and shaved, save for his drooping mustache that always tickled her lips. She'd liked that.

"I'll get you more spirits," she said.

He grunted and handed her the glass. She hastened to the dark kitchen, found the lamp, pulled the glass chimney and scratched a match, and lit it. The quart bottle of Crab Orchard sat redly on the table. She poured two, three, four shots. She meant to sleep tonight. It would be a risk. The more he drank, the more he hurt her — unless she could get him drunk. She chipped more of the decaying ice, and dashed in some water.

On the veranda he hefted it, jiggled it, and

chortled at her. Then he poured half onto the deck. It ran, silvery in starlight, out to the edge, and eddied over.

Some cold phantasm shivered through her.

"Dixie, I just want to sleep tonight. I'm tired."

"You sleep too much."

"Please, Dixie, just tonight."

For an answer, that massive hand clamped her forearm again, so hard it hurt. "Don't ever say no to Dixie Lacy."

Her chest ached with dread. "Then, Dixie. Let's make it — you know — nice. You know."

He seemed amused, though he said nothing.

"I mean, like a husband and wife. Like — nice." She realized she didn't have words for it. She'd heard of it, heard of marital bliss, and gentleness. And sometimes she had seen it between her father, Agamemnon, and his women, in the Nebraska railroad towns. "Nice, Dixie. I'll kiss you, Dixie. A real kiss, like a wife. I'll kiss you like a sweetheart."

He rattled ice in his glass, and she heard it land on the deck, a cold clatter. Then he loomed above her and she felt some giant force lift her bodily from the chattering wicker, and haul her weightlessly into Abner Dent's white house and up, up, up.

Much later, she didn't know how long, she lay wearily, unable to sleep, staring through wavy bubbled glass that made the stars blur and wobble, and thought of escape. Escape before she was used to death, before she was worked to the bone, before she died.

Maybe Abner would help her. Abner loved her. She'd always thought it sounded weak, the tender things he said to her when they'd lain together. Weak. But now she wanted them. Wanted every soft word whispered in her ear. Wanted the lingering touch of his fingers on her face, touching her lips, talking to her with touch. Wanted his fierce embrace, the thing that had annoyed her before. She ached for that suddenly, and felt sorry she'd scorned him. She wished she could cry, but she didn't know how. So she lay in the dark beside the hot presence of Dixie, lay hurting and alone and staring at nothing.

Zimmerman didn't want the heifers.

"Sorry, Dent. I'd get in trouble with the DHS if I took them."

"Mind if I pen them while I hunt around?"

"While you sell to my competitors," Zimmerman grumbled. "Well, all right, but don't say I never done you a favor."

The twelve-hour day shift had ended with piercing whistles from the mines above, and as Abner stepped out on Main, he encountered weary men everywhere, begrimed Cousin

Jacks, or Cornishmen, Irish, Germans, Italians, who'd found the mines a way to gain a foothold on a new life in the New World. Other men, less weary, trudged up the hill toward the Spotted Horse, the Collar, the War Eagle, and Alpine, as well as the giant Maginnis Mill at the upper edge of town, whose twenty stamps thumped through the valley like a spastic heartbeat.

Abner had no trouble peddling one heifer at Joe Dennison's hotel, as long as he would take mine company scrip in payment, which was all right. It was negotiable in Maiden. He scribbled a bill of sale and peddled the other heifer to the restaurant for cash. A town with a thousand hungry men in it would eat two heifers in a hurry. He took his seventy dollars of cash and scrip to Bollanger and Boissoneault, the largest mercantile in Maiden, bought a battered Winchester carbine, an ancient revolver, some .44 caliber cartridges, a blue cambray readymade shirt and duckcloth britches, a riveted canvas saddlebag, a jackknife, blanket and slicker, some camp gear, and provisions: beans, coffee, sidepork, and more. Bollanger accepted the Maginnis scrip readily enough, and Abner kept back about five dollars in green-backs, against the future. He loaded it all onto the yellow gelding, feeling complete again.

Dusk had settled early, as it always did in the choked valley. Blue sky above, sun on the ridges, but lavender in the bowels of Maiden. Abner dropped the yellow horse at the livery barn and headed back to Montana Avenue, for a shearing and shave if he could catch the old barber there. He had to wait while the dour tosspot sawed off the locks of four miners, but after supper time Abner had been shaved and shorn, witch-hazeled and powdered, washed and changed.

A chill rolled into Maiden evenings, even in summer, but the lavender half-light lingered well into the night this time of year. Four dollars. Enough for a four-bit feast, a few whirls at the hurdygurdy if he felt like it, and some serious guzzling. He hadn't treated himself to anything so grand in years, having poured every cent into the ranch — and Eve. Tonight he'd forget her and Dixie Lacy, but tomorrow — he'd do something.

After a meal of boiled-everything, he wandered through quiet streets, waved at the city marshal, and drifted toward the hurdygurdies, some odd tension driving him in that direction. He chose the old place, The Star, and entered at a moment between dances when quiet prevailed. The girls, in their tinselled full-skirted dancing costumes with daring necklines, worked the bar, flirted with miners who stood in clusters, beer mugs in hand. Abner stood just inside the door watching them, watching the painted smiles, hearing the false laughter and tinny gaiety of the place. He studied the girls, seeing paint and hard eyes and a weariness he'd not seen in younger days, when all he wanted was a whoop-up. Maybe he'd been an innocent after all, he thought. And yet, these ladies didn't practice a scandalous profession, at least most of them didn't. But they were for sale anyway, two-bits a dance. And they sold themselves with all the fake gaiety and guile used by women more sordid.

He scarcely recognized a face among them, and knew that even in the brief lifespan of his marriage, these women had come and gone several times over. Few stayed long. Some married, some drifted into darker professions, and others just took off, with some urge inside to dance in every hurdygurdy in the West. A few made it into proper society if they were demure enough, sweet enough, prim enough. Most didn't, and often they encountered the sort of ice among married women in town reserved for those in lower professions.

"Abner Dent!" exclaimed a tall blonde one, pushing toward him.

He peered at her blankly.

"You remember me, don't you? Hildegarde?"

He did. He'd whirled her a few evenings, before he'd met Eve.

"I'll buy you a drink," she said.

"You'd buy me — that's a surprise."

She steered him toward a corner table, far from the lamps that lit the dance floor and the bar.

"It's a line," she said. "You get them to the table that way and they buy drinks anyway. A man can't stand to have a lady buy him one. I get tea that looks like whiskey and they get some watered stuff."

"You're buying," he said.

"I'd like that. But you'll have to agree to tell me about Eve. About you and Eve."

"I won't agree to that."

She grinned, rose, headed toward the bar. He'd liked Hildegarde. Tall, rawboned gal with a faint accent and a wiggle when she walked. He saw the wiggle had vanished with age. She reappeared carrying a tray with two glasses of water and two shotglasses filled with amber stuff.

"Real Kentuck," she said, smiling faintly. She poured her shot into the water, and lifted the glass. "Here's to you and Eve," she said. "We haven't seen you in years, Abner."

She waited for news, her head cocked, her gray eyes expectant.

"I can't talk about it, Hildegarde."

192

"Is it bad, Abner? Just a yes or no, and I'll stop."

"Yes."

Music clattered from the upright piano. A derbied gent with a green sleeve garter tickled a palsied melody from it, and miners stomped toward their ladies.

"Want to dance, Abner?"

"No." He'd started feeling bad and wondered why he had wandered into this place of memories.

"Let's go for a walk. You don't belong in here."

"They'll be mad at you — taking a customer out."

"I'm too old to care."

He followed her to the door, and into the dusk, which eclipsed the piano and the stomp. He followed her as she leapt a rill and clambered up a naked slope beyond, until they panted on a low plateau a hundred feet above, with the town glowing below.

"That's better," she said. "Look, Abner, I know all about you and Eve. They all come in, the Judith cowboys, and tell us. I could have told you, never marry a hurdygurdy girl. But sometimes it works. Sometimes I think — we're worse than the women in the cribs. I know how to get every cent out of any man. Let them think I'm all starry-eyed and in love. Yes, Abner?"

"You promised," he said.

"I promised not to ask you any more. I didn't say I wouldn't talk about it."

He turned to go down the slope.

"No, wait. I'm telling you things. Telling you what most cowboys figure out. We fake everything. We fake what you want. Eve was better at it than any of us, and she got rich, almost. A fake, Abner. I am too, but I'm too old to change, and I don't hate myself for it anymore. I give them some lies for their two-bits. A dream, maybe. A dream of a house and a wife and a — a lover and a hug. I'm a fake little wife for two-bits."

"You could marry, Hildegarde."

"I'm too honest. I'd end up like Eve. I'd do it, squeeze a man dry, from habit. From the habit of digging into pockets every night, making promises I won't keep; saying — saying things that suggest — that lead them on. And I'm making eyes at them and letting them peek at my bosom and I'm thinking about money, like another two-bits, four-bits, dollars until I go home. We're like that. But the miners, the cowboys — they don't ever believe it. You didn't believe it."

"I thought Eve cared for me some."

Hildegarde laughed. "This business ruins us worse than — the other kind. So what if we don't — take men to our rooms? This is worse. At least the girls who take men give them something for their money. We give them a dance, yes. But we squeeze drinks from them, make promises, plead and push and pull and pretend we care, and lie. We're worse. We're worse by far. We give men lies and take more from them than the other women, the bad women."

"You're pretty hard on yourself, Hildegarde. Men have fun there, or they wouldn't come. They've bought a good time and don't feel bad afterward."

She smiled affectionately, and slipped her hand into his.

"We make them think it! I know just how to make men think they're having a grand time, think I love them, think they're the best man in the place. Hard on myself? You don't even know what that means. I know how to be hard on myself, but I'm too old to change. I'm telling you, Abner. Hurdygurdy women are the worst. Worse than any honest — whore."

"No, Hildegarde. Don't talk about yourself like that."

"I will! You're still blind! You don't see! I'm trying to help you!"

"Help me?"

"Yes!"

He didn't fathom it, and eased his way downslope while she followed silently through thickening night. He walked her to the dim-lit door of The Star, and she opened it to the cascade of piano music.

"I tried to help you, Abner," she cried, and closed the door behind her, until the world lay muffled to his ears.

Chapter Thirteen

Abner stood in the muddy street not knowing where to go. He realized he had no place to go; he was utterly alone in the world. The dance hall girl had tried to tell him something, but it didn't seem to be anything new. From the bowels of The Star, faint rumbling reached him, the stamp and scuff of boots, along with the muted rattle of a piano.

It bewildered him. He walked a few feet toward the livery barn and stopped. He could saddle his horse and load up his new outfit and leave . . . for someplace. He could unroll his new blanket and slicker and make a bed at Zimmerman's, as he used to. But he didn't belong there anymore either; he had no more business with the butcher. He had a few dollars; he could rent a hotel room. That brightened him momentarily, but after a few steps he dragged to a halt. He'd better save his cash.

He wondered what had become of Hungry, who'd disappeared back in the Belt Mountains. Probably in one or another saloon here. He could scout them. The métis boy was his only friend, only ally. He started for the Highgrade Saloon, and stopped. He didn't want to find Hungry. Not now. He stood in the uncertain dark, at a loss for direction, aching to walk someplace, anyplace.

He stood in the honkytonk street feeling the bottom drop away from him, sensing the collapse of everything he'd built. His sheer aloneness hit him like a falling anvil. Homeless and alone in an alien mining town. The muscles of his legs ached to carry him somewhere, he could feel them walking him to the livery barn, walking to his yellow gelding of dubious title, springing him up and out upon the stupefying dark.

The next moments he could not understand, and later couldn't remember, but he knew himself to be crumbling inside, his very lifeforce bleeding out of him as if from an opened artery. He'd lost. Life had ended for him, young as he was. Somehow he hadn't felt it when Dixie Lacy drove him away. Hadn't felt it when he confronted Trump and took a horse and gathered two of his beeves. He'd staved it off while he peddled the beeves and outfitted himself and gobbled slop and tried The Star and listened to Hildegarde tell him that a dance hall girl could be worse by far than a whore. He knew he'd staved it off, refused to look into the abyss, denied the deepening dread that kept eating at him — until now.

He'd slid from cattleman to vagrant. His remaining cattle would somehow disappear, even while pastured with those of fairly honest neighbors. They might not be sold, but they'd end up in ranch cookpots, and the calves would be mavericked. He'd become a vagrant saddle tramp now because of — a woman. He wanted to bury himself in the night, and his legs willed it, but his seared soul wouldn't let him, so he stood paralyzed. A dance ended and silence sifted from The Star, soft as crickets.

He understood that he'd fallen into utter paralysis, with each impulse to go somewhere blocked by its fierce opposite.

"It's you, Dent," said Francis Matz. "I been watching from across the way. You all right?"

Abner stared.

"Had a few too many, have you?" Matz asked. The marshal didn't wait for a response, but bored in and sniffed Abner's breath, muttering at the result.

Abner couldn't speak, and sensed the man's presence as if from the bottom of some terrible well.

"You ain't all right. Any fool can tell that," Matz said, puzzlement on him. "You riding back tonight? I think you'd better not set a horse . . ." He scratched at an armpit. "Say — you ain't been over to the opium fiends —"

"No," Abner mumbled.

The exasperated marshal eyed Abner irritably, and gave up. "Well, Dent, I don't want

199

no lying on some store porch like some vagrant. If you wasn't you, I'd nab you for a vagrant."

"Vagrant," said Abner.

"Dammit, something's wrong. I can wake up Doc Puechner."

"I'm all right. Just alone is all."

"Where's that métis boy?"

"Around."

"I'm taking you over to the livery. You got your outfit there?"

The marshal wasn't asking. He pulled Abner along, down the gulch to lower Main, where the weathered board-and-batt barn hulked in the night. The hostler had blown out the lamp.

The walk had restored Abner to the world.

"I'm all right now, Francis," he said. "I'll get my soogan and bed down in the loft."

Matz eyed him sharply. "First time you said anything I could cipher. All right then. I'll let you be. But see doc tomorrah."

Abner nodded and watched the man shuffle into the gloom. He settled into a plank bench in front of the livery and absorbed the darkness, the acrid horse smells, the muffled clatter of saloons, and far up the gulch, the relentless heartbeat of the Maginnis Mill's stamps, crushing quartz the way men like Trump and Lacy stamped human beings to rubble.

He rode down the long twisty teamster trace from Maiden to the Judith country, not knowing what to do. He liked the yellow gelding because it never stumbled, the way half the horses he'd forked did, and he liked the feel of his new outfit tied behind the cantle, but he didn't know where he would go or what he would do when he got wherever he ended up. He couldn't think of that, so he enjoyed the June sun, already high although he'd been only two hours on the trail.

He could do anything. He could clear the country, start somewhere else. He could stick around and fight Dixie Lacy and his shadowy men and probably end up buried somewhere, with a cutbank caved in over him. That seemed as good a fate as any, and better than most. He asked himself what he wanted, and discovered he didn't know. He'd been too busy all his life to ask that. He'd worked and scraped by and never asked where it led or what he'd end up having. A ranch, a wife, a family, a place in the basin. He hadn't probed beyond that because there was always the calf with scours or a heifer needing help, or a locoed steer, or the bronc to be broke, or some thieves stealing his beeves he had to go after.

This long downhill grade took him toward the Judith Basin, and when he got there he'd make the next decision. A while later, when he pulled up the gelding about where Warm Spring Creek broke out of its foothill valley, the decision was forced upon him. He could either cut around the back of the Moccasins and look up his neighbors and tell them about Lacy, or he could ride south, toward his ranch. He sat the pawing horse, pondering it, and found the answer fast enough. He didn't want help from his neighbors. Ben Hruska might listen kindly, but the rest wouldn't. They'd smirk behind his back and Trump would laugh. If he went to his neighbors for help, they'd take it as proof that Abner Dent couldn't do a cattleman's job. It would only confirm them in their perception of him. He didn't like what they were saying about him — but maybe they were right. Maybe he wasn't cut out to ranch the Judith country. Maybe they understood what he was better than he did, he thought gloomily. If he ever hoped to get along in the Judith Basin, he'd have to prove something to them, and that meant doing whatever he had to do all alone.

He turned the horse south, a decision made. He sensed the fatefulness of it. At the crossroads, he'd taken the left fork, and his life would never be the same. At least it was a decision of some sort. He still didn't know what he'd do, but he'd ruled out something, getting his neighbors to bail him out. He didn't feel good about it, but neither did it bother him. What did rise through him was the good surefooted feel of Trump's yellow gelding, jogging eagerly along, carrying him as if he were a feather. That at least seemed real, while all the rest, these large decisions, made little sense.

He pushed aside his gloom and concentrated on making time to — somewhere. At the south end of the Moccasins, he found himself faced with another choice. He could leave the trace and cut southwest toward his white house, or he could stay on the two-rut road and let it carry him down into Lewistown, a rough trading crossroads set in the valley of Big Spring Creek. He couldn't imagine what he would do once he got to his house — he'd probably be chased away, if not shot on sight, so he turned the gelding south, faintly aware that another decision had been sealed.

The gelding never wearied, but neither did Abner push the bronc, and whenever he hit a creek he stopped and rested the animal, while he lazed in the racing shadows and darting sun of a windy June afternoon. He loved the Judith country, and marveled once again at the bending green bunchgrass shimmering under the westwind, and the purple peaks around him, their mysterious flanks black with pine. The Judith country was a strange mystery that made him ache and yearn for unknown things. He rode through his own country feeling homesick, and couldn't fathom that, feeling homesick here where he'd put roots down. He couldn't come to any decision about anything, but he felt the land tug at him, until he wanted to get down off the horse and hug the earth and press it to his breast.

He raised Lewistown around supper time when he topped a long roll of prairie north of the village and began a soft mile-long descent toward the huddle of log buildings clustered along a wide dirt street that defied the compass. Southwest of town along Little Casino Creek stood a dozen tattered lodges made of decaying buffalo cowhides that could no longer be replaced because the buffalo had vanished. There were always Indians around Lewistown, unlike the mining camp high in the Judiths. Just south of the main road lay Reed's Fort, where the tribesmen, Blackfeet mostly, traded their last robes and skins for knives and axes and powder, and begged because they had to now.

Abner couldn't fathom what he was doing in Lewistown, but it didn't matter. He was here, really, because he'd avoided the other basin cattlemen, and because he didn't want to ride toward the white house. Of such sundries was his life made now, but he didn't care. He enjoyed this place. It was fast becoming a ranch supply center for the whole basin and seemed less alien to him than Maiden, with its polyglot mining population that scarcely knew a cow from a coyote. It hulked lifeless in the afternoon sun, except for a few dusty horses tied to hitchrails, dozing hipshot while they waited.

Abner walked his gelding down the somnolent rutted street, past the gray false-fronted mercantile that snaked back, past a log saloon, and a raw yellow board-and-batt hotel, Fergus House, unpainted, its knots bleeding red pitch, past a low gray-log livery barn with a sagging roof and a bearded hostler lounging on a stump in front. Past a gingerbreaded house calcimined white, with a picket fence around it, and a freight yard with swaybacked wagons penned inside, like caged whales.

It struck him that he had no place to go here, either. And the town had changed. He had always seen it through the eyes of a cattleman ranching a long day's ride west. It had been a friendly village, eager to do business. But now it hulked solemnly, eyeing a vagrant with its unblinking eye. A vagrant? No. No one in the village knew his life turned upside down out in the Judith grasses. He was still the cattleman here. His imagination had wrought the change, and yet he felt it, felt the town's scorn of him. He wondered if his account at the mercantile remained open; whether Gus at the log livery barn would board his yellow nag and keep a tab, as he always had.

He reined the bronc and stood in the center of the caked street, amazed. Everything that seemed different had been in his head, a phantasm. He'd imagined it. He also realized that he still didn't know where to go. The hotel, with cracks opened by drying lumber, cracks so wide the outside stole in? He settled for the livery, knowing Gus would let him unroll his soogan up in the loft. But he had no reason to be there, no reason to be anywhere, no business. Vagrants had no business.

He found the hostler dozing under a hairy saddle blanket in his little cubicle to the right of the wide double-doored entrance. Gus peered up at Abner with ice-gray eyes, and grunted.

"You, is it?" He unfolded a sagging body that lacked a right arm below the elbow, a souvenir of Bull Run. His deft ability to handle horses, feed them, clean stalls, bridle, harness, and saddle horses with one good arm and a stump, had flabbergasted every cowboy and horseman in the Judith country.

"I'll board him," Abner said.

"Trump's," said Gus, eyeing the brand. "Mine now."

Gus grunted, surveying the hard-muscled animal and its load of fresh gear.

"You been outfitting."

"I lost the other," Abner said. "Mind if I unroll my soogan in the loft tonight?"

Gus grinned. "Cheaper'n hotel and warmer."

"Thanks, Gus. I guess I'll fetch some vittles."

"You looking for that breed boy of yourn?"

"Is he here?"

"You looking for him or not?" Gus asked, testily.

Abner intended to say no, and found himself saying, "Where is he?"

"Livin' in sin."

"Hungry?"

"Too hungry. Yeah, he fetched himself a hideyhole in the Injun lodges beyond Reed's, and he's got him about three little squaws all at once." Gus grinned suddenly. "Makes a man envious. Got courage I ain't got."

Abner gawked. "Hungry? My Hungry?"

"None other. I figured you's come to fetch him back out to your outfit."

"I — uh, I guess I'll go find him."

Gus nodded. "I figure the boy's about blown his pay and you'll have no trouble. He buys a quart or two of redeye, and he and them squaws have their nightly — what do they call them things — festivities."

"Which lodge, Gus?"

Abner got directions and walked southwest along well-trod paths, past the log trading post, and out toward the tattered brown cones rising along the narrow creek. At the third one he paused, scratching gently on the doorflap. From within he heard giggling.

The flap parted and the wide amber face of a Blackfeet woman appeared. Then it disappeared and Hungry peered out.

"Come in, Mister Dent," the boy said, politeness upon him almost as if he knew this meeting would happen at this moment.

Abner slid into the brown dusk, and discovered the company of three thin women awash in tan and purple calico, their straight jet hair hanging loose, and Hungry, who eyed him with a strange glee.

"These here are my wives, Mister Dent."

"Wives, Hungry?"

"Sort of. Long as I got beer money anyway. Want one?"

"Hungry — I've got one back at —"

"Mister Dent, you don' know nothing about women."

Chapter Fourteen

Marvin Trump kept hearing rumbles. Lucius Marcullus Washburn, the only fat cowboy on earth, told him he had been riding the Louse Creek country and had come upon three skinny old men, all armed, shoving seventeen Bar D steers toward the Dent place. They said they worked for the Bar D. Washburn had judged them to be hardcases, and asked nothing more, fearing for his skin. He told Trump that the gents were distinctly unfriendly.

His segundo, Rooster, on the other hand, had been over on Big Spring Creek where it skirts the Moccasins, and had found some late calves branded with that lazy questionmark — calves suckling Hruska cows. And others of his boys had spotted heifers, steers, calves, cows — the whole ball of wax — sporting both the Bar D and that questionmark . . . a brand no one claimed. Helena officials had scoured the brand books for that one and had come up empty-handed.

That whipped fool Dent had thrown in with that rustler Lacy. It was so obvious that Marvin Trump began fuming and muttering about nooses and hemp. And that damned Dent hadn't returned the yellow bronc. Trump had been so startled when Dent walked in, saddled up, and rode out, saying the bronc and the outfit belonged to him now, that he'd let it happen. Now Trump cursed himself for that, standing there, gawking at that skunked fool, and letting it happen. He should have clobbered Dent, just as he flattened him in about two seconds at the roundup. And no one had seen Dent's lumpy hide since. The wife-whipped man had slunk away, probably cowering in his big white house and hiding behind Dixie Lacy's power now. A fool and a crook.

Marvin Trump was not a man to lament such events. Rather, he exulted. He loved to push, and now at last he could start leaning on Lacy himself. He knew it'd come to that, push and lean between himself and Dixie Lacy. And before it was over, Lacy would be swinging from some cottonwood, and Dent beside him, and that golddigger of his wouldn't waste a tear on either one.

One hot morning, as June melded into July and afternoon heat bled the prairie of its moisture, Trump decided he was going to have a look himself. He thought to take Rooster along because the banty man could face down any three hardcases that Dixie Lacy might hire. Just Rooster. Certainly not Lucius Marcullus, who staggered broncs and sweated lard and left peculiar fruity odors behind him in the outhouse.

"We are by gawd going to pay Dent a social call," he told the foreman. "Saddle up and take a carbine. No, take the Sharps rifle from the cabin. I want some range if we need it."

"Social call," Rooster muttered.

Trump lifted his two hundred forty pounds onto the back of a ribby claybank stud — he prided himself on riding studs — and they set out before dawn, to exploit the fleeting cool. As soon as the sun cleared the Judiths in the eastern haze, it hammered all day long, pounding hot heavy light into man and beast and sucking juices from them until any sane rider would head for cover. And there wasn't much cover in the basin.

They raised the white house three hours later, a ghost schooner riding the browning prairie. Trump's spirits soared with every clop of hoof at the delicious prospect that lay ahead. This time he wouldn't lean on Dent. He'd dent Dent. And if Lacy hung around, all the better. A man, at least. And almost a match. But only almost. Marvin Trump knew that Dixie Lacy boozed too much, lived too hard, and had a soft gut.

As they approached they spotted a couple of drovers day-herding beeves close to the home place. And a third man lounged up on the windmill knoll, measuring them, a rifle in hand. It didn't surprise Trump at all. He'd figured it out. Dent had thrown in with Lacy. That hurdygurdy woman had driven him to the ground, and he wasn't man enough to deal with it, or her. She'd be out on the veranda, as usual, whining away the hours.

"Those fellers are Lacy's, I figure," he said.

"Sure not Dent's."

"Between 'em and that iron-tit, they'll clean out every honest cattleman in the basin — just for starters."

"Looks that way. I figured Dent would slide into something like that when he hit bottom. No telling what a woman can do to such a feller."

"We'll take the measure of it. They don't want trouble; they just want to be let alone, so we'll go on in there and have us a look. We might sorta ride toward all them beeves, just to read sign, Rooster."

They cut right, steering toward the herded beeves. Trump's horse stumbled, and it riled him.

"I'm going to shoot this lunkhead if he don't walk right. He's the third stumbler I've had in a year."

Trump shifted his bulk violently, and the claybank faltered again.

"Look at that, will you," Rooster said, flap-

212

ping a hand at a cow and calf. "The question-mark on that calf, and a blotch on the cow. That's running iron work."

It was indeed. Trump spotted more evidence, and by the time they turned toward the malevolent white house a half mile off, he had gleefully made his entire case.

He put his claybank into a lope and watched dark sweat blacken the withers. Maybe the animal needed some lessons, such as running on a blistering day. Rooster tagged lightly behind as they swept into Dent's yard and headed for the hitching posts at the front of the place. From the corner of his eye, Trump spotted a weathered old man lounging at the breed's cabin, and another sulking in the shadow of the barn aisle. And every one wearing a popgun.

He grinned wolfishly, his eye fattening on the sights. They hauled up, Trump sawing on his reins just to sore up the claybank's lips some. It couldn't be better. Abner Dent, woman-whipped, and a yard full of hard men. But it wasn't Dent on the veranda, and not the black-haired tramp either, but Dixie Lacy, shiny black boots on the rail, his back deep in the white wicker, looking like he owned the place. It puzzled Trump.

"Social visit," said Lacy, his eyes mocking.

"Neighborly," said Trump.

"Lots of shade up here. Who'd make it ninety degrees at ten?"

"Where's Dent?"

"I ran him off, tail between his legs. Left the country. Maiden, maybe. The Bar D's got a new owner."

"You run him off?" Trump could scarcely believe it.

"Takes a man to squat on government land."

"You pay him something?"

"Nope, I carpetbagged it. I carpetbagged this house, his beeves, and his woman."

"Carpetbagged? I don't know the word, Lacy."

"Took, I took it. Like that mess of Yankee carpetbaggers that came down on Texas and the whole Confederacy after the war and stole it from us. See those gents? Carpetbagged. Every one a Texan, or southrun anyway, his holdings carpetbagged. Those Yanks like you swarmed in, set up their crooked legislatures, raised taxes, and then bought up the places that were tax-delinquent for pennies, because none of us had a dime, just worthless Jeff Davis dollars that wasn't Yankee money."

"You're saying you stole this outfit, Lacy? Rustled it?"

"Carpetbagged. Learn the word, Trump. The Bar D's my registered Texas road brand, so I carpetbagged Dent's herd. The Lazy Questionmark ain't registered by anyone."

That puzzled Marvin. "But anyone could register it and claim —"

Dixie Lacy's chortle stopped that reasoning cold.

"You're just a common thief. Dent had squatter's rights. We all got squatter's rights. We'll have our outfits when we get surveyed. And by God, your running irons have been doctoring more than Dent stock."

Lacy grinned amiably, his wild eyes dancing. "The house drew me. Damndest house I ever did see, Trump. Fit for a Texican who's been carpetbagged. Only it takes a man to keep a house like this, more man than Dent. So I got my sights set higher, on the whole basin. Got my sights on yoah outfit, yoah beeves, Trump. Got a lust for yoah beeves. Got an eye for Pelz cattle, for Hruska's stuff, and the rest. You got any objections?"

Marvin Trump sat his restless claybank amazed. The man was announcing his intention to steal every animal in the Judith Basin and drive off the owners. Beside him, Rooster sat calmly, chewing plug, his hands conspicuously parked on the saddle horn.

"You can leave easy, or you can leave hard, Trump. I figured you'd be around one of these days. You can take the message to the rest."

Trump beamed, enjoying this. "This is gonna be fun, Lacy. What have you got here, five or six men?"

"And one hurdygurdy girl." Lacy looked amused.

"She'll wipe you out."

"Dent didn't know how to handle her. I do. She takes some using."

Lacy lowered his shiny boots to the enameled deck of the veranda, and stared dreamily toward the shimmering mountains.

"That fella behind you, lounging around the bunkhouse, he's Two — we don't have names, and I don't know their names. He's a Texas cavalry vet that got carpetbagged. He hung on until eighteen and seventy-one, before they got him on taxes. Up there by the windmill — with the Winchester — he's Five. He says he's a Louisiana infantry vet. They stripped him fast; limped home after the war and he'd already lost a rice kingdom to some Yankee West Point lieutenant with an eye for good land and the authority to write military occupation orders. They arrested his parents and then him for sedition and incitement to rebellion. His ma and pa died of typhus in a stinking hole, and he almost died of it. By the time he got out, his land had been confiscated and resold. Even the old tombstones were yanked out of the plot, so's not to remind anyone of

216

anything. All my men have a story like that. And they live with it every hour, every day. Up here you got no memories, but we do, Trump. Four, out there, he came home and found his wife used and mad. Some Yankee sergeant. Four, he filed a lawsuit anyway, so they charged him with inciting to riot, and he rotted in a hole for six years."

Marvin Trump shifted in the saddle, wondering about it. It made a good story, but this was eighteen and eighty-four.

"Bull, Lacy. That was almost twenty years ago."

"Took us a while. Every man here hung on, tried to live proper after we got carpetbagged and starved out. When we finally got together in the Indian Nations, we tried a few things and failed. Took time. We got long memories, Marvin. We drink memories, toss them up and drink them down again. That one over there, Three, when he drinks, his memories fill his skull and he's right back in Hattiesburg and it's happening again and he's screaming. We don't let him drink. But sometimes he does, and then he gets dangerous. We all got memories like that, and fifteen, twenty years is like yesterday."

"We'll see," said Trump, still enjoying himself. "Can't say as I ever heard a rustler boast before."

"Carpetbagger, Trump. Not rustler. Carpet-bagger." Lacy's gaze bored through Marvin and pinned him to his saddle.

Lacy stood up suddenly, while the wicker chair crackled behind him, and somehow he seemed to fill the veranda, owning it with his very presence. Marvin Trump watched, aware that the man who'd commandeered the white house had the easy tread of a lord, possessing his domains and chattels with some violent force that seemed palpable. Behind that fickle smile and careless posture lay an alert intelligence, apparently fueled by some ancient rank injustice. Such men, blistered by the past, turned lobo in the present.

"Social call," said Lacy, mocking again. "I have some of Dent's good Kentuck. A little early, you might say, but what are neighbors for? Excuses. Neighbors give us our excuses, eh? I'll have the woman pour. Dent's whiskey and Dent's ice. Dent was a builder, you know, making ice-houses and cutting the ice. Never wasted a minute."

"Mrs. Dent? She's still here?"

"I use her," said Lacy. "That's all she understands."

"I suppose she prefers you to Dent. A man, I mean."

"No, she'd like to flee." Lacy's eyes flared madly again.

"She's a prisoner, Lacy?"

"All women are more or less prisoners. Dent never knew that."

Marvin Trump pulled a stiff leg over the rump of the claybank, and slid to earth, springing sore knees a moment. "I never turned down good Kentuck, Lacy. Especially Dent's."

Rooster took that as a signal to slide down from his bronc and tie its reins to the hitching post. "Don't mind if I do," he muttered.

Lacy vanished into the silent house, while Trump settled himself into a commodious wicker armchair. Rooster chose to settle on the white stairs. The shade felt splendid. Soft zephyrs traced the length of the veranda, probing through the wicker to cool his damp shirt and britches. The broncs slumped in the brilliant heat, pestered by vicious black horseflies. Off on the horizons lay the Snowies and the Little Belts, undulating in the heated air like mirages. No wonder the Dent woman hunkered down right here, he thought. It was plumb pleasant, even on a brutal day, and the grand vistas settled the spirit.

He heard the vague thump of doors back in the house, and the rattle of something, but no one came. He stretched out his legs, the way Lacy had done, cocking himself back in the armchair, feeling like a lord. No wonder

Lacy had stolen the place. It amused him, suddenly, the thought of Lacy simply moving in and driving Dent out, simply walking in and saying Git! and watching Dent git. Lacy was a man he could get fond of, if Lacy weren't a thief. Trump wished he'd thought of it first, moving in and telling Dent to git!

Out in the browned-off ranch yard, Dixie Lacy walked to the bunkhouse, leaving spirals of dust with every step. He muttered something to the man there, who whirled off toward the corrals beside the barn. By the time Lacy topped the veranda stairs and settled beside Trump, the armpits of his prim white shirt were brown with sweat and dust.

She emerged from the front door silently, provoking Trump's curiosity. Was this Eve? She wore a party dress of yellow silk, but it looked bedraggled and stained. She carried a tray with a bottle of Crab Orchard, a bowl of chipped ice, a cut glass carafe of water, and several glasses, and didn't look at any of them. She set it on a wicker table and stood, her gaze fixed on Dixie.

"Pour," said Dixie.

She did, silently. Two fingers per glass, some ice, a splash of water. Trump studied her, amazed and envious. Lacy had turned her into something useful. Silently, she handed the sweating glasses to the guests, her eyes averted.

220

"Right nice of you, Missus Dent."

"She's not Mrs. Dent. I carpetbagged her. She quit being Mrs. Dent long ago, when I came visiting."

"Dixie, don't —" she muttered.

His boot slid outward, hooked between her legs, and yanked sideways. She staggered and tumbled in a heap, the smirched yellow dress twisted around her.

"Told you, Eve. Never say no to Dixie Lacy."

Trump studied it, amazed and delighted.

"Serve the rest of the drinks," Lacy said. "Eve doesn't have a last name. Maybe I'll call her Eight. She's nobody."

Silently, Eve pulled herself up, rubbing her left calf. Trump discovered bruises he hadn't seen at first, faint lavender marks on her forearms and neck; red puffiness along a jaw. Got what she deserved, he thought. Lacy was man enough, unlike Dent.

"She's coming around," Dixie said, as if Eve weren't present. "She didn't take any breaking; least none that sweated me. That Dent, he just don't know a thing about ladies."

She returned to her serving, her gaze averted and low.

"She's getting plumb useful. Cooking, cleaning. Even makes our bed now, pulls up the counterpane. Dent used to do it, pull up the sheets and blankets and counterpane. Son of a gun, can you feature some whipped Jack like that? She's still lazy as a jenny mule, and I hardly know why I carpetbagged her. Mostly because she was Yank and lived here. She sort of came with the house, like a stove. I had my eye on the house a long time. Maybe if she don't shape up some more, I'll share her. I been thinking of letting my men carpetbag her. They get antsy around here, no place to go."

"Dixie — you wouldn't!" she said. Trump thought it was the first hint of emotion he'd seen in her.

Dixie laughed, enjoying himself thoroughly. "I do what I choose," he said. "Now git."

She fled into the silent tomb within, and Trump chortled. This Lacy was some buck.

Off to the west, Trump spotted some commotion. Through a haze of golden dust, he could see several beeves being herded toward the house by two mounted men.

"Time for the entertainment, gents," said Lacy. "Never say I don't give my guests a high old time. Drink up, and we'll start the show."

"Show?"

"Carpetbagging," said Lacy, a peculiar anticipation lighting his face. "I am the world's best carpetbagger."

From the barn, two men carried a smoking

brazier by its legs and set it down on the yard before the veranda. Within it charcoal glowed hotly, heating two short running irons.

Suddenly Marvin Trump had an inkling of what this show would be about, and his stomach turned over. He sipped, but the whiskey stuck in his parched throat.

The drovers were herding a dozen or so steers onto the brown grass of the yard, and Trump knew even before he could read their brands, what they would be. The Lazy H. Marvin Trump's own. The steers bawled, not liking the murderous heat, but the sweat-drenched drovers pushed the cattle ever closer, until the beasts milled and lowed just below the veranda rail. Trump read his brand on each animal, and sank into the wicker. He glanced furtively at Lacy, and found the man's gaze bright and intent upon him, his faint smile radiating pure joy.

"Some show, eh, Trump?"

Marvin Trump thought to shoot the man and then thought better of it. Behind him, a gaunt gent with a pair of holstered revolvers leaned against the house. In Lacy's own lap something blue glinted.

Down below, two men whirled braided rawhide loops over the head and heels of a steer and dropped the stretched beast into the dust. Another whipped a piggin string around its legs. Another lifted the red-hot running iron from the brazier, and performed his artistry on the bellowing creature. The acrid scent of burnt hide drifted upward. When they loosed the bawling steer, the Lazy H had become a blotched mess, and below it lay a Lazy Questionmark.

"I didn't plan this for today," Lacy said. "Too hot. But any day's a good day for carpetbagging. I found that out in Texas, where the heat didn't slow 'em down none."

Trump thought he could admire a son of a bitch like that.

Chapter Fifteen

It took a moment for Abner to accustom himself to the gloom of the lodge, but when at last he could see, he found himself gazing at a weathered mother and two daughters, both probably in their teens. And in spite of their redeye-induced grins and giggles, all three had starved down to bone, so that their patterned calico blouses and skirts hung loosely over bony frames. The lodge had been stripped of everything other than grimy blankets, and the old buffalo hides that formed the cone seemed so frayed they could not last much longer.

They'd traded everything they had for food, and perhaps were selling themselves now for a pittance to fill their bellies just one more day. That had been the fate of the tribes when the last buffalo disappeared, Abner knew. He felt a pang of guilt because he'd shot buffalo himself, wanting the splendid Judith bunch grasses for cattle, and the Blackfeet removed somewhere, anywhere. He'd heard the reports of mass starvation over on the Piegan reservation because the government failed to feed them and the Indian agent didn't care. But he'd been more concerned by the occasional theft of beeves by Indians than by their dilemma — until now. Their circumstances horrified him.

Hungry must have seemed like a gift of the gods to them. He still had twenty-eight or thirty dollars when he rode out of the Belt Mountains after abandoning Abner, enough to dull the hunger-pain for a couple of weeks, with quarts of redeye and a bit of food. Even now they passed a single tin cup among them, filled with the amber hell from an uncorked green bottle tilting precariously on the dirty blankets. Drinking was the only thing left to them, and it felt better than food because it dimmed the future.

"These ladies are Blackfeet, and they love me up," said Hungry. "They call the Cree, like my mother, the Lying People." Hungry thought that was funny, and chuckled. "I can hardly talk with them, but we get along. I tell them what I want and they tell me what they want."

The women watched blankly, smiling, not understanding more than a few words of trader's English. One handed the cup to Abner, but he shook his head. She looked offended.

"You must be about out of money, Hungry."

"I yam. This is the last bottle."

"Then what?"

"Then maybe I hunt muledeer or kill raccoons."

"You have nothing to hunt with."

"That don' stop me, Mister Dent. The women, they make things."

"Are these women — selling themselves, Hungry?"

"Only to me — for now. Cheaper than Mrs. Dent, eh?"

Abner angered at it, but felt pierced by the stark truth of Hungry's boozy observation. Mrs. Dent had been expensive beyond all imagining.

"You don' know much about women," Hungry added.

"You can watch your tongue!"

The women studied them, not understanding, grinning amiably.

"I don' know their Injun names," Hungry said. "So I think of saints. Genevieve — that's the mother; Marie, that's her over there, and Cleo, eh?"

Marie squirmed around the circle of the lodge until she sat close to Abner, and then hiked her skirts over her knees, revealing smooth young legs.

"Marie, she's cozying up to you. You can have her if you want. Maybe give her two-bits. We'll go outside if you want."

"Hungry! I'm not — tell her no —"

227

He shrugged. Marie grinned and muttered something in her own tongue.

"She says, Anytime."

In fact the slender girl aroused Abner, but he bit back his feelings sternly. "Hungry: why didn't you come with me to the white house?"

He shrugged. "They kill breeds. They don' want no witnesses. So I says, Hungry, you want to live, and I come here. How come they don' kill you, eh?"

"I don't think Dixie Lacy's like that, Hungry."

"You don' know women and you don' know Dixie Lacy." The cup arrived in Hungry's hands, passed by Genevieve, and he sipped steadily a moment.

"Hungry Billedeaux, you'll kill yourself with that."

Hungry shrugged.

"You're out of money. You've got to do something now."

"I don' have to go to a reservation. Breeds don' have to. If I make these my women, they don't have to either, unless they want. I still got the lineback dun, picketed up the creek. We can go somewhere."

"The dun?"

"Yeah, and these women, they got three, four ponies. We can all go somewhere. You and me and them."

Abner started laughing. He couldn't help it. In Lewistown they still thought of him as a cattleman, instead of a vagrant with no more home than this tattered lodge. Hungry laughed, too, and pretty soon the ladies howled, for want of anything better to do. Abner decided that was a homecoming. Abner Dent, former cattleman with a house that was legend throughout the Territory, at home in a tattered lodge on Little Casino Creek, hard by Reed's Trading Post.

He peered out into the night. "Hungry, listen. I'm starved. I'm gonna walk back into town for some vittles. The mercantile's closed but maybe the restaurant's still serving and I can get some grub. You all should be eating, not drinking. If they're shut, I've got some chow in my outfit at the livery barn."

"I ain't hungry. These ladies don' want nothing."

"That's because — you shouldn't give them that stuff!"

Hungry shrugged.

Abner stepped out into the night air. Along the northwestern horizon a transparent blue lastlight defied the spin of the globe, giving him all he needed to walk north to Main Street. The women and Hungry disturbed him, living hand-to-mouth, with a future consisting of exactly nothing. Like his own future. He thought he might keep them all afloat awhile by stealing his own cattle from Lacy, one by one, and selling them here or in Maiden. The thought disgusted him. He told himself sternly that Hungry was no responsibility of his; that he'd let Hungry go days earlier; that he had even less responsibility for those Blackfeet women, no matter how desperate their condition. That's what the government was for, to take care of those displaced people.

The July night lay soft and dry as Abner made his way toward the settlement along the cottonwooded bottoms of Spring Creek. He could smell the juniper and pine and sagebrush scents rolling down the mountains on the night breezes, and they stirred something mysterious in him. He loved the Judith country so much something in him choked up. He possessed it jealously, never satiated, a lover of land so magical that his love was always unrequited, and he always wanted more of the transparent air, the blinking white stars, the black-shouldered mountains thick with long-needled ponderosa and fir, and above all, the waving bunchgrass that sprang waist high beside dancing creeks filled with silvery trout. He needed that, and something more that he couldn't put a name to, something elusive the

Judith country slipped to him in dizzy narcotic doses.

On Main, he rattled the door of the restaurant and found it closed, so he walked around to the lamplit window of the kitchen and found its proprietor, Ulysses Graves, washing the last chipped crockery mugs.

A few moments later Abner was two dollars lighter, and carried a dozen boiled spuds and some sidepork in an old Harvest Maid flour sack. He paused at the livery barn long enough to fetch his soogan, and then trudged back through spidery clutching cottonwoods toward the black cones of the lodges. He could not support these desperate souls; not even for another day. He wanted his ranch back. His place. His livestock. His corrals and barn, and the log house he'd lived in before — Eve. Momentarily he hated the white house and all it stood for, including his ruin. Hated it with unreasoning rage, seeing in it the millstone that sank him, made him an alien in his own country. He wanted only to turn time back, to begin again just as everything stood before he'd hankered for Eve and surrendered all he had to her. But there could be no turning back.

At least, not until he dealt with Dixie Lacy, who squatted in his white house, disposed of his cattle, and — climbed each night into the fourposter with Eve. Not that it bothered him anymore. In fact, they deserved each other. He only wanted to drive the pair of them out of that white house, drive them and the white house away, out of the Judith, away.

The log hulk of Reed's Post startled up on his left, and a minute later he swung right, up Little Casino Creek, enjoying the frosting of stars over the devil's cake night. An idea had caught him, threading its unbidden way through all the barriers of his mind, all the censorious things that shouted No! as it took shape. But even while a part of him cried out against such folly, the other part of him saw it as a way of turning the clock back and starting over; a way of driving Dixie and Eve away, away, away. He sensed he might have a future after all, something to look forward to, a chance to recover some of what he'd lost. And maybe even a way to help these people; rehire Hungry, and let him bring this impromptu family of his to the safety and security of his ranch.

He found the third lodge, dark and quiet save for an occasional rustle of cloth and some feminine mumbling. He announced himself and waited until the doorflap parted, and then he slid into a blackness that stank sourly of rotgut.

"Hungry, I brought some boiled spuds and

some sidepork. We can eat the spuds now, cook the other in the morning."

But Hungry didn't answer.

"Sleeps," said a voice in English.

He settled on a blanket and dug into the sack, passing the still-warm potatoes to eager hands. Not much of a meal, he thought, but it would fill them and nourish them. They ate, the three women ghostly presences. And when at last the potatoes were gone, one of the women slid close and hugged him, and he hugged back, aware of hot tears leaking from her eyes onto his collar and neck. He did not know who.

Eve understood Dixie perfectly. She came to know him as completely as the condemned knows his executioner. She fathomed his moods and purposes, and knew they were much like her own. He used her, which didn't upset her at all. In fact, using others was the only relationship she understood, and she had never been able to comprehend Abner's tenderness and generosity, which she always supposed was weakness, or maybe sentiment. But Dixie was just like her, and treated her as she had treated Abner.

That should have made him predictable, but it didn't. She never knew what he would do to her, and that unknowing, along with his occasional cruelties, filled her life with a fine hum of terror. If she resisted him, he beat her. But if she pleaded with him, or even asked a question, he sometimes beat her also. If she failed to meet his expectations, he punished her. Once he twisted her fingers so badly she thought they'd break, but then he let go. She wouldn't be much good with a broken hand, she thought bitterly.

Her life had become an ordeal. He pitched her out of the fourposter before summer's dawn, and then she drudged through a breakfast for seven men plus herself and Dixie; did the dishes; plunged into a round of housecleaning because he wanted the big white house so spotless it ached with newness. Somehow she was supposed to prepare lunch, too — they called it dinner here — but that meal was light because most of the men were out on the range somewhere. And then she had to do it all again for what they called supper. And Dixie made her mend all their clothes, wash them once a week, heating water on the woodstove and stirring the clothes with a wooden stick in a big copper boiler, rinsing them, wringing them out by hand, and hanging them up to dry. Clothes for nine persons. And he made her wash the sheets on her bed, too. The men in the bunkhouse didn't have them, but she had to wash their blankets now and then to keep bedbugs at bay.

At the end of each endless day her body ached, and she fell into bed drugged with a need to sleep, but he pestered her there, keeping her up, robbing her of rest until black hollows formed below her eyes. She neglected herself. If she spent time washing and combing her hair, he would beat her. Sometimes he beat her for no reason, grabbing an arm so hard it left purple bruises, punching a fist into her shoulder, slapping her hard across the face for nothing. He said she deserved it; that it was good for parasites like her. She always seemed to be licking wounds — most frequently gashed lips from his vicious slaps. She wept when he slapped her hard, but he always laughed.

She had no time. Every second was his; he owned her as if she were a slave. She barely had time to brew pennyroyal tea and sip it when she needed to; in fact, she barely had time to count the days. And her supply of the herb diminished alarmingly, but she couldn't send away to Fort Benton for more. And she dreaded what might happen if a child formed in her belly. She feared the prospect of childbirth even more than she hated Dixie's cruelties. She scarcely had time to wash her private things and hang them in the spare bedroom upstairs where all those men wouldn't see them.

Dixie watched and yawned and read her mind. When she thought of escape, he knew it and played with her like some giant cat toying with a mouse. When she wanted only sleep and he pawed her, he repeated her excuses to her before she had time to whisper them.

"I use you. Using is all you understand," he said.

And he knew the ultimate terror, the one thing that sent chills through her body and soul.

"Stop your whining or I'll start sharing you," he said over and over. "The boys need some fun. I'll send you out to the bunkhouse for a few weeks."

"Dixie — please — don't you want me just for you?"

"I'm tired of you."

"But Dixie — you said you loved me, when you used to visit."

Dixie laughed uproariously, until the four-poster rocked and protested. "I say anything to anyone. Learned that from the carpet-baggers."

As the days turned over, she no longer thought of escape; she hadn't the faintest chance. But she toyed with murder. A butcher knife; a revolver. Maybe something in his spirits. But she never went beyond toying with it as she scoured pots and poured steaming rinse water over cracked dishes. Other thoughts kept invading her, tendrils of things she had never experienced. For one thing, the shining house pleased her. She began to take a savage pleasure in keeping it clean, and at times she even went beyond Dixie's demands, for instance mopping the enameled veranda one cool morning. The big white house glowed. Waxed furniture shone. The chimneys of lamps sparkled. Windows gleamed. The pile of the rugs stood high after regular beating, and the hardwood floors glinted. Not a cobweb gathered around the chandelier ironwork or in a high corner. The plank floor of the kitchen no longer stuck to her shoes, and the gum and grease that had layered over everything there had been scoured away, making the kitchen seem as new as when Abner had first shown the finished house to her.

The great house seemed home to her. She'd poured her energy into it, wearing herself ragged, tiring muscles, and now she felt a keen possessiveness. It was hers! For the first time in her young life she'd poured something of herself into her surroundings, and discovered that pain and labor and exhaustion were the coin of ownership.

She caught Dixie enjoying the white house, too, though he tried to hide it from her. His face softened when he walked into the parlor at night and found all the lamps of the chandelier shedding gold into all the bright corners. She sported him running his hand over the wainscotting, and sliding it sensuously along the bannister leading upstairs, and peering through immaculate windows at breathtaking vistas of rolling grassland and purple mountains along every horizon. She discovered him dressing differently, letting his silver-threaded hair curl longer, taking his broadbrimmed hat off inside, and furtively wiping his boots before entering. He was even being careful with cigar ashes, not for her sake but for the sake of the white manor that made him a lord.

Late one evening she sensed a thread of gentleness in him as he sprawled in a parlor chair, staring at his world.

"We have a beautiful house, don't we, Dixie?" she asked softly.

He leapt like a cat at her and slapped her. The flat of his palm sandpapered her cheek, bringing a blush to it, and her left ear rang.

"Not we. It's mine. Not we."

"But — but — Dixie — I'm Mrs. Dent. This is —"

The second blow floored her, and made her head ring.

"Yoah nothing. The house would be a cesspool if I left you alone. Yoah not Mrs. Dent.

Yoah not anything."

She lifted herself from the rose-patterned carpet, feeling less physically wounded than hurt in her heart.

For an instant she thought of fleeing, running, killing him. He knew her thoughts and laughed. She composed her stinging face and thought of Abner, who never hit her, never hurt her, and always was patient. She had to grant him that, anyway. For an instant she yearned for him, but it faded swiftly. She loathed Abner. Dull, plodding Abner who whispered his love and waited patiently. She hated him! She'd never return to Abner Dent.

She sat up, staring narrowly at Dixie Lacy, grinning above her, his polished black double-stitched boots lethally close to her ribs, and felt herself possessed and consumed, and knew life had become better with Dixie — cruel as he was — than with her gentle husband who waited — and waited. She smiled upward, and saw knowing in Dixie.

"Women like it. I've never met one who really wanted to be treated the way she said she did. Forget him. I know what yoah thinking, so forget him. He bored you to tears — away all day and too polite at night. I ain't polite. And I'm here. I send my men out to do chores so I don't have to dirty my hands.

And I'm better company than no company all day long."

She felt the truth of it. Something in Dixie electrified her, fascinated her, surprised her. His utter unpredictability, for one. And recently, even though he used her crazily upstairs, she'd found ways to use him, turning as savage as he, and she'd never experienced anything like that with Abner.

Scared witless, and afraid of another belt, she stood and smiled. "I love you, Dixie," she whispered.

She saw the grin and the fist, and felt the blow shock her ribs and shoot nauseous fire through her, but she felt herself being caught as she fell, and next she knew, she was on the divan and he was pouring whiskey over her.

Chapter Sixteen

All the long hot ride home Rooster kept babbling about what he'd seen, and Marvin Trump wished he'd shut up. Marvin was trying to think. He'd never thought much about things because shoving had been a good substitute. If he couldn't fathom what someone was up to, Marvin simply leaned on him, and that was all it took.

Marvin sensed he'd met his match in Lacy, and it delighted him. At last, someone who'd lean back instead of just caving in, like all the rest. In fact, on the veranda he'd worked himself into a cold sweat wondering if he'd leave the place alive. Lacy toyed with him like a lithe catamount, his eyes yellow with joy at Marvin's discomfort and rage.

Marvin had been forced to watch the blotching of his brand on fifteen beeves of all descriptions, steers, cows, heifers, and a bull. Lacy's men had been artistic, searing strange designs into tormented flesh until all semblance of a readable brand vanished. And then they'd sliced into ears, making random new patterns that further obliterated ownership. And on each bellowing animal they ran a Lazy Questionmark brand below the blotched one.

Trump stared at all this with a bull-rage rising up in him, contained only by Dixie's smug gaze, and the presence of a skeletal armed man lounging casually behind him. Before his eyes, his own cattle were being stolen from him! Hundreds of dollars of his own beef, lost to him! The very audacity of it amazed him — making him witness the loss of his own beef. In the middle of all this it came to him that he wouldn't escape alive; they were letting him witness the theft only because they would murder him and Rooster when it was done — just the sort of toying with terror that Dixie Lacy enjoyed.

But when at last the brands had all been blotched and the hurting beeves driven away, and the gear removed, Dixie had smiled.

"An entertainment. Branding's always vaudeville. I hope you enjoyed yoah visit, gents. I always welcome company."

And with that, Marvin found himself clambering into his burning saddle, and Rooster beside him, riding into the furnace winds of afternoon. Not for a mile did Marvin Trump relax, and with every step of the horse he expected a rifle bullet to sear him out of his saddle. That's when Rooster started babbling, almost incoherently, apparently having experienced the same terror and astonishment.

"I said shut up," Trump snapped, and the

wiry man subsided, letting his bronc walk slowly northward in the brutal heat.

The more Marvin tried to make sense of what he'd seen, the more flummoxed he became. Lacy's men weren't altering a brand into something new; they were blotching the brands, and adding a Lazy Questionmark that belonged to no one, and altering earmarks into random nothingness. It dawned on him that he hadn't really watched theft, exactly — not a thing he'd witnessed transferred ownership from himself to Lacy — but simply the destruction of ownership. Trump could no longer claim a beeve with a blotched brand that totally obscured his mark; but Lacy couldn't claim it either. Lacy had called it carpetbagging. But what earthly good was it?

Trump slid so deeply into his reverie that he failed even to teach his claybank manners, so it plodded along as slowly as it could get away with, while Rooster sweated remorse. Trump knew he had to lean on Lacy, lean hard, but he didn't know how. He fantasized loping back and pounding Lacy to pulp, and then whipping every one of those skinny rebels working for Lacy. Go back and pound them like fenceposts. It pleased him, the images forming in his mind's eye.

"All them Rebs was armed, and I figured they'd plant me for sure, six feet under,"

Rooster muttered to no one in particular.

It tugged Marvin back into hot reality, and his fantasy vanished. "I'll figure this out; you just mind your business."

Rooster laughed cynically. Marvin had never heard his segundo mock him, so he stood up in the stirrups, wanting to look impressive. Air cooled his crotch and he forgot about smart-alec employees.

He felt sweat dampen his armpits and river down his brow and neck. They were a long way from his spread. Funny how that veranda stayed cool and pleasant, even in the heat. Big houses had some sort of comfort about them, he thought. He'd like one of them himself someday. But not if it wiped him out, the way it'd destroyed that dumb Dent.

Fifteen beeves lost before his eyes. How many more? The terror prickled through him. What if Lacy intended to blotch all his beeves? He couldn't sell, couldn't ship! The Stockmen's Association worked closely with the railroad, and the Northern Pacific hired some tough dicks to check brands when beef was in the shipping pens. The NP never knowingly shipped blotched brands or any brand on the cattlemen's blacklist, or any unregistered brand. By God, if Lacy blotched all his beeves, he couldn't get an animal to market, or get paid! The sheer terror of it laced through him.

"Rooster, he'll blotch us all. He'll blotch every cow in the basin! He'll wipe us out, me and Pelz and Hruska and Perce. And him not stealing a beeve, at least slapping a brand on that he's got recorded in the books. So he'll sit on his porch and watch us, and laugh. By God, I never seen the like!"

Rooster eyed him coolly. "That Lazy Questionmark ain't worth spit. Anyone that registers it's going to get strung up from the nearest cottonwood limb. Lacy's dumb. You can't burn a brand next to a blotched one without you get into trouble."

Rooster annoyed him. "That don't help none, and I don't want your half-cocked advice. Them cows, no one can tell apart. Who's to say what's mine and what's Hruska's and who's to say we're swearing the truth? Lacy ain't stole a beeve, far as I can see, except maybe Dent's. All he's got to do is say they ain't his. You're dumb as an ox, Rooster. If you had brains, you'd be running the outfit, not me."

Rooster smirked. "He'll drive you out, since you can't sell, and then he'll figger how to peddle all them blotched ones. Maybe a deal with an Injun agent somehow. They're all hungry as cooties."

Trump kept silent. An idea was tickling at

245

him, something at the back of his skull that wouldn't quite take shape. "Maybe he don't care about owning," he muttered.

"Don't care about owning? He wants everything! He stole Dent blind, even his worthless woman!"

But the idea hung veiled in Marvin's head, irritating him with its elusiveness.

He couldn't fathom Dixie Lacy, but he could lean on him. When he rode into his own ranch yard, things were going to explode, he thought.

Two hours later they steered their weary, alkali-caked horses up to Trump's log cabin. He leapt down onto sore legs, and began barking orders even before he and Rooster had cared for their horses.

"Washburn — where's that fat bum?" he roared, knowing he'd find the porky cowboy lazing in his bunk, reading a Ned Buntline novel. But Lucius Marcullus Washburn was studying petticoats and chemises and bust enlargers in a catalogue while perched in the two-holer.

"Washburn, you reading that catalogue again? Lissen, that Lacy's rustling this outfit blind. All the outfits. I want you to ride on over to Hruska and the rest, and tell 'em — Lacy's blotching brands. Just blotching brands. I don't have men enough to go hunt down every cow in the basin, hundreds of square miles, but all of us together, we got to get our stock close to our home places so we can watch it."

"I can't come out yet," said Washburn.

"Well you hurry up and ride. Take your bedroll because you'll be out a coupla days."

The response was a grunt.

He found Rooster unsaddling their tired horses, and brushing the brine off their hair.

"Rooster, we got to act fast. We're going to have one hell of a roundup. I want to gather every animal in the basin including the ones that Lacy's close-herding down there. That'll take men. But we'll get every one, including Dent's Bar D, and those blotched ones they're herding down there while they heal up. I don't want a single beeve anywheres that Lacy can get his mitts on. We'll herd them all up here, and keep a guard from all the outfits on them day and night. I don't want to see a beeve within twenty miles of that white house. And get the broncs, too, including Lacy's. Get everything that moves."

"That's a tall order, Mister Trump."

"Start it rolling. I'm sending Washburn to fetch the others."

Rooster stopped his combing of the clay-bank and pulled a packet of cut plug from his shirtpocket. "You figgered out what

247

Lacy's up to? It sure beats me." He pinched off some plug and laid it under his tongue. "This here claybank's got hotted up fetlocks. Feel that," he said, running a hand over the flared joints in the legs.

"Quit fooling with that stumbler and get a gathering put together. We'll leave at dawn; I want the boys outfitted, the cavvy brought in, and all the rest. And I want them all armed. Those Lacy men looked like trouble."

"We don't want shooting wars," Rooster said. "That bunch isn't like Dent. They'd shoot back, I figger, especially if you want us to fetch all those beeves we rode through this morning."

"When they see us all, they'll run. They're seven plus Lacy. We're forty-some, all told, amongst us."

"You sure you know what you're doing? You figgered what Dixie Lacy's up to yet? Because if you haven't, we might just get our tail in a crack."

"It's coming to me," Trump muttered.

But it wasn't.

It had amused Dixie, the way Marvin Trump sweated out his terror on the veranda. Trump fully expected to be led off and shot, along with that wiry foreman of his, and buried for all eternity under some caved-in

248

cutbank somewhere. The way Trump had eyed Two, who lounged behind him on the porch, had been a sight to see. And Rooster, too. The pair had turned pale, and then green-fleshed, and sat squirming.

Amusing. Just as amusing as their puzzlement at the spectacle they witnessed. Blotching brands. Not theft, really, but loss of property. They couldn't fathom it; couldn't fathom Dixie Lacy and his men. They would puzzle it all the way back to their outfit, and probably never even come close, even though Dixie had virtually told them, given them all the clues they needed.

He settled into his wicker to enjoy the afternoon. Not even the day's mounting heat destroyed the shaded comfort of the veranda, if a man had a little whiskey at hand and a slave to tote and fetch. Marvin Trump, the local bully, pale as a ghost. That would entertain him for hours. The man'd go back there and start gathering cattle; probably alert the rest of the cattlemen in the basin. They'd puzzle over it, miss the obvious, and make a defense. It had always been like that.

What they would never fathom, because it seemed to run against human nature, was that Dixie enjoyed destruction. All his men did. He wasn't stealing anything except maybe Dent's stock, and that was only because of the sheer coincidence of having the same brand. No, Dixie was still fighting the war, and so were his seven men, and their obsession was to destroy. The Lazy Questionmark brand was nothing but a huge joke. He didn't intend to register it, and find himself hanging from the nearest cottonwood limb. No. The brand evoked mystery and mockery, and all his men enjoyed it.

Two of his men were surely crazy. He didn't know whether the war itself, with all its horrors, had deranged them, or its aftermath, but they were perfectly mad and irresponsible. Three others had simply lost their will, having seen and suffered too much: gentle parents thrown into prison for alleged sedition and rebellion; stripped of property and life; sisters and brothers buried after being thrown into the streets and lanes by bluecoated Yanks. The damned Yanks had marched in from the North, looted and confiscated, destroyed reputations of honorable men, laughed at suffering. So three had lost their will and become perfect puppets. If he commanded them to shoot themselves, they'd do it promptly. The two others were perfectly rational, like himself, but Devil's lieutenants, also like himself, enjoying the darkness because they'd been robbed of light. Six's three sisters had been ripped from their home and installed in a bordello for Yankee enlisted men. Seven had been a doctor who was prevented from caring for the sick and wounded after Sherman's destruction of Atlanta. Not that he could do much, with no supplies, but he couldn't even bandage and comfort the screaming, the dying, the miserable, the women in childbirth. And so these two, like himself, had made their own pacts with the Devil, scorned the tattered ideals of goodness and mercy and love, and found dark joy in the aimless ruination of the world. Both were perfectly rational, like himself. And also like himself, fully absorbed with spreading hell on earth.

They all called him captain although he'd been a sergeant and Two had graduated from Virginia Military Institute and had been a colonel of volunteers. For them all, the War of Secession had never ended and never would. They'd drifted from place to place in the unpoliced West, like ghostly Quantrill's raiders, destroying whatever whimsy led them to destroy, and then slipping off to destroy something else.

These Judith Basin ranchers would never understand it. Never grasp that Dixie enjoyed chaos, and his mission was to spread suffering like some demonic Johnny Appleseed. It would be beyond their fathoming that they

251

faced mortals who scorned worldly gain, ranches and cattle and roots, wives and children, esteem in their villages, luxuries, trips, pleasures, comforts. Utterly beyond Trump's imagination. But about the time the basin ranchers did fathom it, he would trump their hard-won wisdom: Dixie had discovered the Promised Land after decades of wandering, and he intended to settle down here. The great house enchanted Dixie. After twenty years of wandering like Moses, he'd found something he cared more about than wrecking Yanks. He'd suddenly become a lord of a plantation, with servants at his beck and call.

Which reminded Dixie that it was time for more amusements.

"Woman," he bawled.

Eve appeared at the front door, anxious as always, wiping flour-dusted hands on her dirty skirts.

"Yoah obedient, aren't you?"

She nodded, dread in her. Whenever he toyed with her the fear in her face became palpable.

"You'd never rebel now, would you? Run away?"

"Dixie —" she murmured.

"I've been reading your thoughts, Eve. You were hoping Marvin Trump would see your sad condition and rescue you. That he'd go fetch all the ranchers and come here and save you from me."

"No, Dixie, I didn't —"

"Don't ever say no to me. That's what you were thinking, wasn't it. Yoah got a possum mind."

"Dixie, don't hurt me —"

He frowned. "If you obey, you don't get hurt."

She nodded nervously.

"Here," he said. From his black holster he slid his long-barreled Colt .44 revolver, a weapon he'd scarcely ever fired. He handed it to her butt first, its scrimshawed ivory grips thrust toward her hand.

"Dixie —" She bridled at the sight of it.

"Take it. Shoot me. See, it's loaded. You've thought of shooting me for weeks, shooting and running away. Now's yoah chance. In fact, I insist, and you must obey."

He thrust it at her, and she grasped it gingerly, as if she were touching something too hot to handle. She stared at it, transfixed, paralyzed.

"I told you to shoot me!" he yelled.

"But Dixie, I —"

"Of course you can. You've thought of nothing else for days. You've wanted to steal it, slip it from me at night. You've walked to it in the middle of the night. All right then, if you won't shoot me, shoot yourself."

"Dixie!"

"Of course you can. Easy. Put it to yoah forehead and pull the trigger."

She gaped at him, and then at the glinting blued device, and finally hefted it, dread in every movement. She peered at the front of the cylinder and found bullets nestled in their tubes. She lifted the hammer fearfully and found a cartridge under it and eased the hammer down in terror.

"You've disobeyed me. You know what that means."

"Don't, Dixie. I don't want to —"

"Yoah afraid to. Yoah afraid of me. Yoah a pismire. All the rest of yoah life, I'll use you. Others will use you. Yoah nothing. You have no mortal will."

Her lilac eyes burned, and she lifted the revolver slowly. He turned, facing her. She lifted it higher, and it amused him, the emptiness in her. Vacantly she lowered it again.

"Yoah getting to enjoy slavery, woman. I can see it. Nothing escapes me. You like to clean the house."

"I do what you ask."

"That's the trouble. You don't even rebel. Here —" He sprang up from the wicker and wandered inside. "You like this palace too much now that it shines."

He wandered into the parlor, and with a hard sweep of his hand he sent a lamp sailing. The chimney shattered, and coal oil seeped from the brass reservoir into the ashes of roses carpet.

"What are you doing!"

"Making yoah life miserable." He sprang toward the dining room where a set table awaited the men. He swept Haviland china to the floor, and glasses and silver. It shattered and tinkled and clanged and shivered. It rolled and died, shards of nothingness. "I'm the Devil's lieutenant," he said.

"Dixie, don't!"

He wandered into the kitchen and found bread rising in tins. He tossed them at her. She dropped the revolver and the tins, too, and they clattered to the floor. Tears welled in her eyes, and it entertained him.

"Here," he said. He lifted the square cannister of flour, yanked off the lid, and dumped it upon her, letting the white powder bloom over her jet hair and her bodice.

She stood, paralyzed. "Oh! Oh, God! Why, why, why, Dixie?"

"Because you liked it."

She slumped, sobbing.

"Keep the gun. You haven't the will to shoot me. You'll have it and not use it and know you ain't worth spit."

Chapter Seventeen

The idea kept hurting Abner's mind like a bee-sting. It was madness but it refused to go away, and festered in him, sending its poisons out into his soul.

He might loathe that white house now, but once he'd loved it, taken pride in it, delighted in the wedding gift he was able to scrape together for his bride. So long ago. It still was his! He'd overseen the construction, found carpenters in Maiden and lured them away from the boomtown. He knew every board and square nail. He'd ordered fittings in Fort Benton, and had them shipped up the long, long Missouri from places as far away as St. Louis and Independence. He'd sold mother cows, wincing at the terrible cost, but hoping that a little sacrifice would be the blood and sweat shed to make a dream come true.

No territorial banker would finance such a thing, especially on federal land, so he'd driven cows to market after he'd driven steers and calves and heifers, and somehow scraped up almost five thousand dollars, a princely sum for a princely house.

And now he intended to burn it to the ground. It oppressed him. It had not been the fruition of a dream, but the beginning of a hell. And it crushed him with its cost and weight and gloom. Now it was the magnet that drew Dixie Lacy to it. He could have no other reason for settling there. The house itself lorded over the basin like an English squire's country home, its very presence telling the world that all the affairs of the Judith country were settled within its rooms. That's what drew Lacy. Not Eve. Not the Judith country itself. Lacy could as easily have started his own outfit and herd in that half-empty country, but he chose to commandeer the house. And that was reason to burn it to the ground. Lacy would leave once the place had been reduced to ashes. And if he took Eve, all the better. Abner would start over, he and Hungry, in the humble log cabin, and then the sun would shine again.

He fought this demonic idea fiercely. No one burned his own valuable property! Surely it was madness. Everything would go, including the one thing he cared about, a tintype of his parents which set on the rolltop desk — his sole link to his heritage. He would have no way of sneaking in there and snatching the image of his parents from under Dixie Lacy's nose. The place had been guarded closely, and those men of Lacy's weren't greenhorns.

Would Lacy really leave if he were burned

out? Would he drive off Abner's Bar D cattle with him? Or would he merely move to the bunkhouse and continue on? Abner had no answer, but some deep intuition whispered that if the house burned, Lacy's enchantment with the place would die in the ashes. As for Eve, she'd merely make it an excuse to flee, with or without Lacy.

But there remained the practical difficulties. It was one thing to dream of creeping up to the house some dark night and lighting a fire. Quite another to hone such a pipedream down to reality. Most disturbing of all was the possibility that he might kill someone. As much as he despised Lacy and Eve, he had utterly no wish to consign them to death in their beds. But the more he thought of that, the less likely it seemed that anyone inside would be trapped. Lacy often had a night guard, either out at the windmill knoll, or up in the cupola. One quick alarm and Lacy's men would boil out of the bunkhouse and put out the fire.

At least they would if they had water. The storage tank on the knoll had a valve he could turn off — if the guard didn't spot him. He'd not only have to shut the valve; he'd have to break it somehow. That would still leave the river, less than a hundred yards distant. Which meant he'd have to destroy the buckets on the place somehow, also without being caught by the night guard. There'd be some in the kitchen beyond his reach, and one or two in the shed.

And how would one set a house afire, especially with a guard watching the night? It struck Abner that burning a house would be no easy thing. Dew on the wood might foil him; the efforts of seven or eight people, even without much water, could swiftly end it. It would take time to heap kindling and paper against the wood and hope the shiplap siding would catch. What's more, the siding didn't come all the way to the lawn. The mortared rock foundation rose several feet from the ground. That meant he'd have to start the fire inside the summer kitchen, which formed a leanto structure on the back of the house; or on the veranda, which he didn't want to do because he wanted to leave an exit for Lacy and Eve. It would have to be the summer kitchen.

He paused amid his reverie to consider his madness. He blinked it away and stared around him. The lodge lay silent in the dawn gray. Hungry and his ladies slumbered, sleeping the sleep of the innocent instead of planning arson. It was all madness. He shoved the fantasy aside, not wanting any part of it, and stared into the dim starlit sky where the smokehole at the apex of the lodge gave him a glimpse of the universe. Burn his own costly house? How could he even think of such folly?

Coal oil. Only a liberal application of coal oil would ensure that the job got done. Anything else, a fire of paper and kindling, they'd extinguish in a hurry with water from the kitchen reservoirs. Burning down a house would be no small enterprise. But coal oil might do it, coal oil splashed widely across the summer kitchen, on siding, maybe in the kitchen itself if he could sneak in. And then what? He'd start the fire with sulphur matches, and the flames would crawl, and expose him instantly. He'd be a target. He might just as well paint a bullseye on his chest — unless the guard was up in the cupola and couldn't see anyone close to the walls of the house. He'd need to stash a fast horse somewhere — and that was another thing. He'd have to free the ranch horses, drive them off so that he wasn't followed afterward. The thing kept getting more and more complex.

"You're thinking of something," said Hungry. "I can tell."

"I'm thinking of burning down my house."

Abner heard a wheeze from Hungry's direction. "You just don' understand women," he said.

"I'm serious. I'm going to do it."

"Find another woman. I got lots. I'll share these if you like."

"Hungry, dammit. I'm going to do it."

He heard a giggle and the rustle of a robe.

"I'll share one. Then you don' think of burning down your house."

Abner heard groans and giggles that could only be amorous, and bolted up, shedding his blanket and grabbing his boots. Outside the doorflap cold air lanced at him. He sat on damp ground and tugged his boots on and ran a hand over the stubble on his cheeks. He'd turned into a tramp these last days.

He'd need gallons of coal oil, he thought. He could get it at the mercantile if his credit was still good. No one seemed to know what had happened at his place, and maybe he could put it on his account. If not, he'd have to find more of his beeves and sell them. He could trade a steer for tins of coal oil. Gallons of it. Maybe ten gallons. Enough anyway to foil a lot of men.

It disturbed him. All his life he'd tried to build, to add, to create, to grow. Never destroy. It felt shameful, this thing, this destruction of thousands of hours of carpentry; of wood and nails and shake shingles, of milled hard-wood railings, of brass knobs, and lead pipes, and white enamel. It disturbed him so much he was sure he'd abandon the whole thing when it got down to the reality, the night journey to his outfit, spreading the kerosene, turning off the valve on the knoll, and all the rest. He'd cut and run. Guilt would lance him. Guilt and cowardice. He could never summon courage enough to do anything like this.

Shots would blaze at him from the bunkhouse. Some wild coincidence would upset everything. Some hand in the bunkhouse would choose that critical moment to step outside to relieve himself. Or it might rain, the chance cloud undoing all he'd done, as if to say that no man could go against nature, destroy just for the sake of destroying. The ghosts and spirits of every carpenter who'd labored on that place would cry at him, dance around him, protest his every step toward the house, knowing his dark intention to reduce their prideful labor — many had worked lovingly to build that place — to nothingness.

But he had to drive Lacy away. He loved the land under that house, the good earth, rich with the grasses of the basin. He loved the view from the veranda, the low blue mountains and the puffy clouds they caught; the endless seas of rolling land, land so rich it'd support a hundred thousand cattle. He wanted his land back, the land he'd slept upon and clutched and sifted through his fingers.

The land caught his soul and held it. The land healed him, and would heal him of the wounds Eve had left inside. He could not have the land until he drove Dixie Lacy away forever. And Eve too. He could deal with all the rest; he could deal with Marvin Trump when the time came. So it came down to that: Dixie Lacy or himself. One or the other would walk away from this, but not both.

The northeastern sky lightened, and the first hint of blue drove the murky gray away. A new day. An ordinary summer day, but a momentous one because his mind was made up, and he'd do what he had to or die trying. But he didn't think he'd die. And the dawn he was witnessing in the sweet clean air signified a dawn in his own life.

The Judith Basin ranchers, hastily gathered on Wolf Creek with their roundup crews, found themselves stunned witless. Better than ninety percent of the cattle they'd gathered had been tampered with; brands blotched, earmarks altered to random nothingness. The ones not altered tended to be Dent's Bar D beeves, and even those had the peculiar Lazy Questionmark burnt into their flesh. Most of this had happened within the six weeks since they'd completed the spring roundup. They hadn't any way at all of telling who owned what beeves.

"We might go by the spring tallies and rebrand," Ben Hruska said, staring somberly at a vast mass of bawling longhorns no one owned. "Just parcel them by tally and put the irons to them."

"We ought to string up Lacy and that whole bunch," Law Perce muttered. "And Dent, too. He seems a part of it since his critters weren't blotched."

"I don't think he is, Law," Hruska said. "That's Dixie Lacy's Texas brand. He boasts of it. The fact is, Lacy hasn't stolen one beeve from us, far as we can tell, unless he's got that Lazy Questionmark stashed in some brand book somewhere. But it sure looks like he stole Dent's beeves."

"We'll see," said Leo Pelz, ominously. "Dent was in trouble, that woman of his. I wouldn't put it past him to throw in with Lacy."

"It's got me buffaloed," Law said. "Why would anyone blotch brands? All he's doing is making life tough for us. Now no one can claim the beeves, including Lacy. He's got no more handle on 'em than the rest of us."

"It's enough to string him up. He can claim they ain't his from now to doomsday, but he needs stringing up," Marvin Trump said. "He did it. He showed me and Rooster. We saw it happening."

"I don't know that you can string up a man who ain't stole anything — far as we know," Hruska said. "Maybe if Abner's got a complaint and can prove it —"

"We can string up Lacy and everyone with him, and Dent, too, if we feel like it. What's to stop us?"

"The law," Hruska muttered. "And seven or eight Lacy men who look mighty handy with guns. These boys here, they're drovers. We got the advantage in numbers, but I don't suppose any of them is a killer or would stomach a necktie party, even if we could catch Lacy's outfit. They know Lacy has no claim to these animals. I think we'd better go slow."

"Buncha babies," Trump muttered. "All a bunch of nannies."

"I think you'd like to take that back, Marvin," said Perce sharply. "I think you'd just better."

Trump glared at them truculently. "You're a bunch of cowards."

Perce boiled toward Trump, but Hruska stepped between them. "That's enough. We got to figure what to do," he yelled. From around the circle of cattlemen the nooning drovers stared.

"If you hens don't go after Lacy, I will."

"Look — Marvin — stringing up Lacy doesn't solve much of anything," Ben said

265

amiably. "We've got a hell of a tribulation. We can't sell these beeves. We can't make money. We can't prove we own any of them. We can't ship them. You know what the railroad does; they don't bend on that for nothing. We can't find a buyer who'd take them. We're busted and stringing up Lacy isn't going to un-bust us. You're broke, Marvin. You hardly own a cow."

"I own as many as my spring tally says."

That struck Ben Hruska as pretty bull-headed, but that was nothing new for Marvin Trump.

"I think we'd better get a territorial lawman here. When we tell him what happened, and what we want, he can maybe give us a clean bill on our beeves," Hruska said quietly.

"What's the association rules?" Perce asked.

Hruska knew, and could hardly bring himself to say it. "The Montana Stockgrowers Association rules say that blotched beeves become the property of the association itself, and will be sold by the association to pay for range detectives and legal costs against rustlers. We all signed it; we're all committed to it."

"But that's for an occasional stray, or a few they get from rustlers. This here is our whole stock, except for whatever Lacy's got down there on Dent's ground . . ." Pelz said.

"They can't take our entire herds from us!"

266

"They can. They're pretty near law, since the territory goes right along with the association. It may be a private club but what we wrote up for rules is what gets enforced by the territory, the sheriffs, the railroads, and the buyers," Hruska said. "We've got to explain it and work something out."

"Yeah, with Lacy sulking around causing more trouble. If we don't fix him now, he'll fix us. I'm a-going over there right now, and any pansy that wants to stay here can stay here," Trump yelled.

Hruska sighed. He'd been watching a small moving knot of animals a mile off, as had several of the drovers, and now the knot had transformed itself into several horsemen, five at least.

"Maybe you won't have to, Marvin."

Transfixed, they studied the expanding figures of horsemen floating over shining green prairie toward them. Lacy on his blood bay, unmistakable. And his men, as obscure and anonymous as ever. Hruska peered around at the drovers, dreading trouble. A few were crawling toward their soogans. None were armed; six-guns were a nuisance during a gathering. Only Trump was heeled, and he stared wolfishly, his intentions written plain on his face.

"Don't, Marvin. Don't be a damn fool," Hruska said.

267

But Trump smirked.

"Suit yourself. You're alone."

Lacy looked somehow dashing, as he always did, under his wide-brimmed hat. The four men with him carried double-barreled scatterguns across their laps, and wore a pair of revolvers. One had a holstered third revolver slung over his saddle horn. They could throw awesome amounts of lead in seconds, which was not lost on any cattleman or drover who watched the horsemen walk in and separate into a military-type line, each rider about twenty feet from the next in murderous array. Lacy himself had a shotgun across his lap.

"Afternoon, gents," he said, surveying them all. His gaze fastened on a drover, one of Pelz's boys, sidling toward the wagon. "You. I don't think so."

The drover halted, frozen.

"I see you've been studying brands. Very interesting. No one owns anything," he said amiably.

"We can fix it. We got our tallies and we'll get the law," Trump said. "You figgered you could steal our entire outfits, but you're too clever to do it right."

"Steal? Steal? These aren't mine. I have no claim on them."

"You think you do. You're going to register that Lazy Questionmark, or maybe you got it registered in some other place. Only it didn't work, Lacy."

Dixie Lacy seemed to enjoy Trump's truculence. "Sorry, but I've got beeves of my own. These aren't mine."

"You're gonna make 'em yours somehow. Unless we put a stop to it. That's why you blotched 'em — so you can grab them some fancy way. You're a thief and a coward, Lacy."

Hruska winced. Trump was prodding, with some sort of crazy courage that could get him killed.

But Lacy grinned, wild light dancing in his eyes. "No, I wouldn't say so. I'm a carpetbagger. That's different. I wouldn't steal from you, Mister Trump, not when a man can carpetbag."

"What's that mean?"

"Why, it means I use the rules rather than violate them."

"You blotched all them beeves."

"Carpetbagged."

Hruska's tension seeped from him. This seemed to be a talk session, not a shootout. "Maybe, Mister Lacy, you'd care to explain all this? Blotching brands will cause us some problems, but nothing we can't resolve with the help of the association."

Lacy lifted his hat and ran a hand through

thick brown hair, and settled the hat again. His curious gaze wandered through the crowd, settling alertly on this man and that, as if summing them up and drawing private conclusions.

"I'm a range detective by trade," he said. "These gents work in deep cover to prevent theft. Actually, I'm a principal of the Rocky Mountain Range Protection Service, headquartered in Denver City. I have a man there you can contact. We're here to make sure yoah blotched beeves don't get sold. They don't belong to a living soul. Not to me, not to anyone except maybe the Montana Stockgrowers Association. We're going to protect public property, just in case you take notions."

A red rage built in Ben Hruska. Trump stared at Lacy, popeyed.

"We'll be making sure these blotched beeves aren't sold or removed from the Judith country until their ownership is settled," Lacy said. "It may take years. The courts will have to settle it. It might even take some lawmaking. Right now, the Stockgrowers Association owns all these. Who'll get what is a very complex question."

"I knew you were a thief," yelled Trump. "How're we gonna survive even six months?"

"Carpetbagger, not thief. I enforce the law and keep the rules, Trump. We-all call it

270

carpetbaggin'. And after you-all leave the country, busted, someone will claim the increase. Put a hot iron to all those slick little calves next spring. That's carpetbaggin' and nothing else. Meanwhile, these detectives here'll make sure there's no stealin' public property."

Trump looked ill, but he still resisted. "What's that questionmark brand, Lacy? That yours, too?"

"Nope. Not mine. That says nothing and means nothing."

"Then why —"

"Consult the Devil," Lacy said. "Only he knows."

Ben Hruska calculated swiftly. Without cash from the fail shipping, he'd have to lay off his entire crew. Without cash from a spring shipping, he'd sink, heavily in debt. And so would the rest. Especially with these "detectives" putting Lacy's brand on the spring calves, and threatening anyone who had hung on through the winter. Legal theft, he thought. Barely legal.

"Carpetbaggin'," said Lacy, reading minds.

Chapter Eighteen

Eve wept, mixing her tears with the soapy water she was using to scrub the rug. But her desperate wiping didn't help much. The rank smell of kerosene permeated the rich rose-colored nap, and nothing she did seemed to help. She collected shattered Waterford glass in the parlor, shards of Haviland china in the dining room, and debris in the kitchen, all the while weeping until her eyes hurt and tear-streaks coursed down her hollow cheeks and into her damp bodice.

She couldn't stop. Some convulsion gripped her as she struggled to restore order, some defeat that flooded her soul and then her eyes. It wasn't just the china that had shattered, but her soul, too. Everything within her was broken to bits, mind, body, and worst of all, hope. Shards of hope lay prostrate about her like the carnage of war, and with hope broken, so was her spirit. She couldn't stop, any more than a breeched dam could stop a flood. She swept and mopped and grieved each plate with its blue filigree, its beauty forever smashed.

For two hours she wrestled with the chaos, until at last the place looked decent again. She couldn't understand the depth of her anguish or how she'd come to love a sparkling house that glowed proudly. All she knew was that she'd been forced to toil, to wear herself to the bone, until her entire body ached and her heart cried for release, and the result had been a dazzling house that delighted her, waxed and scrubbed, polished and washed; with snowy sheets on beds, sweet-scented towels, a fragrant kitchen with delicious odors rising from it. . . . Smashed.

Supper time approached, and she couldn't bear the thought of feeding those men. That part remained drudgery, the endless cooking and washing dishes and scrubbing their clothes. They would file in, these men whose names she didn't know; who peered at her with vacant eyes. They would wolf down her heaped food and leave, barely speaking, and at the end of each of these terrible meals she felt hollow, as if something had been sucked out of her. She'd been denied even their company; even the pleasant talk that usually accompanies a good meal. And at the end, she would face a whole table full of dirtied dishes and hours of cleaning up.

And now she couldn't stand the thought of that. She leaned on her broom in the kitchen, everything restored as best she could, and felt her spirits ebb. She dropped the broom and staggered to her room, still leaking tears, and threw herself across the fourposter. Her mind whirled crazily. She loved the white house and hated it. She had discovered pride in keeping it up, but hated being Dixie's slave. She hated and feared Dixie, especially in his mad moments such as this, but he made her feel alive and sometimes made her laugh when he wasn't hurting her. She remembered Abner with yearning, remembered that he had always treated her as an equal with free choice, not as a slave. And yet he remained dead to her, inert, and she couldn't summon any feeling about him. Some moments she hated them both.

She felt the tears wet her cheek and exhaustion consume her. Supper. Past time. It didn't matter. She slid into a torpor and at last her sobbing slowed. That's when Dixie burst in.

"Where's supper? What's the matter with you? Get up."

But she didn't.

"I told you never to say no," he said, and with one lithe bound he lifted her off the soft bed and let her fall to the carpet. She groaned and didn't move.

"Yoah not fooling anyone."

She didn't move.

He kicked her and she felt her ribs explode, and pain lance outward, but all she did was groan.

"I know the racket," he said. "If I didn't use you, you'd use me."

She didn't fathom that, and his voice seemed a mile away. The left side of her chest ached, and she felt the pain pierce into her shoulder and down her arm, and crawl across her stomach. She knew she had to sit up, or that black boot would smash her ribs again. Wearily she twisted up, until she sat, staring up at him.

"That's better. Yoah hardly worth kicking. Get supper. My men are waiting."

"No," she whispered, surprised at herself.

Some wildfire kindled in his eyes, turning them yellow and feral.

She'd come to some kind of crossroads her fogged mind couldn't explain. She wouldn't cook. She would not clean up after his crazy tantrums. Whatever he destroyed would stay destroyed. She wouldn't slave over a hot stove for madmen. She wouldn't wash their britches and underthings, pounding them on the Howard washboard until her arms dropped off. She would come and go freely. She would keep house, but not if he bullied and ragged her. She knew something had happened within her. She'd come to some sort of ending. She wasn't what she had been. She didn't scorn labor and she didn't complain.

She knew she hadn't been much, and she

knew she could do better. She'd always known, somewhere in the back of her mind, that people who worked hard, didn't complain, didn't use others, and gave more than they received, lived well and happily, and were finer than her kind. He'd done her a favor of sorts, forcing her to work, but slavery wasn't really a favor.

Her tone must have startled him because he paused, no doubt weighing how to torment her next.

"This house is mine. You and your men must leave now."

"Well, aren't you the lady. Worthless parasite making lady-talk."

"I was that," she said quietly. "But now I'm not. You're the parasite. You're nothing. Too empty to rebuild your life after the war hurt you. You've been nothing for twenty years."

He listened, startled, mockery building on his lips.

"Are you going to walk down to the kitchen or do I drag you?"

"Drag me."

He lifted her easily, and she felt herself being thrown over his shoulder, felt her clammy chemise stick to her as he trotted down the stairs and dumped her on the kitchen floor.

"Get busy."

She did nothing, waiting for the blows. He would kill her, then. He loomed above her, a poised puma ready to strike.

"No," she muttered.

The boot caught her skull, yanking it backward. She saw blinding light and felt her neck twist. The second caught her ribs again, and others landed on her legs and pelvis, and then she felt the slap of his palm across her face, and felt blood ooze from her nose. Pain exploded like shellbursts, going white behind her eyes, streaking up her legs, catching her belly, filling her with nausea, never stopping, the battery of some gray army, until she couldn't see and couldn't hear and couldn't feel and blackness slipped too slowly through her hammered body.

She drifted through a screaming dark, aware of nothing but pain and the hurt of her breath. She slid in and out of nothingness, until at last she returned to herself and knew she lay in a bed, and a man with a goatee was staring at her. She knew him. He was one of Dixie's men, one with vacant eyes and an occasional mad glare.

"I'm a doctuh."

"Go away. Let me die."

She drifted off again, vaguely aware of hands on her, moving her, cleaning her. Some vast wheeling eternity later, night and day, she came into herself again, and he still sat beside her.

"I'm a doctuh," he repeated.

"Let me die."

He laughed, with the noise of brittle paper crumpling. "Saw a lot of those," he said. "Better'n you."

She ignored him. The pain lancing through her told her she might live, and she couldn't imagine why. Waves of nausea flooded high in her, and relentless aching tore through her body. She tried to lift an arm, and couldn't. Sheer mad pain raked her when she tried to move it. Broken ribs. She lay helpless and at Dixie's mercy.

The next time she opened her eyes, her gaze confronted Dixie's. He stared down at her, mocking, observing with catlike fascination.

"I warned you."

"Get out of my house. You and your men."

He seemed amused. "I thought you hated this house. Too big, too lonely."

"I was free," she whispered.

He reached down and grasped her jaw, turning her head one way and another. "My, you're beautiful. You color up so nicely, yellow and purple. And swollen up where you lost the tooth."

"Leave or I'll kill you. Sooner or later."

He grunted. "You lack will."

278

She wished she could rise from her bed, but she couldn't, and lay helpless, waiting for him to leave. Her mind wasn't on him, but on will. The last time he said that, he'd dared her to shoot him. That time, she'd known her weakness and terror. The revolver still lay in her chifforobe, and now she had will, even though she could scarcely move a muscle.

"Yoah taking notions. I think I'll share you. I thought to keep you for myself, but you've got notions. I'll fix those. Tonight you'll pleasure them all, over there. Then you'll stop taking notions."

"No, Dixie . . ."

"You don't cotton to it? Ah, that's good."

"God, no, oh God." Tears rose again, as a desolation more terrible than anything in her life engulfed her. "Let me die, Dixie, let me die."

"You never were one for work," he said. "But tonight you'll work."

She stared up at him with blurred sight, scarcely believing she'd heard him, scarcely believing this was her Dixie.

"Yoah nothing," he said.

That was the last she remembered until the shouts and wavering orange light and eddying smoke awakened her.

It took planning. Even more, it took persuasion. Hungry had no wish to tag along and get himself shot at by experts, with a lot of firelight making him plain. Even less did Hungry want to shoot at any mortal.

"I yam not the killing type, Mister Dent."

"I don't want you to. I just want you to pin those gents in the bunkhouse with a few shots into the logs. I don't want them rushing out and pouring river water on the fire."

"You're crazy," Hungry said. "Burning that house."

His insolence chafed Abner.

"Look, I'll give you a bill of sale for a Bar D steer."

Hungry muttered, thought, and accepted. That was over a month's wages.

Abner bought the four gallons of kerosene at the mercantile, putting it on his account. And then he lowered the shining tin cannisters into two burlap bags. He didn't want the metal glinting in the dark.

They rode out of Lewistown early one afternoon of a July day. The moon would set about one in the morning. No clouds built in the sky, threatening to undo what Abner intended to do. They rode due west, with the rectangular tins of kerosene clanging gently in the burlap sacks. Neither spoke, and there was nothing to say.

Blue light lingered along the northern

horizon when they approached the Judith River and the house just beyond. Abner called a halt, and they waited about a mile from the river until true dark settled. They slid off their mounts in river brush on the east bank, and Abner led Hungry to a spot where he could lie surrounded by brush, but within carbine range of the bunkhouse and the cupola, where a night man probably watched. They picketed the horses, but Hungry would stay close to them just in case they tried to bolt. Firelight and gunshots could panic the animals.

Abner studied the cupola, and could see no one up there peering into the night. Perhaps Lacy had relaxed the guard. A sliver of moon lay low, delaying everything. Abner itched to get on with it, but even that crescent of light would be enough to reveal him to an alert sentry. So they waited, swatting mosquitos and other humming things that whispered around them.

The place seemed quiet enough. He sensed horses in the corrals and meant to free them to hamper pursuit afterward. He stared bitterly toward his bedroom window, silvered in the thin light, where the moon's rays pierced into his bedroom and onto the sleeping forms of Dixie Lacy and Eve. When the moon perched at last on the horizon, turning orange before it slid from sight, he nodded to Hungry, lifted the two burlap bags, and edged toward the river. He could have ridden across and spared himself a cold soaking, but that would have made a lot of noise. Instead he lowered himself into the stream, feeling icy water soak into his boots and then up his jeans, feeling his feet slip on the bottom, feeling the water churn up to his thighs and then down his legs again. He clambered out in the midst of thick choke-cherry brush, a hundred yards or so south of the ranch buildings. He stepped out from the river brush and froze, waiting to see whether he'd been spotted. He wanted to run, but he made himself stand quietly. Nothing happened.

He walked north along the river, the house looming ominously at his left, an evil thing disturbing his thoughts and making him jittery. He lowered the two bags without making noticeable noise. It occurred to him that he hadn't planned for a dog. A barking dog could ruin everything.

He edged north and west, circumscribing an arc that would keep him away from the house but lead him toward the knoll where the windmill and reservoir stood — and perhaps a sentry. He studied the area hard, seeing nothing in the deep dark, but that didn't mean much. A man sitting on the ground, his back against the tank, would be invisible. He worked his way slowly up the grade, sensing that no one watched him, and finally he peered over the rear of the tank. Nothing. He caught his breath. His heart pulsed unnaturally.

The valve lay on the other side. He crept around the tank, seeing nothing. The valve stem thrust upward, cold iron with a small wheel upon it. He grasped the wheel and turned it slowly. It shrieked. He yanked his hands away from the icy metal as if he'd grabbed a puma by the tail, and flattened himself. No dog barked. Nothing. He waited another two minutes, feeling his heart thump the earth under his chest, and then tried the wheel again. It shrieked in pain, a plaintive chatter as rust loosened under his twist. He paused. Still no trouble. It would take a dozen spins to close that valve, but he had to do it. He'd moved the wheel barely a quarter of a circle.

He steeled himself for a full turn, and twisted frantically, hearing the steady howl as the resisting iron rod fought back. It seemed enough to bring men out of bunks and chase ghosts and set horses to neighing, but toward the end of that revolution the howling abated into a grumble. He stopped, sweating, and peered around. He could scarcely see, but knew every horse in the corrals stared at him, giving him away.

This time he forced himself to wait several

minutes, and then turned the valve again. It muttered but didn't howl, and in another moment he'd shut off the water. They could turn it on again. But one of Hungry's missions was to scare away anyone running toward the valve. Bullets would be persuasive, he hoped. He felt certain now that no sentry lurked this night, and walked easily around the back of the bunkhouse and barn, to a rear pasture gate, which he slowly opened, trying to keep it from creaking. The horses eyed him nervously, ready to bolt.

The bunkhouse door swung open, and Abner froze. A form emerged and wandered a few yards. Abner heard the sound of liquid falling. If the man was at all observant, he'd see the horses all staring westward, where Abner stood like a post at the opened gate. The man wandered to the corral, studied the horses, and then wandered inside. Abner wondered whether they'd all boil out and start shooting. He'd be caught cold. But nothing happened. Clock-ticks later, Abner relaxed a bit but didn't move. He waited what seemed like forever, and then slipped into the corral, quietly herding the horses around its perimeter and out. They didn't drift far, but enough to give him and Hungry an edge.

After that it seemed easy, at least at first. He swung around the circle, keeping well away from the ghostly house, and found the burlap bags. These he carried gently straight toward the summer kitchen. The building seemed huge in the dark, an evil mountain radiating a hellish white glow into the night, making his hair prickle. He knew he was choking down terror. He paused in the lee of the rear wall, close now, too close to be seen from any window or the cupola. He trembled inexplicably, and a hundred whispered voices within him told him to flee. Told him he would commit murder and the blood of those inside would be upon him. But he wouldn't. He'd give them an exit from the front door. And Hungry's shots would awaken Dixie and Eve.

Trembling, he edged toward the summer kitchen door. He found the knob and pulled gently. The door was unlocked and swung open lightly, as if charged with his trembling energy. He stepped in, waiting for his eyes to adjust to the deeper gloom, remembering where tables rested, the laundry tubs sat, the wash stove hulked. Oddly, the place stank of kerosene. He thought it was his own.

Silence. He slid one rectangular tin from the burlap and twisted off the cap. He found the other tins, as heavy as cannonballs, and opened them also, wondering at their odd preternatural weight. His hands weren't working;

that was it. His muscles weren't functioning. He poured, hoping the kerosene wouldn't simply leak between the floorboards to the earth below. He hadn't thought of that. But it puddled on the enamel. He sensed it more than saw it. Boldly now, he emptied other cans higher up, letting the gurgling kerosene run down the siding, collect along the doorway. Then finally he poured out the last. There'd be a wall of fire thirty feet wide crawling up the wall.

His breath gusted unnaturally. In fact he was holding it in. Light it and run. Dodge around the corner and into the shadow, so he wouldn't be spotted en route to the river. He found the matches in his shirt pocket and pulled out one, but his hand felt paralyzed. Should he do this monstrous thing?

He scratched it on the stove. It flared wild, blinding him with its amazing light. He lowered it into the kerosene, which caught swiftly. Smoky yellow flame raced in either direction, hurting his eyes.

The kitchen door boomed open. Lacy in a night shirt, revolver in hand.

"What?" he said. "You!"

Abner leapt at the man, catching him as he stepped into the summer kitchen. Lacy landed hard on the wet planks, breath grunting out of him. He sprang up, right into Abner's fist, and they tumbled through the doorframe. The revolver exploded. Dancing flame swirled upward. They landed on the kitchen floor together, clawing viciously at each other, each soaked in kerosene.

Chapter Nineteen

Live or die. Abner knew instantly that the former sergeant had been schooled in the roughest company. Lacy's knee jammed upward, aimed at the groin, but Abner twisted, and felt the murderous blow hammer his hipbone. It would have doubled him over, finished him in a moment. Lacy went for the eyes, trying to claw Abner's eyeballs out of his skull, but Abner jammed his face into Dixie's head and bit an ear, feeling his teeth mash through lobe.

Lacy's massive fist pounded Abner's kidneys, shooting nauseous weakness through Abner, and then Lacy's fists slugged at Abner's head, popping it back and forth like a punching bag. Abner jerked up, shoved a forearm into Lacy's throat and pressed, feeling the man gasp for air under him. Lacy bucked, driving his torso high, lifting Abner upward and away, and then the sergeant rolled, tossing Abner off. Catlike, Lacy sprang up, sending kitchen pans clattering. Abner stared up, dazed, seeing wild orange light leaping, sucking hot tendrils of smoke into his aching lungs. The whole summer kitchen roared. Vaguely, he heard shots and shouts.

Lacy darted toward his revolver, which lay at the doorjamb, inches from a wall of fire. Abner swung his legs hard and tripped him just as Lacy leaned down. Lacy toppled like a great tree, through the door and into the summer kitchen. He shrieked, an eerie howl, as his soaked nightshirt turned into a torch and burnt his flesh. Lacy leapt to his feet and bolted outdoors, his back an inferno, a man fleeing from the devil.

"Don't," Abner yelled. "Lie down and roll!"

But Lacy screamed toward the river, a yellow torch, howling through the blackness. Abner watched aghast, his head pounding and his whole body pulsing with vicious pain. Lacy, still shrieking eerily, landed in the river with a distant splash, and then Abner heard only the sound of sobbing. Alive, but burnt. How alive? Abner didn't know. He hadn't planned on this. Everything had gone haywire.

The rear wall roared at him, bellowing doom. Abner stood, paralyzed, his body aching, and then drifted through the kitchen, his own familiar kitchen, into the dining room, the parlor — where his rolltop desk occupied a corner. The tintype. The one of his parents he expected to lose. He paused, wondering how the odd detail caught him just when he should be running from Lacy's men, leaping onto his horse and fleeing with Hungry.

The tintype. Light danced eerily in the windows. Smoke eddied through rooms, layering in cool air. He yanked open the roll top and began pillaging, finding the small metal image at last. A bonanza. He slid it into his wet pocket, aware of more shooting, hoarse shouts. And something else — a wail that sent shivers through him. Eve's voice, wailing down the stairwell. Let her wail. She deserved to wail. But he couldn't. She was obviously frozen with fear up there, and would need leading out, like a blindfolded horse in a barn fire. He sighed, and bounded up the wide stairs, two at a time. The whole house thundered, and the smoke thickened, razor-edged inside his aching lungs.

She lay in the fourposter, howling like a wolf on a January midnight.

"Eve! Get out now!"

She stared at him, stunned. "Abner!"

"Get up!"

"I can't."

"Get up now. There's no time left!"

She caught smoke, and coughed terribly. "I'm hurt. I can't move — Abner . . ."

"Get up, Eve."

She sobbed.

"You still want me to do everything," he yelled wildly. But he slid his hands under her and lifted. She gasped and he could feel her body shudder in his grip.

"Broken ribs," she muttered. "Dixie — almost killed me."

"Serves you right," Abner snapped. He carried her dead weight through the door, into a wall of smoke and heat, coughed his way down the stairs, feeling dizzier by the second, hit a cool draft of fresh air in the foyer, and plummeted out onto the veranda. Behind him the house roared and shook, a monster consuming all within.

Ahead, the world danced. Shivering yellow light caromed off the barn and bunkhouse. Men in white longjohns ran aimlessly, shouting. An occasional shot racketed from the east — Hungry shooting. And with every shot, these dancing ghosts dropped to earth, pinned by terror.

Eve groaned, still a dead weight in his grasp, unable even to lift her arms. Too bad for her, he thought. He staggered down the veranda steps onto the lawn, feeling it buck and heave under him, and carried her another forty or fifty yards to a safe place. Behind him flame thundered and cast wild light out upon the blackness. He set her on the cold grass, his duty done.

"There. No one died," he said. "When you can, get off my place."

She groaned, and crumpled into a convulsing ball, weeping.

"Take me," she whispered.

"Take yourself."

"He'll kill me."

"He's badly burned."

"I'll die. I can barely move. Take me, Abner."

He'd never seen her sob like this, never seen her helpless and destroyed, and he pitied her momentarily.

"His gang will take care —" Which reminded him that he stood in plain sight, utterly vulnerable to a band of vicious cutthroats, well armed. "I'll see you around," he muttered.

"Abner, Abner, he tried to kill me because I'm not . . ."

He didn't hear the rest. Lacy's gang had vanished, either into the bunkhouse or somewhere else, maybe hunting buckets. Too late. The house had become a torch. For an instant he saw the proud cupola engulfed in a chimney of fire, watched it die high above him, watched it tilt slowly, and fall into the roof, and watched the roof cave into the upstairs, sending a pillar of sparks up into the blanketing black.

Then he understood. Lacy's men weren't hunting buckets. They knew. They'd plunged out into the dark hunting horses, and when they found and saddled them, they'd come

292

after Abner. He left Eve on the grass, sobbing but safe, and trotted eastward toward the river, hoping Hungry wouldn't shoot him.

"Hungry, it's me," he called, yelling into the blackness of the river brush.

Nothing answered. Behind him a rising thunder boomed, and a wave of heat rocked him as he trotted. He turned, seeing the great white house cave in on itself, like an anvil cloud lit up by its own lightning. Done. He'd succeeded. He threaded into the river brush.

"It's me, Hungry," he said, growing more and more terrified of the boy's trigger finger.

He reached the bank and waded in, feeling swift icy current tug at him. It felt good, and he realized he'd been hurt in a dozen places. His wet jeans had no doubt saved him from a lot of burns.

The groaning that rose almost at his feet sent a jolt of terror through him.

"Dent."

Abner gaped around, discovering Lacy a few yards downstream, a dull white mass of flesh in the water.

"You killed me, Dent."

Lacy's gasping pierced Abner.

"No mortal should suffer pain like this. My back's fried meat."

Abner waded toward the panting, groaning man.

"Shoot me, Dent. For God's sake, shoot me."

The flowing water blurred the white flesh. Lacy sat up to his shoulders in it. He had lost his hair, and the back of his head seemed blackened.

"Get it over with!" Lacy gasped. Then the man sobbed, a racking noise more terrible than anything Abner had ever heard.

"I — can't do that, Lacy."

"You always were a coward."

Wild rage built in Abner. "Call me any damned thing you want, Lacy. I'll have my place back, and you off it. Call me what you want when you're running."

"For God's sake shoot me. I can't — this is — no man —"

"I'll help you get out. That cold water's going to kill you if nothing else does. Eve's out on the lawn and I'm taking you there. And I'll fetch someone out from Lewistown with some laudanum. But I'm not going to shoot you."

Abner waded toward Lacy, intending to lift him out.

"Don't touch me," he shrieked. "Don't touch me."

"Mister Dent."

Abner whirled at the sound of the soft voice, and spotted Hungry standing on the far bank in the wavering weeping light.

"Help me, Hungry. He's burned."

"He don' much want help, Mister Dent."

"For God's sake don't touch me!"

"Can you walk, Lacy?"

"Shoot me. I can't stand this."

"Can you walk?"

"What does it matter?"

Abner scarcely knew what to do. He stood knee-deep in the flowing current, trying to find some sense in things.

"I won't shoot you, Lacy. But I'll leave a carbine on the riverbank."

"Do you think I can hold it? My hands are pulp. I haven't any fingers."

Lacy's voice faded into nothingness as he spoke.

"Lacy! I'm dragging you out and going for help."

"Never mind," the man mumbled. "Pain's going away. Go on, Dent. Leave me be. Cold water's fixing me up . . . feeling fine."

Abner sat his horse on a rise just across the river, riveted by the spectacle before him. He knew he should flee. They'd come after him and Hungry any moment. But he couldn't. His house, his own house, once his pride and joy, was dying before his eyes, shrinking and folding into ash, like his marriage. Its yellow

295

deathlight illumined the land with a ghostly glow for a mile around, making everything visible. It tugged at him, his place, his paradise, his heaven turned into hell.

"We'd better git, Mister Dent. Unless you figure we're a match for seven hardcases."

"In a minute, Hungry."

Men were drifting in from the outer darkness leading horses, but they seemed in no hurry to give chase. Others, half-dressed now, hollered for Lacy, and trudged along the river seeking the fire-bitten man they'd seen screaming toward water. Abner watched the searchers narrowly, knowing he sat within range of their weapons. In the murk he heard splashing and shouts, and nothing that sounded like Lacy's voice. Beyond, near the bunkhouse, men brought still more horses, a dozen of them, and tied them to the hitchrail there. It puzzled him.

"They don' seem in a hurry to catch us, Mister Dent."

"They can't find Lacy. Lacy held them all together with that way of his. I think they don't know what to do."

Three searchers began working downstream, sometimes visible and sometimes obscured by dark brush, calling for Lacy, but Dixie Lacy didn't reply. At the bunkhouse men toted gear out to the horses and threw packsaddles over several animals.

"Leaving! They're leaving, Hungry."

"Looks that way. Except for Mrs. Dent."

She lay huddled on the lawn, a white lump, unmoving.

"She's hurt somehow. Lacy did it. She got a lesson, I guess."

Hungry peered at him. "You just don' understand women, Mister Dent."

"I sure don't."

The searchers gave up. Abner watched them trudge back across the wide sweep of lawn, and jaw with others in the wavering light. Nearby, the house tumbled to earth piece by piece, the amber light fading to orange. Nothing stood except some fieldstone chimneys. Because of a southwesterly breeze, no spark had ignited the barn or the bunkhouse. Even across the river, Abner could feel radiant heat warm his face and dark shirt. The yellow horse shifted unhappily under him, wanting to go. He tugged its reins gently, not wanting to.

In the dying light, men saddled horses and loaded packs onto other horses, cleaning out the old log bunkhouse. Leaving, then. Leaving! It dawned on Abner he didn't need to head for Lewistown, didn't need to flee. He was coming home to the place he loved. He would walk the earth he'd made his own, feel his roots reach into it, see his mountains from the window of his log house. His!

"I yam feeling safer by the minute, Mister Dent. I thought they'd shoot my hide."

"It's not safe. We don't know where Dixie Lacy is. We don't know what they'll try. We'd better stand guard tonight."

"You're fixing to take the place back, then?"

Abner smiled. "And hire you if I can. I've got a heap of debts, and I don't know how many critters — something anyway. But I started with less."

"What about her?"

"I'll take her to Maiden or Lewistown tomorrow. Whatever she wants. If they don't steal the wagon from me."

"— And you can find a nag broke for harness."

Lacy's obscure toughs rode quietly south into darkness, but Abner didn't move. The fire died, leaving only bright coals and a powerful heat that still radiated out to them.

Abner waited a while more, not wanting to expose himself and Hungry to a spiteful sniper. Then he splashed the yellow gelding across the river and up onto the lawn, bypassing Eve. She annoyed him. Her very presence on the place soured his return. Still, he thought, she couldn't help it. She could barely move. But he'd take care of all that in the morning.

The old bunkhouse smelled of sweat and tobacco, but seemed remarkably clean. Who were such men, to keep a place as polished as an army barracks? Abner carried his lamp to the far corners, finding not even a dustball. Who were they, these men who had drifted silently through his life, in and out, like ghosts? Who was Dixie Lacy and what had he wanted?

He realized he was thinking of Dixie as a dead man, though he had no proof of it. He felt sorry, suddenly. He hadn't wanted death, and had planned this whole night carefully to avoid it. But it had come. Surely Lacy was floating down the Judith River, or was snagged somewhere in its many shallows.

"I guess we can settle in, Hungry. This is better than I thought."

"I got wives to look after, Mister Dent."

"Wives? Wives?"

"Yeah. You know. On Little Casino."

It startled Abner. "I didn't think — I thought we could just pick up where —"

Hungry chortled. "I ain't pickin' up. You don' understand women. I do."

Something sagged in Abner. "Well, I was hoping you'd stay and —"

"Who says I yam goin'? I can use the wage. Only I got to fetch the women and bring the lodge. We'll have the lodge."

Abner gaped. "The lodge?"

"Yeah. And maybe we can build a cabin for winter. We got plenty of time, eh?"

"Hungry, you devil! How many are you bringing?"

"All three. Them ladies can cook like hell, too. Maybe they'll work for you, eh? I'll give you one if you want. Three's more than a man needs. Share the wealth. I got three, you don' got any. You can take the mother since you're an old man. Her Injun name means Buffalo Cow Makes Water, but you can call her somethin' else."

"Hungry!"

But the lad was stripping gear off his dun and toting it inside.

Some instinct told Abner to keep his horse saddled and ready to run, so he hitched it at the rail and walked out on the lawn, step by step, toward the silent white figure huddled there. He would do his duty. That's all that remained, duty.

He stood over her, and watched her stare up at him in the dying light.

"You saved my life," she said.

"I don't know why. Do you want a tarp or a blanket or something? I can carry you to the barn if you want."

"Abner? I tried to tell you —"

"I'm not interested. Keep it to yourself.

Tomorrow, maybe, I'll drive you somewhere. Take your pick."

"I tried to tell you — I'm willing to —"

"I don't want to hear it. So Lacy hurt you. What did you expect? Man like him. Users, both of you. Neither of you ever heard of marriage vows."

She wept. "I tried to tell you —"

"Hungry says I don't understand women. He's right."

"The barn," she whispered.

"All right." He lifted her gently, surprised by her groaning at the slightest movement. She'd taken a terrible beating, and her face and body puffed unnaturally.

The black cavern of the barn aisle confused him, and he felt his way along, looking for some clean place to set her down. She wept, and he felt her tremble through her thin white night dress. It dawned on him she didn't have a stitch to wear, and as usual, he'd have to come up with something.

He didn't know where he was taking her. He didn't know whether manure filled the stalls. He wandered through the inkiness, bumping posts, cursing softly, hurting her.

"Oh hell, I'll take you to the bunkhouse tonight. You've spoiled my place and my life for years, so I guess you can spoil it one more night."

She wept.

He found his way through the huge rectangle of a barn door, and carried her through starlight to the bunkhouse, where light glimmered in the shining glass window.

Hungry stared as he brought her in. "Barn's not a proper place," Abner said roughly.

Lacy's men had built several wood pallets, and Abner settled Eve on one.

"It's hard," she said.

"You were always one to complain, weren't you."

Tears leaked from her eyes. Hungry watched, curious.

Abner unfolded a saddle blanket and tossed it over her, and found another for a pillow.

"I could keep house for you, Abner. I can cook. I can clean . . ."

"Sure you can. I'm taking you out of here tomorrow. And you or I or both of us will see a lawyer."

"I can cook, Abner. I'll do everything . . ."

She peered at him intently, her swollen tear-streaked face lifted toward his.

That damned Hungry sat on his bunk grinning.

"I don't know what's so funny, Billedeaux."

"Like I said, Mister Dent. You don' understand —"

"Shut up," Abner roared.

Chapter Twenty

The early summer sun didn't awaken Abner, but the soft gabble of voices did. He sat up, sensing he'd slept deep into the morning, and clawed at the holster that lay near him. They'd come back and by God he'd give them a fight. He glanced around his familiar cabin, orienting himself to a place he hadn't slept in for years.

No Hungry. The lad must have slipped out while Abner slept away his exhaustion.

But Eve, awake and staring. Her battered face shocked him. The flickering light of the fire had subdued the swelling, the purple and red bruises. She met his gaze and said nothing.

Abner wheeled out of the bunk and slid to the small window, taking care not to invite a bullet. Horsemen stood around the smoking pile of ash, pointing and shouting. Not Lacy's strange obscure crew, but neighbors. Trump, like a bull riding a horse, Pelz, Hruska. And some drovers. That blaze must have been visible for twenty miles, he thought.

Men approached the bunkhouse now, with revolvers drawn, supposing Lacy's men were in it. Abner lacked time to dress, but buckled his black holster belt over the white long-handles he wore summer and winter, and swiftly opened the door.

"It's you, Dent," said Lucius Marcullus Washburn.

"Who'd you suppose?" Abner retorted, irritably.

A few men grinned at Dent's peculiar costume.

As usual, Trump pushed through the gathering spectators on his horse, being the biggest frog in the pond.

"What the hell happened? Where's Lacy?"

Abner stared at the man, feeling disgust rise in him, feeling the time had come to settle a lot of things. "What happened is my business," he said curtly.

"It's my business. The house is gone and that's my business, Dent."

Trump's naked intent to possess the house someday lay thick on the morning air.

Abner stepped off the stoop, feeling grass stab at his bare feet. He stopped just a foot or two from Trump's horse, and stared up at the big man. "Marvin," he said softly. "It was my house and I burnt it."

"Burnt it! Are you crazy?"

"No, I never felt better. It's like a millstone off me. Now you've seen what you came to see, so go along to your outfits."

"Just a minute, Dent. Where's your partner, Lacy?"

"Lacy's probably dead, and you can take that back."

"I don't take nothing back."

"Lacy died accidentally. His men left. I'm repossessing my place. Does that satisfy you?"

"You killed him?" Trump's gaze turned wary.

"No. It was an accident. I tripped him when he was reaching for the gun he'd lost while we fought. He was soaked with kerosene and fell into the fire. He's in the river somewhere. Snagged or drifting."

"Lacy's dead? That thorn in our side?" asked Ben Hruska, sounding utterly amazed.

"How could that be? Him with all those nightriders?" Pelz asked. "You have help?"

"My man Hungry, some kerosene, and a match."

"And Lacy caught fire?"

"It could have been me."

"Lucky break for you, Dent." Trump laughed, but no one else did.

"I didn't want anyone to die."

"Especially a rustling partner, eh, Dent?"

"Get off your horse, Marvin, and say it again."

Abner felt a wildness infuse him; felt his heart begin to race; felt his fists itch. Trump had seventy or eighty pounds on him, but Trump was going to take the licking he'd earned. And Abner was going to take back the respect he'd lost.

Smirking, Trump slid off the saddle, his gaze on Abner's bare feet. Abner knew then he could expect a vicious boot on his toes.

"I say you're Lacy's partner, Dent," Trump said, balling his big fists.

"That's enough, Marvin," Hruska said. "A man doesn't burn down his house without a reason."

Trump bulled in like a sore-toothed grizzly, intending to flatten Abner and end it as fast as he'd ended the other fight.

Abner sidestepped, yanked his revolver, and buffaloed Trump, cracking the barrel hard over the big man's skull. Trump staggered.

"Evens the odds," Abner muttered. He whirled and leaped on Trump's back, running an arm around Trump's windpipe. He squeezed, feeling all the hardness of the years of ranching in his bicep as he rode Trump to earth. The man roared and gasped and tried to roll Abner off, but Abner hung on grimly, choking air out of the blocky rancher. Trump pawed and kicked, but nothing he did loosened Abner's steely grip, and gradually Trump's wheezing slowed.

"Dent! Let go!" Hruska roared.

Abner didn't. He'd had enough of Trump for two lifetimes.

"You're killing him! Let go or we'll tear you off."

The thunder of blood in Abner's head stopped thought, but Hruska's yelling finally reached him. He relaxed his murderous clamp.

The man wheezed on the ground, sucking air.

Abner stood, slowly. "Anyone else?" he muttered. It seemed a stupid way to settle things. "Anyone else thinks I was in with Lacy?"

"No one ever thought it, Dent," said Pelz. "That was just Marvin, being bull moose."

"You licked Lacy and those toughs!" exclaimed Hruska.

"I lit a fire."

"Whatever you did, it worked," said someone or other.

Trump, beet-faced, rolled upon his knees, still sucking air like a beached carp. They stood silently, watching the big bull of the Judith Basin pull himself together.

"You don't fight fair, that lick with your gun," Trump complained.

Abner laughed shortly. Others did, too.

"I'm not done with you, Marvin. Stand up."

The man unfolded slowly, and stood panting, hanging onto the skirt of his saddle.

"You owe me. We're going to settle for those bulls."

"I didn't take nothing. We put your brand on them."

"You stole value."

"Aw, it was just a joke."

"The joke will cost you twenty grown steers."

"Twenty steers!"

"That's a fair exchange. For using my bulls."

"Seems fair to me, Marvin," said Pelz. "You took something from Abner, any way you count it."

Marvin Trump glared at them all, one by one, from pig-eyes, and found only stony determination in every cattleman and drover.

"All right."

A small change seemed to filter through the men. Something eased. A few cowboys grinned.

"I guess that about wraps it up, Abner," said Ben. "You got some beeves around that weren't blotched. Lacy had a Bar D registered in Texas. I figure he marketed a bunch of yours somewhere, and we can't help that. The rest of us got a problem with those blotches, but we've sent word to Helena to send a man out. If we don't get a sale okayed, we'll go under, every one of us. That's what Lacy wanted. Wanted us to pull out. Quit! He didn't care. He'd let them blotched ones breed, and put his mark on the calves. Maybe slip a few blotched steers to anyone that wanted beef. By God, he came close. He'd be king of the basin!"

"And those half-mad men of his would be sitting on your spreads," Abner said. "War-ruined men. Didn't care if they destroyed or built. At least until Lacy got the itch to start up an empire — with a carpetbag trick."

"If the Territory okays it, we'll form a coop-erative, get the Territory and the railroad to let us ship, and we'll divide up the sale according to the tally books from spring. By God, they've got to help us ship, or we'll still go under. We'll cut you in on some, Abner, because those extra bulls of yours helped us all."

"That will suit me," Abner said, dourly. They'd all kept Trump's little secret from him, even Ben Hruska.

"I never did like it much," Ben added, glar-ing at Trump. "But we'll all make it up to you."

Abner nodded.

"I guess you're staying in the country, Abner?"

"I'll rebuild. Pay some debt fast as I can."

"If you don't mind my asking — what happened to her?"

Abner nodded toward the bunkhouse. "Injured. By Lacy, not the fire. I'll haul her to Maiden soon as she's able."

"Sounds plumb sensible."

Men laughed, and Abner resented it.

"I have work to do," he said dourly.

"This is some story, Dent burning down that house, driving Lacy off," Pelz said. "Damned if anyone'll believe it. You, of all people. Abner Dent."

"You'll start believing now," Abner snapped. He felt sore-toothed mean.

They took the hint and turned their nags. Trump clambered aboard his slowly, his face still beet-colored. Abner watched him unblinkingly.

"This place will never be yours, Marvin."

Marvin Trump nodded and sawed the reins of his claybank, while the animal fought the cruel bit.

Abner watched them ride off, gawking at the black mound of char, with tendrils of smoke still lifting from it. The stink of ash still oppressed the air. In a day or two he'd paw through the mess and salvage metal fittings. And in a few weeks he'd start hauling ashes to a coulee. But now he had work to do and no one to help him, because that damned Hungry had vanished. Lacy's gang had used up most of his prairie hay, and he would have to cut and stack tons of it to winter his horses.

He wandered aimlessly through the barn, assessing his losses, enjoying possession of his own property. Harness still hung from pegs, and his sickle-bar mower seemed intact. He'd try to find his pair of drays. He wondered how many beeves he had, and what his debt amounted to. He'd started with less, though, and he'd build again, and sit on his front stoop and see the purple mountains and the waving green grasses dotted with his beeves again, and ride the sweetwater creeks again, and sweat and cuss beside the rest of them at the roundups again, because that was his life, and he would build it better than before.

He delayed as long as he could, counting losses and making plans, and then he faced the cabin, and her.

He found her lying on her side. Her cheeks glistened, and he knew she'd been crying again.

"You ready to go?"

She turned, painfully, to stare up at him with lilac eyes that once enchanted him. "Where?" she asked softly.

"Maiden. Anywhere."

The tears came again. "I can hardly move. He broke my ribs. I can feel them. More than one."

"You pick friends like yourself."

"I need — I hurt so much. Could you wait?"

"No. Not for you."

The wetness streaked down her puffed cheeks. He couldn't get used to her looking like that, swollen and bruised purple. "I'll need a dress. Everything's gone," she whispered.

He had forgotten that. And didn't care. "You can take the blanket."

"The blanket? You'd take me to Maiden in a nightgown and a blanket? And leave me there like that?"

"Yes. I've got to find the draft horses. They'll be along the river somewhere. I'll find them and harness them. Then we'll go."

"Abner — I can't — I'll die."

"That's the risk."

She sobbed softly, seeing her fate. "Just a few days? Please, Abner?"

"No." He wasn't going to let her toy with him again, and by God, she would be out of there just as fast as he could harness the spring wagon.

"Abner — I'm . . . sorry for everything. I failed you."

"Don't. Use your wiles on some other sucker. You've never been sorry in your life."

"But I am, Abner. I am!"

"Tell it to the next fellow." He turned to leave.

"Abner — if you take me to Maiden, like — like this — there's only one place I could go. Please don't make me —"

"You already belong there. You joined that sisterhood when you entertained Lacy."

She sobbed then, and he stood unmoved. No woman's tears would ever move him again.

"Are you hungry?" he asked. He hadn't fed her. Hadn't even brought her a cup of water.

She nodded. "And I have to — I have needs."

"Waiting on you as usual," he said dourly. "Nothing's changed."

He slid arms under her and carried her to the stinking privy back behind the cabin. It was rank with the usage of seven men, but that was her problem, not his. He set her down and left her, heading for clean sweet air. Later, at her summons, he carried her back, hearing her groan at every step and jostle.

"Could you wash me?" she asked, dully. "I can't even lift my arms to my face."

"This is familiar," he retorted. He dropped her onto the hard bunk again, knowing she'd groan. But he kindled a fire and bucketed water from the river, and started it heating. He'd wash her. He'd see her bruised body. She was no more desirable to him than a dead fish. She was unclean inside, and no scrubbing would fix it.

Her tears had slowed, but not her pain.

"When I'm better I could cook and keep house," she said. "I don't mean — you know — married. But I could work. Dixie made me. I know how. I could earn my keep."

"You always knew how. And it did no good. Forget it."

Neither spoke, but thoughts loomed large in the old log cabin, and they avoided each other's eyes as Abner waited for the little stove fire to heat some water. He didn't have soap, but he had a scrubbing rag.

"It won't change your mind, and you won't hear," she began softly. "But I need to say something. You always treated me like a grown woman, an adult, even though I was acting like a girl. You respected me, gave me my freedom, and I — I didn't know how to accept it. I know you — you loved me, Abner. I didn't know what love was. I know you showed me love, by being patient with me, and forgiving me as long as you could."

He didn't care what she was saying, and shut it out.

"Dixie treated me like a slave. He treated

314

me like a little girl. He took away my freedom. He didn't love me. He didn't respect me. . . . And he made me work. He beat me. He was cruel. If I didn't work, he'd almost kill me . . . and I deserved it."

She lapsed into silence, while they waited for the water to warm.

"I deserved how he treated me," she repeated softly.

"Forget it. We're going to Maiden."

"He used me and hurt me. But he made a woman of me. I don't like drudgery. No one does, except maybe a few women. I don't like cooking and washing and mopping and dusting and sewing and — cleaning the water closet. But I did it. And I took pride in it. I wasn't proud of anything else, but I took pride. You saw the house! I made it shine! I could do that for you, Abner. Just be useful, is all. Just earn my keep and feel like I'm giving something."

"It's too late." Abner stuck a finger into the pot and found the water lukewarm. Good enough. Let her shiver. He lifted the castiron kettle and hefted it to her bunk, and found a rag. She watched him silently.

He sighed. "Don't get notions," he muttered, and pulled her nightdress up. And gaped, horrified at the damage Dixie did. Scarcely any part of her torso had escaped

Dixie. Great purple and yellow bruises coiled over her belly and hips and breasts. Her skin had been lacerated everywhere, leaving dried blood in gashes and cuts. Her left ribs bulged, bones out of place and protruding just under the flesh.

"My God," he muttered. "Why didn't you tell me?"

She was weeping again.

He washed her gently and then bound her ribs with a winding cloth he fashioned, tying it as tight as she could bear, while she endured, stoically. All thought of taking her to Maiden vanished.

"I'll fetch a readymade dress and some things for you in Lewistown in a few days," he muttered.

He found a straw-filled tick that seemed free of bedbugs, and slid her onto it, and made a pillow of sorts of a folded blanket. Then he fed her, spooning some oat gruel into her gently. She slipped into sleep almost instantly, and he pulled an old horse blanket over her, though the day would be warm.

He spent the midday sorting through his supplies and equipment, taking stock. And checking on her every little while. She awoke in the afternoon, and he cared for her again.

"You gave me everything you had, and I

returned nothing," she said. "I didn't know what love was."

"No, you don't," he agreed.

She awakened again in the evening, when the sunlight lay flat across the valley, gilding the mountains to the east and south with amber light. It had always been a moment he'd loved.

This time, as he stood on the cabin stoop, he spotted movement far to the east, caught by the sun. He watched it curiously, until he knew. Hungry on the dun. Three Blackfeet women on dark ponies, each carrying a bundle. And a fourth pony dragging a travois loaded with lodgepoles. Abner smiled. His outfit wouldn't be lonely. He watched, mirth rising in him, and he laughed. How strange it felt to laugh.

He turned inside, and found Eve staring up at him. "Hungry's coming — with his family."

"Hungry?"

"Three Blackfeet ladies and a lodge." Abner grinned.

She managed a smile, through puffed lips. "I'd like to get to know them."

He frowned, reading her mind. "Servants."

She looked stricken. "No, Abner!" She sobbed again, and Abner couldn't fathom it.

She composed herself, wearily. "You'll send me away, and I deserve it. But I'd like to try. Just work for you, if you'd have me. I owe you a lot. Our marriage is — gone. But I'd stay and help. Would you let me give? I've never given. All my life, I've never given. It means a lot to me now."

He stared. "Give? You?"

She nodded, tears still welling up. "Love is giving and I want to love."

She peered up at him, a terrible earnestness engraved in her battered face, and it touched something in him.

"Let's give it a whirl," he said. "If you can stand someone as ugly and stubborn as me."

"You're not ugly, Abner Dent. I've never seen a man more handsome."